Joseph McInerny

Powderhorn

TANGLEFINGER BOOKS • NYC

This is a work of fiction. The author, in an attempt to evoke the time and place in which the story is set, has employed language that may be offensive to contemporary readers. The sensitive reader is asked to accept the material in its context.

Cover photo: Bianca Preusker,
used by permission.

Tanglefinger Books NYC
ISBN: 978-0615650838

Under a full moon on a wind-blown October night in 1935, he buried the girl's body in the Powderhorn Park. Her unmarked grave is still there, I guess, in a spot shaded by tall cottonwoods, close by the baseball diamonds and the horse-shoe pits. I don't know the exact location. He only described it like that, and said she was laid in the ground with prayers. Telling the story, he seemed to think that, me being a woman, I'd take some comfort in that — the prayer part. Like it would make the tale less awful. He didn't know that I myself had stopped making prayers long ago.

Horton Moon was alone at her grave that night, and to this day he mourns as if he'd buried his own self with those prayers. He once said that she was "the one," and maybe he really believes this; it's easy, I guess, for a man like Moon to cast everything he's got onto a person who died before she could see him for what he was.

He was a flawed man. He used to like to say he loved too much. But who doesn't think that about himself? It's the oldest line in the book. Usually coming out of the mouth of a man who doesn't know how to love at all. Anyway, Moon was flawed. Nobody contested that. He was ignorant about things he shouldn't have needed to be taught. Maybe it was all, as he would tell it, because his brains were scrambled from love. I don't know. Who can know what made him tick? I wasn't inside his head, so I can only guess. In any case, he made a hell of a mess of things.

He got some bad breaks, and the few good breaks he got he threw into the wind. But that's true with most men. Maybe true with most women, too, I've got to admit. Anyway. The real story isn't about the breaks he got or the messes he made. It's about how he changed, or tried to. I mean, it's small potatoes if a saint does the right thing, or if a philosopher finds his place in the world. Moon was no philosopher, and anyone who came within a hundred feet of the man could tell you he was no saint, yet he still did better than most in figuring things out and he worked, I think, to rise above his nature. In the end, he certainly did all right by me and mine. And he tried, in his way, to straighten some of the other matters out. He did have the decency to bury the girl in what he thought a proper manner, to say a prayer before he threw the dirt in over her bones. And just the fact that he was there, in the Powderhorn that night, says more about him than I can. Maybe he wasn't such a dope about things after all.

Minneapolis, Minnesota

1934

One

At the Frenchman's, I've got a nice warm yellowy feeling in that place just behind my eyes and I've got a just-filled glass on the bar in front of me and I've still got more than a dollar left in my pants pocket.

Peterson beside me is telling a story about golf. It's a long story, going on longer than it should, I think, but Peterson's a true friend and I'm not about to cut in on him in what I'm guessing is about the middle of his story.

Peterson's just now taken up golf. It's a game I don't understand. But I don't understand very many games, and I'm forever confounded by the ability of men to talk and talk and talk about games they've played or games they've watched being played. It's a mystery to me, the appeal of these games. Now, Peterson might just as well be telling me about a Greek play he's read — telling me in *Greek*, I mean — or explaining a new theory about ways to measure distances between the planets.

It means nothing to me. But Peterson's a true friend and he'd loan me a dollar as quick as I could ask for it, and so I sit and I listen to the story he tells. It seems there is a park on Lake Hiawatha where they play this game, and Peterson spent the afternoon on the course hitting the ball about and I can't for the life of me follow whether he played his game well or not. He seems to be happy in the telling, though the story he tells is one of misery and frustration.

He is describing a situation in which he was forced to swing his club at a ball that had landed behind a tree. "It's a physical impossibility," Peterson says happily. He's one for using queer expressions of hundred-dollar words. Physical impossibility. I watch Elsen drawing beer and I find myself wondering, for the first time really, about how a fella named Elsen runs a place called the Frenchman's. Elsen's a Swede, and his wife is, too. I seem to remember that he has a grandfather who's Norwegian, and Elsen once told me that during the war he was integrated into a British unit for a time, and I know he's traveled as far as Canada on summer fishing trips, though none of these facts does anything to explain the Frenchman name. Peterson goes on — too long, as I say — and then, without really coming to a point as far as I can tell, he stops and asks me:

"Is the work steady?"

For a moment he's caught me. I've been listening but not really so, if you know what I mean. And I have to sip at my beer and lick the foam off my lips, stalling like, before I think that he's asking about Albert and the plumbing. I nod. "It is. Why?"

"Just asking. It isn't always."

"No, it's not always. But it is now. I'm steady with Albert."

"He's promised you work?"

"He hasn't promised me anything."

"Fuckers never do. Never will." Peterson's long face, blue in the hollows of his cheeks, is expressionless. But his voice is changed. It's a change I don't like.

"But there's work," I say quickly. "I can see enough to know that. And I'm good. No reason Albert won't keep me busy."

"And no reason he will, Hort. You know that as well as I. As long as you work for the boss you're only as good as the boss tells you you are."

"I'm steady with Albert," I say. I want Peterson to stop talking in this line. The fact is, I'm *not* feeling so steady with Albert of late. He's been acting queer on the job, being short with me for little things. And, Lord knows, I need to stay steady with him. I've been behind on the rent three months running now.

"You're steady with Albert for now," says Peterson. "But for real security, a man needs to be his own boss."

"If the work goes away, it goes away. And then I'll be broke whether I'm with Albert or on my own."

"So it's a question of ambition?"

"Peterson. Will you stop with this nonsense? Speak straight."

"Horton?"

"What is it you're talking circles around?"

"An idea."

"So I thought. Let's hear it."

"Not so fast. It's still just an idea. Not really a talking-out-loud thing yet."

Ach. Peterson. His ideas. I can guess the gist of what he is on about anyway, going on ideas of his from the past. Maybe he's got a crooked scheme on how to claim the reward this St. Paul millionaire, Steven Linen, has put up; on posters all over town, Linen's offering a reward for the return of a servant girl who ciped a bunch of stuff from his mansion. Or maybe some acquaintance of Peterson's has recently come into possession of certain goods that could be purchased for pennies on the dollar, or maybe Peterson himself has come into possession of some such goods, and it is a question of helping him place these goods with the right fence. Peterson is full of ideas like this.

I've listened to Peterson's ideas in the past. I admit it. I'm no altar boy. We've done jobs together. Midnight stuff. I've driven cars for him, shook down some pansies with him, moved property. Small stuff, good for beer money and not much else. But that was all when I was a kid. When I was a kid, I did all sorts of nasty things, took all kinds of stupid risks. Peterson doesn't seem to be able to get that I'm not a kid anymore.

"I ain't interested," I tell Peterson.

"Ain't interested in what?"

"In your idea."

"I haven't told you my idea."

"Then I'm not interested in hearing you tell it."

"Okay. That's different. You're not interested in hearing it."

"No, I'm not."

"Fine."

"I'm steady with Albert."

"For now."

"Yes, for now. I'm steady with Albert and I've four babies at home and Annie's likely carrying a fifth now, and I ain't interested in hearing ideas of yours."

"So I heard you say, Horton. You ain't hearing none of it. I'll shut up."

"Please do so."

"Done."

We two sit there drinking for a good minute then, the only sound between us our glasses being taken up and set back on the bar and, once, Peterson picking a cigarette from his pack and asking Elsen to pass the match cup.

"They say putting's the thing," Peterson says after the minute has passed.

"Putty?" I ask him, confused.

"Putting. Hitting the ball short."

"What — golf?"

"Golf."

I slump on my stool and reach for my own cigarettes. I light a butt and breathe out the new smoke. "I don't know golf, Peterson. I really don't."

"Listen. I'm saying. People who know say that putting is the thing." His face is not changed from before, and for all I know he is still talking about his "idea," or maybe he is finishing the story he had been telling before, about the day at Lake Hiawatha. I can't tell. "Everybody thinks, when they take up the game, that you just whack the ball as far as you're able. And that's part of it. But, you know, a large percentage of the game — a *huge* percentage — is putting. Short distances. Finesse. It's a French word."

"I know finesse."

He glances sideways at me, then back at his beer. "So it's finesse. It takes a light touch. A sure touch. It's harder than hell to get it right."

And I'm thinking now that he *is* back on the day at Hiawatha and so my brain is going away, too. Peterson talks and I smoke and I start to thinking about Annie and how she might be up with our fifth, and how, if she is, the money at home is going to be even tighter than it is now. And it's tight now. I'm thinking about the times, calculating. Annie's been begging off sick most mornings lately, but there was once two weeks ago when I came home drunk and I got ugly on her, and another time last month when we did it sweet, hiding under the blankets on a weeknight after the kids were down. It doesn't matter to the baby whether you do it drunk or sweet, of course, but I find myself wishing this one is coming in from the sweet.

"Did you not hear what I said?" Peterson is asking me now.

I did not. My cigarette is halfway in my mouth and I freeze there staring back at Peterson and then the smoke stings my eyes and I wave the cigarette away and then shake my head.

"I didn't hear you, no," I say to Peterson. "Very sorry."

"Where were you?"

"Just here," I say. "I was thinking about something, though."

"Are you still?"

"Am I still what?"

"Are you still thinking about something? I mean something other than what I'm telling you."

"No," I say. I feel drunk now, all at once, and it's an awful feeling. I suck on my cigarette and fight to clear my head. "Go ahead. I'm all ears."

"I was telling you about the vending machines. The candy and gum dispensing machines."

"Oh, Peterson," I say.

"Oh, what?"

I crush out my cigarette and frown at the tin ashtray. "Your idea. This is about your idea?"

"It is." He swallows a mouthful of beer and watches me.

"I can't hear it. I can't."

His voice seems to grow louder, though maybe it's just me. "You can't even hear me out?" he says.

I shake my head. I gather my cigarettes from the bar and pocket them. I leave my beer, not quite finished, and I stand up from the stool. I'm wanting nothing more now but to get me across Bloomington Avenue to home.

"I'm sorry, Peterson, but I can't. I can't even hear about it. It's a physical impossibility."

Two

In the morning I wake up early and it's only Annie and me. The sun is up but only just barely, and it's quiet outside the window at the foot of our bed. The babies are sleeping and none of them has come into our bed during the night. So I reach with my foot under the covers until I touch Annie's foot.

She's awake immediately, and she rolls 'neath the covers towards me and in that early early sunlight I see her smile. She's a small mouth, though nicely formed, and it's a smile that stirs me like first love no matter that I've seen it a hundred thousand times. "Annie," I says, and I touch her nightie with my fingertips.

"No," she says, though without losing the smile. "Let's you and me just lie here sweet," she tells me.

"Give me a taste," I ask her.

"No," she says, "I feel like the devil with the morning sickness."

"Come on," I purr, low like a cat. "I'm not asking you to dance the Charleston, my dear. I'm only asking for a little of what God made man and women to do."

"No," she says again. Her voice is changing, her smile is gone. "It's a bad time."

"It's a good time," I say. "Never been a better time in life."

"No, Horton," she says. "Be kind."

"But I'm the kindest man in Minneapolis," I tell her. "And I'm hard and hungry and what's more I'm your husband."

"Now, don't be that way," says she. "'I'm your husband,' indeed," she says, mocking, and I can hear in her voice right away that there's more beneath the surface than I can know.

"Well," says I, "I am indeed." I say this like I mean to convince her but, really, the fight is on now, and there's no question of my getting any anyway from this point on.

Annie comes out of the gate full speed, her voice quiet but her words tumbling out fast, reading my history back to me. The suddenness of her attack draws a few nasty words from me, defending, but it's not long before the fire goes out of me and I settle back on my pillow. The truth is, I don't care to fight. There were times, back in the days when Annie and I were new together, when we'd fight like mad. But we loved like mad, too, so it all evened out. Now I can't get it up for a fight anymore, and I'm the first to admit that it's a sad, sad thing.

Annie is going on, her voice below a whisper so's she won't wake the babies, calling me a bastard and reminding me of times I've drunk too much or hit the children or walked to the Frenchman's saloon instead of staying for dinner with Annie's sisters. Surely she must see that I'm not fighting back, but she does not let up her end.

"You're a good-time man, Horton," she says, "and when it's a party you're the first to dance and the last to put down your beer. But, now, life's not just one long party, is it? And when there's children to feed or a sick baby to hold or even just, for the sake of Jesus, a wife who needs conversation at the end of the day, you're nowhere to be had. So don't tell me you're my husband like that or I'll spit right back at you that I'm your wife. And then you'll be sorry to hear that there's a lot more a wife demands than a rut in the dark when she's sick to her bones carrying another of your babies. Just because you're hard and hungry. I'm hungry, too, you know. And I can tell you this: I've a hunger for something you're not offering up. So don't whimper to me about hunger, Horton Moon."

So Annie says this and I lie there, my head on the pillow and my eyes on the ceiling, and I try to think about the cracks in the plaster above me and I try to think about the first birds sounding in the trees outside now, and I even try thinking about nothing at all. But all I can think about is what Annie is saying, and that's hell to think about this early in the morning before the day has even properly begun. I mean, where does the day go from here?

*

On the Lake Street line the westbound car is filled and so I hang off the back platform and get a touch of breeze as we pass through the hot morning.

I can smell the dewy late-May night clinging still to the pavement between the streetcar rails — the sun hasn't risen the tar scent yet. So there it is, mixed in with the electric burn that I always love — the night scent, a trace of the hours before and all the dark, cool, quiet that had lay over the city before the day broke.

There's nothing in the world like the promise of morning, when a whole day lies ahead and the streetcar is filled with folks all freshly washed and coffee-breathed, pressed close together on the rocking car like they're nudging one another encouragement. But, for me, there's always that other thing in the morning — the remembered night. When it's early enough, like it is now, you can still get a whiff of it through the growing light.

It is May and the summer is coming upon us already. When I read the newspapers I read large-lettered headlines about banks shutting down and businesses closing and jobs lost. Mostly I don't read the papers. Last year was the repeal, but I'm a man who likes a drink and I can tell you that I didn't need to read the papers to know that the Prohibition had ended. The banks run out of money, but I have no money in the bank and so that means nothing to me.

The newspaper stories of joblessness mean nothing to me, either. The smart fella says that the only sure things in life are death and taxes. Well, there's a thing or two more that's sure in life, and for them things there's indoor plumbing — and for that reason I'm not losing my job. I'm a plumber. Albert has kept me on, and I see no reason that he'll let me go.

Ah, shit. Trouble in the front of the streetcar. We've stopped at the Park Avenue stop, taken on more passengers, but we're not moving. I swing out on my pole, hanging over the side to get a look. Old man and a kid trying to con their way on. Good luck, old man. I know this conductor. He's tough as a goat. The old man is trying to convince the conductor to let the both of them board on one token, but the conductor is shooing him and the kid away to the curb. The car starts moving on. I take a look at the two of them as we roll slowly forward. The old man is cleaner than most bums, and the kid — maybe he's a Mexican — is good-looking. Fresh haircut. I suppose they're not really bums. The old man and I lock eyes, and it gives me a start to see how calm he looks. No anger. No shame. It seems that going about without even enough change in your pocket for streetcar fare is normal these days.

Like I'm feeling for a rabbit's foot, I jam my hand in the pocket of my trousers and I squeeze a small fistful of coins. I've got mine. I pull out a pair of dimes and lift my hand toward the old man and the kid on the curb.

"Cheers," I say. I drop the dimes into the kid's hand as I pass. "Next car will be by in ten minutes."

Newspaper headlines and bank failures and breadlines and poor bastards turned off the streetcar aren't spoiling my good mood this fine May morning. I've got my life, I've got my job, and I've got my Annie. Yes, she had her words with me this morning at first light, but we made up, in our way.

It was later, in the kitchen. Annie was making sandwiches for the kids' lunches. I touched Annie in the place on the underside of her arm, where I know she likes to be touched, and I came in close behind her and nosed away the heavy curtain of hair that covers her ear. Annie wears her hair down, and it's grown to her shoulders, and so her neck and her ears have, for me, become rare pleasures. So I came up close to her ear, which is lovely and small and smells of private places not often seen in daylight.

"My girl," I whispered low.

She dropped her chin and made a kind of backwards sigh — breathing in rather than exhaling — and though I couldn't see her face I knew she was smiling now.

"Horton," she said, speaking my name in the old way, in the soft tones.

"There's not a girl in the world can make a sandwich like you can."

She made a noise, a kind of giggle.

"I mean it."

"It's a rare art," she said, playing along.

"The way you handle that baloney roll makes me mad," I whispered. I was teasing her with the crude joke, but the fact of the matter is I was actually becoming light-headed just to feel the delicate curves of her ear so close to my lips, with my eyes closed and the scent of her hair filling me. I was swooning.

"You're a very naughty boy, Hort," Annie said.

"I am," I said.

I brushed the tip of my tongue along the soft lobe of Annie's ear. At this, Annie tilted her head just one degree further toward my open mouth, and she settled her weight backwards, pressing her ass into me.

"I do like naughty boys," she said, dropping her own voice to a whisper.

I folded my arms around her. I breathed in her hair. I began to rock my hips sideways, humming a tune in her ear that we could dance to. A new Gershwin ballad that we'd heard a radio orchestra play the night before last. I stroked my hand down the length of Annie's right arm. Faint, unstifled animal sounds were rising in her throat. I reached her hand and closed myself over her and she turned her hand over, opening. Our fingers found their places, together.

Then we both heard Lundquist the milkman, on the back stoop — making his rounds late, he was whistling a soap-powder advertising jingle.

This broke the mood, I guess, as Annie laughed out loud and wriggled out from under me. I let her go and I leaned myself against the kitchen countertop beside her.

"I do like to dance with you, Annie," I said. Her hair had fallen forward again, covering her ears and the private parts of her face. But it made me glad to see the way the color had risen beneath her freckles.

Her eyes, the color of Christmas nuts and just now flashing vivid with life, came up at me from her work at the breadboard. "There's no man on this earth can make me dance like you can," she said. Then, like she'd caught herself, she changed her tone and her eyes went back down to the sandwiches.

"Though if that's your idea of dancing," she said, poking at me playfully with her elbow, "we may need to unplug the radio when the children are around."

Oh, my Annie. We do have fun together, even now.

When Annie and I were young, we drank whiskey over chipped ice like a pair of New York millionaires. We danced. We dressed. Annie was a famed beauty, the youngest of the four Thoms sisters, each of them fairer than the one before and none more splendid than Annie herself. She had dark, waved hair and legs like a showgirl. And I was Horton Moon, with my motion-picture-star face. I lived at home with my folks and I spent my weekly pay on neckties and shoeshines. Everywhere we went people looked up from whatever they were doing to see us. Annie and Horton. People whispered our names. Whether we were stepping through the crowd on the lawn of Powderhorn Park on the night of the Fourth, or dancing on a cleared dancefloor at Slip Powell's Cedar Avenue speakeasy, we were the shining center of attention. We were better looking, and younger, and happier, and more in love, than everybody else in Minneapolis then. When I married Annie, the neighborhood turned out on the sidewalk in front of the church like it was opening night of a Hollywood film.

Hang on, now. What's this? Climbing on the streetcar at the Portland Avenue stop. A beauty. Black Irish. Tall and slim with no hips. Not my type, but. Dammit will you get a load of those eyes. Sparkle like polished stones — like whatta-ya-call, onyx is it? Black Irish. Lovely hair. Straight as a china-girl's and all chopped off in a brand-new bob. Skin as pale as bone. Mouth painted in red. But the eyes. Jesus, the eyes on a girl like that could drive a man to do things. Sparkle so black in that white, white face. Like to touch the back of her hair where the barber shingled it in.

Ah, well. Shake it away, Horton. Take a big deep noseful of the ozone from the wires over the car. Clear your head, clear your heart. You've already fallen in love once today, with your own Annie, and once a day is all that any man should ask. Still. I can't help myself.

Even in the beginning, when Annie and I were new together and we were living like movie stars, I never lost my weak heart. I mean with regards to other girls. A wrinkle in a skirt, a spot of sunlight on a plump cheek, a shine in the curl of a new permanent wave. Any one of these could set me off, and then I was fallen for a stranger. Even with Annie Thoms as my bride. Can you imagine?

It's a sickness, I know. The priests have told me. I've confessed most every one of my fallings to a half-dozen priests over the years, and at first the fathers will say some such about distractions or yearnings, but then when I explain to them that, no, I'm talking about falling in *love* — with the rain of rose petals and the Bing Crosby songs playing through my head and the whole deal — well, then, the priests tell me, that's just not normal. This I know. I've fallen in love again and again (like for example, just now, I can easily imagine my future years spent staring into the black eyes of Slim there, in the streetcar's third row, right), but, seven years after we spoke our vows, Annie herself still makes my heart swell close to bursting with a smile in the bed at dawn. I mean to say, I fall in love with strangers but not nearly as frequently as I fall in love, again and all over again, with my own wife. Such is my condition. I've nothing to feel guilt for, but if you don't think what I feel is pain then you've never fallen in love. It's hell. The crooners go on about the heart, but I can tell you the heart is the least of my worries; my pain is constant and dull and it's in my stomach, my head, my shoulders, my back, my arse. I can't think straight most days.

Okay. Enough. On a fine morning like this, who can be bothered with unhappy thoughts of failings and aches? Not I. I just hang on to my life the same way I'm hanging on to the back rail on the streetcar. I'm on the streetcar on my way to work and on my way to all that the day ahead holds, and all you can say about *that* is that it's not promising to be a walk in the roses but, at least, the sorrows of the day to come are not yet known.

Three

Ah. There's a fine one. Trim in the waist and broad in the bottom, the way I like them. Good hair. Bit of red in it. Always nice. And glasses. Funny how most fellas don't look twice at a girl in glasses. Take a look at this one and you see there's not a thing wrong with a girl in glasses. Some girls, it suits them. Their faces. They might even look a bit off without the glasses. Like the glasses kind of finish the face. This one, here, is like that.

Behind the glasses I can see she's got a good face. Strong bones. Not all oatmealy and blah the way some girls. Sharp, this one. Look at that. Her hands. A bit rough, I can see even from here. Working in the shop, most likely. Nothing wrong with that. Nothing wrong with that at all.

Lake Street is a grand street at noon on a Tuesday in May. A fella can lean on a wall in the sunshine and enjoy a smoke. Burp up a taste of fried potatoes and sausage and beer from the lunch. Watch the girls go by. Yes, sir. A grand street.

Pass on by, girl. Another comes into sight. Big girl. But a dresser. Respect that. A girl can be big or small or lame or what have you, but if she dresses herself with care it shows something good about her. A man can respect that. This one. Arms on her jiggling like a couple of undercooked hams. But the dress is nice. Blue. The color suits her exactly. Brings out the high blush in her big moon-face. Lord, think about that one. On the top, if it were my call. Think of a big thing like that riding you — my god. Easy, Horton.

Now. Hello, there. What's this? Washed-out skinny blondish thing in a five-year-old smock just smiling at me like we're all alone on the backside of the moon. Lot of nerve. Who's she think she is? Her big brother ought to smack her one. Teach her to smile at gents on the street. Still, not half bad. Okay — half bad. But half good. I like her smile. She's got a fine mouth.

There's always something, isn't there? I mean, always something on a girl, something to look at twice. Some's got hair and some's got eyes and some's got an ass like a hundred-dollar whore and some's got a fine mouth. Or maybe it's just that I've got the gift of seeing. I always see something, but maybe it's just me.

It's my dumb luck to work here on Lake Street at Lyndale Avenue, where Albert's got his offices on the second floor over the ladies' haberdashery. The place next door sells ladies' boots, and then there's the hairdresser next door down, and there's a milliner across the street, with her window full of summer bonnets. It's a constant parade, the crossroads of south Minneapolis, drawing every female with two nickels to rub together for some lunchtime shopping.

The big department stores downtown are twenty minutes further in on the streetcar, and I suppose the ladies who really have it spend it down there. These girls here, slowing to look into the big plate-glass windows on Lake Street, are mostly working girls from the shops and offices nearby, or young mothers who live in the leafy neighborhoods off the Street. Nothing fancy about them. But nothing wrong, either.

This western end of Lake Street is maybe a little tonier than my own neighborhood, the

Powderhorn. On the east side, passing the Powderhorn Park, our Lake Street doesn't have glove shops and ladies' hairdressing establishments with French names. In the Powderhorn, the blocks off Lake Street are just as leafy and quiet, but they're lined with mostly older homes, and a lot of the big old houses — like the sad, sagging clapboard number Annie and I live in — have been split into rented apartments.

But, like I say, the people here at Lake and Lyndale are nothing fancy. I fit in all right. In fact, with my back against the sun-warmed bricks and my belly full of lunch and the girls all around, I'm comfortable as hell.

Lake Street crosses Lyndale right over there at the end of the block where the streetcar is stopped. Where that good-looking girl with the reddish hair and the trim waist and the glasses is, just now, standing at the curbside and waiting for a milk wagon to pass. Cloppety-clop the fat old horse passes and sure as there's Jesus the damn thing drops a load right in front of the good-looking girl. Shit.

Fucking shit. It's a grand noonday in May and the girls are so pretty they're making my blood rise like quicksilver in a glass, and then a fat old milk horse drops a shit onto the cobblestones and ruins the whole thing. There ought to be a law. Remember when I was a kid. Nothing but the fucking horses and the fucking horse shit. Now we've got the streetcars and automobiles, more every day. Saw a horse get whacked by a Ford last week. Broke the legs on the thing and a copper shot it through the head. Good riddance. One less pile of shit on the street. The Ford was a mess, though.

Light another cigarette with the butt of the last. Good to feel the smoke in my lungs and the dizzy at the back my head. Now a group of four sweet fat Wop-looking beauties are coming out of the lunch counter across Lake. Well. Enough. Wish I could stand out here all the day and just watch the girlies and smoke and feel the sun on my arms. But I've got to get back to work. I'm to make a call.

Technically, I'm not a real plumber, but only a man in the shop — when I make calls, it's all off the page. I'm not in the plumber's union. Albert's is an open shop, but he'd catch hell from the union if it became known that he is sending a shop man out to do real line-and-tap work. So he makes sure it doesn't become known.

This afternoon, I'm to make a call at one of the big houses on Stevens Avenue, and you never know what you'll see there. It's always like stepping through the looking glass when you enter the rarified air of those broad southside boulevards. Glynn claims he once made a call to one of those stately homes and was tipped five dollars by a crazy old painted sodomite, just for stopping a leak in the fellow's bath faucet.

*

Henry Gardner broke my nose. Son of a bitch was two ways to down when he landed a lucky — a wide, wild girly swipe that caught me before I ducked. Then I damn near killed him. After he broke my nose, I put him on the ground and I was kicking him and would have kept on kicking him to the grave if the fellas hadn't pulled me off and away.

I think of Henry Gardner every time, like now, when I'm staring in a mirror in some finely's bathroom and I catch a look at my mug there with the clean white tile and nickel plating all around behind me. Me with my nose all flat, standing in some finely's bathroom.

That's Albert calls them that. "Don't be tracking up the finely's floors with yer filthy boots, now," Albert said to me just today, when he sent me out. "I won't be, Albert," I said back at him. Though what *that* was all about, I cannot say. When have I ever tracked dirt on a job? Albert's all of a sudden taken to bothering me about my work. I like Albert, and I hope he's not turning into a shit. I suppose he's just worried to distraction about money and the times, same as every other soul in the republic.

I hawk up a sick-tasting gob and I spit it into the bowl of the toilet that had been acting up. I flush it away, fast, but just now a face appears in the doorway.

"I beg pardon," her voice says, faraway-sounding, like the sound of the falls coming from behind the mills downtown.

It's a fine face. Swedish, I guess. She's a young one — not yet twenty — and she looks strong and healthy, though her pretty face is a bit roundish. She's not a small girl.

"Is everything all right?" she asks. She looks from me to the toilet.

"Everything's just fine, miss. Terribly sorry to be crude in the house. But I've been a bit sick, I'm afraid."

"Quite all right." She can't meet my eye. She must be new. Probably just hired, fresh off some Wisconsin farm. First job in the big city, working in a house of finelys, and here she walks in on the plumber spitting into the porcelain.

"I didn't realize there was anyone on the floor," I say.

She says, "I just come up from the basement. Mrs. Taylor is in the parlor on the telephone."

"The telephone?" I say. "And who's she speaking with on the telephone, the Queen of England?"

"Perhaps she is."

She smiles when she says this and I like the looks of her teeth. Where's a girl get teeth like that? I can imagine a whole family of Swedes back on the prairie, all of them like her with big white teeth that could take a bite out of you.

I dip my chin and look at her out of the tops of my eyes, the way girls like it — Gloria Dooley used to call it my moving-picture-actor face — and I ask her, "You new?"

"Beg pardon?" she says.

"Did you just start?"

But now her throat goes pink and she gives me a face. "No I did not. Did you?"

"Ah," I say, working my eyes. "Don't be that way. I'm only trying to be social."

But she's not giving me a thing. "You've been hired to work on the plumbing. Please be so good as to tend to what you're here to do."

"That I will do," I say. And if it weren't for the good teeth and the pretty Swedish face, I'd say to hell with her and get back to the job. But she's a beauty, really. Young, but remarkable. I can't help myself.

"Don't be sore," I say. "Please."

"I ain't sore."

"You are. And you're right to be. I spoke out of turn." I do the thing with my eyes. Sure, I'm standing there in stained coveralls with a wrench in one grimy hand, but I've got those eyes, and they're working now, I can see.

"I ain't sore," she says again. "Really I ain't."

"Well, good. What do I know, anyway? I'm just a dumb Mick plumber. Don't mind me."

"Stop," she says, laughing, showing more of those teeth. God, to feel them in the flesh of my neck. Had a girl once years ago, a German girl, who bit when I fucked her. Bit and scratched and grunted like a dog. Beat the hell out of me.

"Are you German?" I ask this one.

"No. American."

"Clever. But really."

"My parents are from Denmark."

"Lovely. You grow up in the city?"

She shakes her head. "Little place in North Dakota."

"And your name is? No — let me guess. Alice?" No. "Becky? Christine? Dorothy? Edna?"

"Will you go through the entire alphabet?" she laughs. "It's Caroline."

"Caroline. A lovely name it is, too. I'm Horton Moon," I say to her. I don't offer her my hand on account of the grease but I tilt my head a bit to one side and that seems to do the trick on her. She shoots her eyes downward and the color goes pink on her throat again, though in a nice way this time.

"And I *am* new here," she says to me. "I began work just last week."

"Well, it seems like a swell place." I glance around the bathroom. The room is about the size of the parlor in my own apartment.

"You live on your own?" I ask.

"You're fresh!"

"I'm curious."

"I'm shocked."

"I'm asking."

"I'm not sure I'm answering."

"Fine, then."

And the two of us keep on like this for a few minutes more. You get the idea. Playing. I like her and she likes me. But then she hears a step on the stairs and she all at once composes her face and smoothes her hair and straightens her shoulders and then she's gone from the doorway. So I'm standing in that white, white room all by myself.

She's gone and then the lady herself appears in the doorframe, low and fat and with a face covered in powder that won't cover up its flaws. I take in a woman's face like a Hennepin Avenue pawnbroker takes in a gemstone, and this one I call a mutt. If she ever had any bones they're gone now, and she's not even old. Pity.

"Did you locate the problem?" the lady asks me.

"That I did, ma'am."

"And are you addressing the problem?"

"I have already, ma'am. You won't be having any more troubles with the water in here, I should think."

"Excellent." She stares at me, and at my hands and my feet and my tools.

"I'll be cleaning up presently, ma'am."

"And you'll show yourself out?"

"I will. As soon as I set things right here."

"Excellent."

The lady goes away from the doorway and there I am thinking of nothing so much as the Dane, Caroline. I start to putting things in place, wiping at the tilework with the unsoiled rag, dropping my wrenches into their bag. Then all at once I just have to stop and I have to hold myself upright with the heel of my hand heavy on the wide ledge of the lavatory. I'm almost dropping down with my feet going out from under me, like I'm losing my balance on black ice, from the feeling of losing her. I ache from thinking about what I've just missed, what I've just lost without ever really having had. I'm twenty-six years old and I've fallen this way more times than I can count, just like this.

It's my weakness, my sickness, my sin. The thing that the priests tell me is not normal.

I suppose it's all balled up with what I said before, about my being able to see something — some thing — in just about every girl that comes across my path. The flip side of *that* coin is that, every so often like now, a girl like this Caroline will come up on me heavier than a barrow full of five-pound bricks, and then it's no longer just about her good teeth or her hair or the sweet curve beneath her starched house apron; it's about Horton himself, stricken, afflicted, brought low and sick with what can only be described as honest-to-Christ love.

Explain to me the sense in that, if you're able.

Maybe someday in the future, fifty or a hundred years from now, some research scientist in a laboratory will figure it all out. The whole thing will be demonstrated to be a reaction between chemical compounds, or maybe the answer's in magnetic electrons and such, bouncing off one another in the air between us. The mystery will be solved. But for now I don't know what it is. Something big has happened between the Danish girl and myself, but I don't know what.

Anyway, Caroline is gone and that's an undeniable fact. Dreams are dreams and facts are facts and the fact is I've got my life. And we've only this one life, any of us. So now the hard darkness, that awful feeling that always comes over me when

I'm going through one of these things, begins to pass over and clear.

I even manage to smile at my sad old puss in the polished glass of the finely's mirror. Ah, well, I think: In another lifetime, Caroline, we'd be the happiest couple in Christendom.

Four

One of the twins, Frankie I think it was, puked all down the front of my clean shirt. So I'm in the bedroom looking for another clean shirt and small Richard is trying to step onto my shoes so's I'll waltz him about the floor like we do sometimes when the radio plays. Only there's no radio playing and I'm in a foul humor on account of the soiled shirt, and I'm standing in my undershirt and trying to get around small Richard to the closet, and I finally lose my patience and give him a swat on the ear. Now he's howling like a half-butchered sow and young Bridget comes running from the hallway to see what the excitement is and then the twins follow and Annie comes so we're all six of us in the little bedroom with small Richard howling and me, daddy, fit to howl.

"What's the trouble?" Annie asks. She addresses not me but Richard.

He blubbers. "Da — Da — Da — "

Which sets the twins off, mocking him. "Da — Da — Da!"

"Shesh, the two of you," Bridget commands her older brothers.

"Shesh yourself."

Annie is reaching for Richard. "Shesh all three of you!"

She takes Richard in close, holding his red face against her skirts.

"Da — Da — Da — "

"There, now," Annie says, into Richard's hair.

The twins keep their end up. Frankie is Da — Da — Da-ing and now Ralphie (I see in the dressing table mirror) takes a poke at Bridget. She slaps away his hand and whacks him hard under the chin. Ralphie starts up wailing.

"Oh, will you never — " Annie is saying, holding out both her hands to keep Bridget and Ralphie and Frankie apart. Richard, frightened by the sudden violence erupting, leans into Annie, and this I can see throws Annie off her balance. She and Richard tumble.

"Annie, dear," I say, managing I guess to be heard over the shouting. I knock the twins sideways with my hip and I step between my daughter Bridget and the spot where my wife and my youngest lay clutching at one another on the floorboards. "Have you not one clean shirt for me in this house?"

*

It's the wedding of Annie's cousin, Billy Toner, and it's quite an affair. After the wedding mass (a high mass, with three priests) there's a sit-down dinner — and not just in the church hall, either, but in a rented room on Cedar Avenue. It's one of those German places with a timbered ceiling and antlers on the walls and banquet tables that seat twenty at a time. I'm sitting at a table with Annie and the kids, along with Annie's sisters and their kids. It's a loud and happy group, kept with some effort just this side of mayhem, what with spilled water glasses and tears over the green beans and young cousins kicking at each others' shins beneath the table. I've got a plateful of potato salad and a breaded veal chop and a tall mug of good, strong, Bavarian beer. And I'm wearing a clean white shirt.

After the dishes are cleared, like we haven't all had enough, the lot of us are marched out the room and across the avenue and down to the Powderhorn Park where, under a darkening twilight sky, they've got a dance band set up in the field above the lake, and paper lanterns hanging from the plane trees.

We've all of us had a lot of the good Kraut beer back at the dining hall, and so we stroll out toward this outdoor dance like it's something we see every day. Like we just belong here.

Coming over the grass and reaching the place where the lanterns and the music are, I make a point of stepping over alongside Jim Dolan, the father of the bride.

"Very well done, Jim," I say, tugging small Richard behind me.

"Thank you, Hort," he says back at me. "But this bit is a gift from Uncle Jack."

"I see," I say. Of course. Only Uncle Jack Morrison could swing a thing like this. Roping off a section of the public park for a private affair. For Jack Morrison, all it took I suppose was a phone call and a handshake.

Annie and the kids and I find a table at the edge of the dance floor and we set about drinking through the bottle of Champagne wine that sits in an iced bucket on the table.

It's a good band, and the place is soon enough jammed with dancers. Everybody's grinning like idiots and laughing and drinking Champagne straight from the bottle while they dance. I'm just watching the dancers and keeping the kids out of trouble, showing them coin tricks and how to make a cigarette disappear up your nose, when Uncle Jack himself makes an appearance.

"Hello, Annie," he says, bending to kiss her.

"Uncle Jack!" Annie rises, meeting him halfway.

Here's Jack, along with his plain-faced, silent wife, Mary. She always looks sleepy. Mary waves at the table full of us, raising her hand timidly, like a child, and then dropping it. She smiles but doesn't say anything. Jack makes up for her.

"And how are these beautiful children?" Jack asks, his voice heard easily over the music. His is a voice used to talking loudly. He touches Ralphie on the head like a bishop giving a blessing. Frankie starts showing Uncle Jack how he's learned to rub a penny into his elbow to make it vanish.

"Hello," I say to Jack. Since he's not going to.

Jack turns to me, the smile on his face stuck in place, unchanged, but his eyes going cold.

"Horton," he says. He turns his attention back to Annie and I can see that the coldness goes from his eyes at once.

Jack and his wife are childless, but he seems to have an especially soft spot in his heart for my Annie, the youngest daughter of his youngest sister. Lucky Annie.

Uncle Jack Morrison is the fucking hero of the Powderhorn. Alderman. About as crooked as a plate of Wop spaghetti. Big, beer-bloated sonofabitch, still talking with an accent like he's five hours off the boat from County Cork. He smokes Turkish cigarettes and douses himself with French toilet water, so you smell him coming five minutes before he enters a room. Him with his hand in a little bit of everything. Street repair crews. Park concessions. He's dirty as hell. Even the Mick accent is a fake, I'll wager. But nothing's ever stuck to him.

Everybody says he's gone up into places too high for the reformers to ever touch him.

There's a history between Uncle Jack Morrison and myself that I maybe need to spell out right here. I don't like Jack. And he doesn't like me.

When I was a young pup of about sixteen, before I'd even met my Annie, I had a run-in with Jack Morrison. He was a big-shot even then, though not as big as he became later. Then, he was a neighborhood boss with the Democratic Party and I was just a punk kid who the fellas down at the party offices used when they needed errands run. I mean the kind of errands they couldn't legitimately run themselves.

Once, there was trouble with a man from the Citizen's Alliance. The Citizen's Alliance was a gang of second-rate Republicans who thought if they shouted a lot in defense of capitalism they might all finally be invited to tea with Mrs. Pillsbury. The Citizen's Alliance man in question had begun making noises about the socialists and the — whattayacallit, Trotskyists? — that were moving up in the Democratic Party. Jack Morrison and his gang didn't know shit about the Russian commies, and they didn't care. Only this Citizen's Alliance clown was starting to publish things in the papers about Revolution and Soviet-style salients in the local wards, and so people who did care about these things were beginning to make moves to look more closely into the party books.

Jack called me in and told me he wanted to send a message to this Citizen's Alliance fella, and so he sent Henry Rourke and myself out to the man's house, out near Lake Nokomis. Now, Rourke was a stupid son of a bitch who was six-and-a-half feet tall and near three hundred pounds. He'd boxed a bit but mostly he just swatted people around on the street. I knew how to hit a man where it counted, too, and so it seemed pretty clear to me what kind of message we were meant to deliver to this good Republican from the Citizen's Alliance.

The situation was laid out that the man was a widower who lived alone in the little house near the lake. Rourke and I went over on a weeknight, after midnight, and knocked on the door. Mr. Citizen's Alliance answered the door in his bathrobe and Rourke pushed his way inside. I stood outside on the stoop and smoked a cigarette, facing out at the nice elm-lined street and at all the nice quiet stucco-sided houses, their lights unlit.

I heard things breaking inside the house. Then sounds like a boot against a side of beef. The gentleman wasn't making a peep, but Rourke was grunting and cursing and saying things, and after a few seconds I made out that he was saying, again and again (all out of breath from the effort of hurting the man), "Jack Morrison! Jack Morrison! Jack Morrison!"

Mother of Christ. Rourke was delivering a message, all right. I had to laugh. But I also had to stop this. I pulled open the door, stepped in, and grabbed Rourke away. It was dark as hell in the room, but I could see the thing on the floor, not moving, that was the Citizen's Alliance man. The man made a moan and Rourke went to kick him again. Then the man wasn't making any sounds at all.

"C'mon, friend," I said to Rourke. I got him out of there.

I don't have to describe the reaction I got from Jack Morrison when I reported back to him a half-hour later. I'd dropped Rourke off at his mother's flat and I'd gone directly to Jack, who was playing a game of poker at the ward headquarters. He left the table and came away with me to the front room, where I told him the tale. I guess the fellas back at the game could hear Jack hit the tin ceiling.

"He said my name?" Jack asked.

I nodded. "More than once."

"The goddamned ape," Jack said. "I thought I sent you along as the brains. What was I thinking? Goddamned kids."

Jack lit another one of his Turkish cigarettes and frowned while he smoked. He seemed to be thinking about something bad.

"Okay," he said, after a while. He bared his teeth at me. It wasn't really a smile. "When you left. You say the man was unconscious?"

"Unconscious, yeah." I said. "That's exactly what he was."

Jack snapped his eyes open and shut a few times and then he took my arm and led me toward the door, speaking to me in a hurried, distracted-sounding way. "Goodnight, young Moon. Goodnight. You've really fucked me up the ass with this."

Whatever *that* meant.

He didn't even bother throwing me a fin or two. Nothing was arranged ahead of time, of course, but I'd figured the job was good for some folding money. But nothing. I spat on the Chicago Avenue sidewalk outside the door and I walked home.

The next afternoon, all the papers had the story about the good citizen from the good Nokomis neighborhood, an upstanding Episcopalian churchgoer and a member of the Citizen's Alliance, who'd apparently surprised a burglar in the night and had taken a beating — and four slugs from a .38 in the head — for his troubles. It made me feel lousy as hell to read the stories. Neither Rourke nor myself had ever even seen a .38, let alone been carrying one that night at the man's house. I suppose it was right then that I decided I'd had my fill of work for the Democratic Party. Jack never did say anything more about it to me, and he never did pay me or even so much as stake me to a free drink. And when Henry Rourke died in a knife fight two years later, Jack didn't even send flowers to the home.

So that's the history. Because I know something about him I wasn't meant to know, Jack doesn't like me — and for the very same reason, I dislike Jack. Add to this mix my having married Jack's favorite niece, Annie. Because even though I've been working a real job steady with Albert for years now, Jack doesn't buy that I'm legit. All of which, if you really want the truth told, sits just fine with me: Jack still looks at me like I'm a punk and a hustler, while I look at Jack Morrison and I see him as exactly what he is.

Just now I get a noseful of Turkish tobacco breath and cologne as Jack bends over the wedding table and talks into my ear.

"Why don't you ask my niece to dance?" he says. It's not really a question.

I move my head away from him. "Got my hands full here, Jack. With the kids."

He's got one of his big red fists leaning onto the table in front of me.

"Mary'll watch the babies," he says.

I look back at Aunt Mary. She hasn't heard any of this. She's just staring up at one of the paper lanterns. She yawns. I turn to Annie and I see that she seems to have got wind of what Jack is saying.

She smiles at me, her eyes bright. Gives a small nod.

So I stand up. "Very good of you to make the offer, Jack."

"Tis nothing at all," he says. He beams at Annie but says to me, in a lower voice, "A dance. The poor girl deserves at least this much from you."

I reach for Annie's hand and make a little bow, like they do in the movies. Sure. Like we're in the penthouse ballroom of the Pick-Nicolett Hotel.

"Daddy and Mama are dancing!" Bridget shouts.

We depart the table amid handclaps and hoots from the children, and we move easily into the thick of the dancers on the floor.

The grass underfoot is soft and the ground gives way beneath the heels of Annie's good shoes. We can't dance properly. No matter. I hold Annie's hand in mine and pull her round the waist closer to me. We step carefully, close together, making our way slowly through the hips and shoulders and elbows of the wedding-dance bodies. We move to the center of the floor, where the crowd thins and the air clears, where the glow from the paper lanterns in the branches of the trees can't reach, where the night is dark and the stars show themselves high above us in the early-summer sky. The kids are on the other side of the crowd now, and if they're still hollering at us we can't hear them. All we're hearing now is the music. The band is playing a slow one. I recognize it from a couple of years ago, when every radio orchestra had it in their lineup; it's a love ballad from one of the Broadway shows. I hold Annie closer to me and our feet stop moving. I press my cheek against hers and sing softly along with the band, singing the love song into her ear. And now nothing matters. No bothers about not having enough money, or about work and Albert and why his temper seems to be turning sour, or about the nuns saying Ralphie is not reading well in school, or about another hungry mouth coming into the house. No, nothing matters now but the song and the stars, and Annie smiling into my ear, and the feel of the soft, forgiving sod of the Powderhorn beneath our still feet.

Five

Sweat stings my eyes and blinds me, and when I wipe with my forearm it only makes everything worse. Now my nose burns and my lips go salty.

"Jesus wept," I say.

"Hot bitch," Albert says, on the stairs ahead of me.

We're not watching our mouths. No finely's this. It's a shithole Franklin Avenue walkup, a stack of rabbit-warren flats filled with poor Kraut couples and their dirty-faced kids. We're on the job for the city on this one.

Seems the cops had to come through last month, after a small-time hood, and they'd shot up the place. The landlord has connections with an alderman and so the city is paying for a fix-up.

Albert and I reach the third floor and we go into the apartment with the open door. Albert goes on ahead into the w.c. and he lets out a whistle that makes me hurry in after him.

The cops must have come upon the bad guy when he was on the crapper. There are blood stains not quite bleached out beneath scrub-marks on the wall, and the porcelain bowl itself is blasted into pieces like a dropped china plate.

"Fuckers shot the bastard on the can," I say.

Albert wipes at his face with a kerchief and nods. "I read the story in the papers. The guy had an automatic pistol. He popped a cop when the cop opened the door on him. Then the other cops shot about six pounds of lead into him."

"Did the cop he shot die?"

"No. Lost an eye, though."

"Pity. Is that the shut-off valve there?"

Albert lowers his tool sack. "It is. Though the man downstairs said this whole line is closed down."

"Good to go."

"Let's get this old piece out first."

"Right."

So Albert and I gather up the broken porcelain and then work the base of the toilet loose from the floor.

When we're finished, I'm as wet and greased as a Channel swimmer, and I go to the kitchen for a drink of water. Nothing in the line.

"I'm going downstairs," I tell Albert. "I need some water."

He waves at me and sits himself down at the little pine table in the kitchen. I see him lighting a cigarette as I leave.

The stairway is hot and airless. No windows. There are electric lights but nobody's turned them on. I skip down in the dark and when I break out into the white blast of sunlight on the sidewalk outside, I already feel better.

I stop and stand for a few seconds, looking around me. There's a butcher shop, its windows hung with bloodsausage and whole hogs' heads, and a bookstore selling German-language magazines. The Powderhorn is probably a fifteen-minute walk from here, but I may as well be in another country.

The building super, a little Kraut with long, white hair, is sweeping at the sidewalk with a worn broom.

"Hey there," I say to him. "Can a fella get a drink here?"

He stares at me without answering and then he jerks his thumb over his shoulder, pointing to the saloon three doors down.

I laugh at this. Not the kind of drink I had in mind. But what the hell. I go.

It's cool and dark in the long front room of the saloon. But this dark is a comfort, not like the dark of the stairwell. Here, the air is getting pushed around by a set of fans placed about the edges of the room. The light eases my eyes and the place smells clean and good. On the wall just inside the door, I see some posters for next week's marathon dance downtown, and one of those posters for the St. Paul millionaire's fugitive servant-girl, and some hand-lettered notes mostly written in German — looks like the typical bunch of work-wanted notices, brass-band concert promotions and lost-and-found slips.

I tell the bartender to bring me a glass of water and a cold beer. I light a cigarette and watch him draw the beer.

He's a young kid. Maybe his father owns the place. He smiles at me when he puts the beer down in front of me.

"*Prost*," he says.

"Here's how" I say back at him.

He smiles at me some more. "You cleaning up after Bill Freund?"

"I don't know Bill Freund," I say.

"He shot the cop. They killed him then."

"Ah. I know the fellow. Shot on the toilet?"

The kid nods. "They murdered him."

"He was a friend of yours?"

"He was a good guy."

"Well," I say. "I'm just a plumber."

The kid goes away down the bar toward some glasses in a rack that he starts putting out onto a shelf. I stare at the liquor bottles lined up behind the bar.

Mother of Jesus. What an ending. Shot on the can. Still, for every dumb bastard taken down by the cops, there are a dozen more living the life. I know. I think of Jimmy Claire, from over on Eighteenth Avenue, who ran numbers when he was still in school and then moved on to floating card games, and now he's living like the king of the world. Owns a roadhouse south of the city. Drives a new Duesenberg and lives in a big stone mansion on Lake of the Isles. And he's never even served anything more serious than a year in reform school. So some get away with it clean.

They say Arnie Sayles' cousin made a million as a bootlegger back in the days. Now he runs his own automobile dealership. Wendell Rasmussen, the pimp, spends five dollars to get his hair cut. John Carr held up a bank truck six months ago and he's still buying rounds down at the Frenchman's with it. So don't play a radio drama telling *me* crime doesn't pay.

Maybe every so often some poor bastard rolls craps and ends up in a police morgue. But there are six sides to these dice, and you don't need to be a genius to figure the odds of the game.

I guess my thinking is sliding along these lines just now because of the talk I had yesterday with Lew Fenster. Fenster is the pawnbroker from Lyndale Avenue. I saw him yesterday on my lunch break about getting a loan on my wristwatch. I got school tuition to pay. Three kids at the church school already and now small Richard will be starting in the fall. Fenster just frowned at my watch and shook his head. A piece of flash, is what he called it. Shiny on the outside but garbage on the inside. So I started in arguing with him, telling him how my brother bought the watch for me in

Chicago, and how it's worth twenty dollars easy. Fenster just frowned at the watch. I started telling him about the kids and the church-school tuition — which I know you never do with a pawnbroker, but I couldn't help it. Fenster shook his head. He tried handing the watch back to me but I wouldn't take it. He held it out to me but I'd push his hand back toward him. Like a backwards tug-of-war. It was pitiful. Fenster finally just put the watch down on his glass counter and turned away from me.

It was sad as hell. Thinking about it now, I still feel like a miserable bastard.

The bootleggers and pimps and holdup men are living large, while the working man is bickering with a pawnbroker to keep his kids in the church school. Now I'll have to talk to Father Pat about scholarship money. I glance over at the posters near the door, and a thought comes that maybe I should make myself a bounty hunter like in the western pictures, wearing a big white cowboy hat and tracking down Steven-Linen-the-millionaire's lost servant-girl for the reward money. Life seems a great load of crap, sometimes.

I spoke to Albert early this morning about money. Talk to Albert, Annie'd said. He's a good man, she said, and he'll listen to reason. There's nothing reasonable, I tried to tell Annie, about paying a man more money just because his wife is having another baby. But Albert's a *good* man, she said to me. Sure, I said.

And so I talked to good Albert and good Albert explained to me that these were no times for giving out pay raises. And — as if my asking was the ripple that lapped against the weak dike and broke the whole damn thing down — Albert then goes on to say that, in fact, he's got to think about cutting back expenses. Expenses are too high, Albert says, and these expenses are nothing but bad news to the future of good Albert's business. And, listening, I get a sick feeling in my gut when I catch on that *expenses* means *persons*.

The persons in the shop are Albert — who I guess doesn't really count as an expense — and Glynn, who's been with Albert since just after the war, myself, and Tony. I'm as quick as the next fellow and so I do the calculations: Tony's just a kid who works for a few nickels a week and Glynn is practically on a partner-basis with Albert, so that leaves me. I'm the expense. Albert's got to cut back on his expense.

I've drunk my beer, faster than I would have liked, and the kid comes back to me from down the bar.

"Get you another?"

"No, thanks," I say.

"Hot day," he says.

"I'm on the job," I say.

"Right," he says, looking away from me toward the door. "You're cleaning up after the cops."

"It's just a job," I say. I don't like the tone of his voice.

The kid turns his face back to me and squints a little. "Yeah," he says. "We're all working on something."

I've got to smile. I see through him. I was his age once, not so long ago, and I can remember feeling like I had it all figured out. Every old jerk who slouched past me on his way through life was a sucker and a chump, making mistakes that I would never make. The kid thinks he's a wise guy.

"What's funny?" he asks me.

I shrug. "Nothing's funny. Your father own this place?"

"Nah. My uncle."

"Good for you. You're set for life."

"Some life," he says. He rolls his eyes. "But I've got something else in the works."

"Right," I say to him, standing up. "We're all working on something, aren't we?"

I pay for my beer. And then I walk out and I go to the building three doors over and I climb the dark stairwell up to the third floor and I help Albert cart down the broken porcelain and the ruined pipes from the place where the cops shot the man to death on his toilet. Down at curbside, we pour the broken pieces of the bowl into the back of Albert's open-bed truck, and I see the white chunks of shattered porcelain rolling out across the steel bed, like dice tossed in a game of chance.

*

The summer has passed all hot and slow like the cottonwood droppings drifting across the flat brown water of the Powderhorn lake. Now it's autumn and the nights are already sharp with cold and the kids need sweaters and wooly pants that I've no money to pay for. Shit.

Annie is heavy with our fifth on the way. She's past the time when she's sick to her stomach and she moves about, back to her old self, quick and sure now.

In September I miss a morning of work with the hangover. First time that's ever happened. Two weeks after this, I fall off walking home from the Frenchman's one night and wake up long after midnight on the ground of the Powderhorn.

Complete blackout. I awake, shivering, covered in a cotton hospital blanket. Later, there are weird flashes of memory, jumpy images in my mind of an old man with kind eyes and a small, soft-faced boy beside him. I make the connection that these are the two I'd seen trying to hustle a ride on the Lake Street car months ago, and maybe its only a memory from then, all twisted out of time by the blackout, but I can't be certain. Somebody covered me in a blanket that night. I know I'm drinking too hard and so I promise myself I'll lay off the gin and drink just beer. And evenings only — no more afternoons and certainly no more mornings.

Mostly I keep to this.

October is sunless and rainy and the weather beats on me. November comes, bitter and dry, and all the trees in the Powderhorn are dead in the cold. When the snow comes, it softens things a little but only a little.

I'm in a funk. I've got bad brains, it seems, feeling like I'm moving around in a grave-deep ditch, distracted only by weird stirrings of a want I can't really put my finger on.

Sometimes I slip back into gin and sometimes I slip back into drinking in the morning. I'm feeling sick from the drink, and from the whole gray time. Christmas coming only makes me sad, as it always has. Ever since I was a kid. Some people get cheery at Christmas, but to me it just brings on a bad stomach. I try not to think too much about the kids and about the presents they'll be expecting under the tree. I try not to think about too much at all.

*

It's a cold Friday noon a week before Christmas and there are three-foot banks of dirty snow at the curbs of Lake Street. I'm going out for sandwiches, trying to avoid the icy patches on the walkway and feeling the cold air bite into my lungs when I pull on my cigarette.

Albert has us all take our turns, some of us going out on the calls and some of us staying back. This week I'm on shop duty. Me and Glynn are up the stairs, shuffling the inventory and answering telephone calls, when Glynn says, Horton my boy, how's about a couple of sandwiches from the Bohunk's? So here I am, slipping across the frozen puddles and feeling like my ears are starting to burn from the winter snapping at them.

Crossing Lake, I come into the sun, which helps a little. Still icy as a bitch, but the sun coming in low from between the buildings across the way at least makes the cold *feel* less cold. I'm glad as hell when I reach the Bohunk's, and I'm reaching for the door when I hear her voice behind me.

"Horton Moon," she calls. I turn.

She is coming across Lake Street, from the direction I'd come, and she holds a paper sack in one hand, which she holds high and waves. She is smiling at me, though it's only a small, half-smile, giving me just a glimpse at the white of her good Danish teeth.

"Caroline," I say.

Then I see on her face a kind of hurt. I guess from the way I spoke her name. But I didn't mean for my voice to sound tired and sad from my having seen her. I really didn't. It just came out that way.

"It is Horton Moon indeed," I say more brightly, trying to make up for myself. "I'm pleased that you recognized me out of my element — as I recall matters, when we last met I was standing in a bathroom with my arm halfway down a crapper."

This gets her laughing, which is good. I mean, she's a good laugher. Not all girls are, you know. Caroline wears a thick, cheap-looking wool cap pulled down over her head against the cold, but she's let her hair down, one long braid draped forward over her shoulder and down the front of a heavy, shapeless winter coat. This coat looks like a child's coat, without any trace of style or flair, and I remember that Caroline only just recently came to the city from the farm. She's still holding her paper sack up in one gloved hand, and she's still laughing her good laugh.

"You are shameless, aren't you?" she says to me.

"I've been called worse. Witless. Senseless. Tactless."

"Stop, you," she says.

"Okay. I'll stop." And I do. I stop talking and I just stand there close to her. Close enough to smell the smell of her breath-cloud in the frost between us, and close enough to practically *taste* the way the winter sunlight turns her thick, yellow hair new colors.

"Well, anyway," she says, not meeting my eyes, in a voice low but clear as a shout into the wind, "it is good to see you again."

"Is it?"

"Yes."

"Well. Yes, it is. Good to see you, too, I mean."

But I'm not sure it is good. I'm not feeling well, just now. Something is off. I'm standing too close to her. I'm a man married for seven years and I've four babies at home and a fifth coming in the spring.

"Do you ever think of me?" she asks.

Now, my first instinct here is to lie. Because what she's suggesting — that eight months ago I met a girl on the job and we exchanged pleasantries for five minutes and then we parted ways and then afterwards I found myself thinking about her more than a normal man would — is so crazy that, even though I know it to be true, I can't say it's so. I mean, to grant her point would be to admit to everything, to confess the whole mess of my life to a girl who, really, is a complete stranger. But of course she is *not* a complete stranger. She is, in fact, the girl in question. What's more, I'm standing close to her and the sound of her voice and the smell of her breath and the thing that she's saying, they're all working together to paint the world in queer new tones that don't make sense in any of the old ways of making sense. In a new way, though, it all makes the most perfect sense in God's universe.

"I — I have thought of you."

"I've been thinking about you, too."

"Yeah?"

"Yes," she says.

There's an intimacy in that last word, and in the way her eyes are playing over my face, that I know is not proper. "Caroline," I say, my voice shaking a bit and my lips feeling parched. "I've got to tell you."

"Tell me what?"

"I'm a son of a bitch."

"Please," she says, making a face like she's never heard the words spoken before. Maybe she hasn't.

"Pardon the language. But I'm — I'm not the way I present myself. See, the truth is, I am married. I have children. I am not in a position —"

Now she stops me by holding up her hand and touching her gloved fingertips to my dry lips.

The bell on the Bohunk's door sounds as it swings outward, interrupting us. A couple of ladies in fox collars emerge. They step gingerly out from the warmth inside, making squeals against the cold. I move away, off to one side of the doorway, and I take Caroline's arm and pull her after me.

I'm looking into her eyes, trying to see some sense in there, some understanding that what'd happened between us before was nothing but a lark. Instead, I see that she's got another kind of understanding.

"Horton Moon," she says quietly. "Are you never lonely? Do you know what it means to be lonely? To be in a city with a hundred thousand souls all around you but to be nothing but lonely — do you know what that's like?"

I nod. Kind of without being able to help myself.

"I think you *do* know what it's like," she says. "I think you understand. I thought that about you the first time I lay eyes on you."

It's a bit mad. Though for the life of me I'm not sure if she's crazy or if I'm crazy or if we're both of us sane as surgeons and it's the world that's gone off. Because, really, being close to her like this feels somehow *right*. The two ladies in fox collars are standing only a few feet away at the curb, discussing whether to hail a taxi or hop on a streetcar.

"Come," I say to her. "Let's get out of the cold." I open the door to the sandwich shop and lead her inside. We stand away from the counter, in the rear near an open barrel of coffee beans.

"Have I been wrong about you?" she asks.

"Caroline," I say. "You never passed from my mind. You never did. It was the strangest thing, but I *did* think of you. I *do* think of you." And now I've got to close my eyes because I'm not at all good at this sort of thing, really. When it's playing games and flirtations, I can do my Hollywood picture-star eyes and stare a girl down till she blushes like a tulip. But now I've just got to close my eyes.

"I knew it," she says, her voice coming at me in a very alarming way that makes me think her mouth is right up against my ear. But when I open my eyes she's standing there just like before.

All I can do is nod.

She says, "I've found you."

"You were looking for me?"

"Weren't you looking for me?"

I shrug and roll my eyes. "Ah. Maybe I was." I'm thinking about the state my brain has kept me in. The funk. The hard drinking.

"So we found each other," she says.

"Well," I say. "Here we are."

Caroline stares with those big gray serious eyes. After a minute she kind of lets out her breath as if she's been holding it.

"Listen," I say. "I'm going to grab a couple of sandwiches. You want to have lunch with me?"

"I'm due back at the Taylor's. I've only just been sent out with this." She lifts the paper sack. "It's a handle to the fixture you worked on at the beginning of the summer. The porcelain has cracked. I'll exchange it. Normally Mr. Dufresne, the butler, would run an errand like this, but he's been sick and I volunteered that I might —"

"I get it," I say.

"I was coming, I was just there, when I saw you leaving the shop and crossing the street. So I followed you."

"You found me," I say. "Just bear with me a tick."

I order a corned beef sandwich for Glynn and a baloney on a hard roll for myself. I could really stand, right now, to grab a box of beer to go from the saloon next door over, but I know Glynn can be a prick about that kind of thing, and so I go to the ice chest and grab a couple of pops instead.

Caroline and I cross Lake Street back to Albert's place, and we climb the stairs together to the shop. Glynn doesn't pay me any mind while I take care exchanging the porcelain part for Caroline, but he looks up from his papers and gives me a face when I begin to walk Caroline out the door.

I give him a face right back. "Your sandwich is right there, on the counter," I say to Glynn. "I'll be back up."

I follow Caroline down to the sidewalk door, and I stand with her in the cool vestibule while she adjusts her hat and gloves against the cold outside.

"Thank you, Mr. Moon," she says. Then, correcting herself, "Horton." She ducks her chin downward and makes like she's going to turn and leave me now.

But I can't just let her go like this. Not after all that business about lonesome souls and finding one another. I'm not sure what I'm doing, but I lunge forward.

"Have you a telephone?" I ask.

"No," she says.

"Well, do you — "

"I'm off work at seven tonight."

"Tonight?" I say. "I mean, seven o'clock?"

"Seven o'clock." She nods.

"Very well. Shall I — ah — will— "

"Do you know a place called Wellington's?"

"Wellington's, the hamburger joint?"

"Yes. On Lake Street at Chicago Avenue."

"I know it."

"I take my supper there every Friday evening. I'm through work at seven."

"I see," I say. Except I don't. I mean I don't really see. I don't see anything, yet I'm going forward fast, like a blind man sprinting at full speed toward whatever it is that lies in his path.

Six

"Do Mortimer Snerd!" Frankie says.

The others at the supper table take it up. "Yes, daddy! Do Mortimer Snerd!"

Frankie, Ralphie, Bridget and Richard are all sounding off, demanding my act. Even Annie joins in, after she stills Richard's hand (he's begun pounding his fork on the table in time with the chant).

"C'mon, Hort," Annie says. "Give us a bit."

I stare down at my plate, scowling at the half-eaten cabbage and the chop. This is part of the act. I give them like I'm not going to do it, and then I jerk my face upwards, doing the Snerd. Howls of laughter all around.

I do Bergen's dummy from the photographs in the newspaper — my eyes half-closed and crossed, my mouth set in a goofy overbite grin.

"Oh, Bergen," I say, my head lolling stupidly sideways toward Annie.

"Yes, Mortimer?" She says, playing her part. She makes her consonants crisp and precise, like Edgar Bergen on the radio.

"I've taken up golf, you know."

The children vibrate with excitement. They are silent as the cutlery. They hang on my every word.

"Golf?" Annie says. She raises her eyebrows and looks to the faces of the children, who grin and snigger to imagine Mortimer Snerd on the golf course.

"Yes," I say. I nod my head and pretend to be distracted by an imaginary fly buzzing nearby.

Ralphie squeaks, suppressing a laugh with a fist pressed against his lips.

Annie takes up her water glass and sips. She watches me, approving.

"It's not an inexpensive game, as I understand it," she says. She really does a remarkable Bergen. She probably could have been on the stage, if things had gone that way for her. My Snerd face slips just a little as I look to Annie — I'm falling in love again with her for this, her Bergen impersonation — but then I catch myself and set my eyes and mouth again.

Still holding the water glass, Annie/Bergen straightens and leans her weight backwards, settling in her chair. "It's a costly hobby, yes. One needs to purchase clubs, a bag, balls — "

"And a second pair of trousers!" I blurt, with Snerdly enthusiasm.

"A second pair of trousers, you say?" Annie/Bergen asks, milking the moment.

"Yes," I say. "In case I get a hole in one!"

The children scream and pound the table till the plates rattle. Even small Richard, who will later ask Annie to explain the joke to him, hoots and shouts with the rest, holding his little hands across his belly as if the strain of laughter will split him open.

Annie leans across the supper plates toward me. She holds her hand out for a shake. "Very well done, Mr. Moon," she says softly.

I take her hand. "Very well done yourself, Mrs. Moon," I say. I lift her hand to my lips and kiss it.

*

Later, when Bridget is teaching small Richard to dry the plates as Annie hands them from the soapy sink, I pause in the kitchen doorway while I fasten the buttons of my jacket.

"I'm off to the Frenchman's," I say to Annie.

She turns from the sink. "Give us a kiss, then."

I go to the side of her away from the two kids and I bend over her shoulder. I kiss her cheek but she snaps her head around, fast, and gets her lips twisted up into mine. She bites into me, playfully, and it's a good ten seconds before we come up for air. Breaking apart, we grin at one another.

"Be good, Hort."

"I'm always good," I say.

She raises one soapy hand and, with her wrist, pushes away a lock of dark hair that's fallen across her eyes.

"Are you carrying much?" she asks me.

"Only a dollar and a quarter."

"Well," she says. "You don't have to spend it all."

"I know that, love."

I spread my palm open over her ass, give it a small brush across, and then I go. Annie's turned back to the sink and the supper dishes.

"Don't be too late," she calls after me, as I pass out the door.

I've told Annie I'm out to the Frenchman's, and I not only walk to Bloomington Avenue and I not only turn left toward the Frenchman's, but I actually do go to the Frenchman's. I stand at the bar and have a beer and a bump and I'm there ten minutes before I pay Elsen for the drink and then I'm out the door toward Lake Street.

Walking west to Chicago Avenue, I go slow. I stop to stare into shoe store windows and I study the cakes lined up in the window of the bakery and I duck into the news stand and I buy another pack of Chesterfields, even though I've a full pack in the pocket of my jacket. There's a barbershop with colored lights blinking in its windows and somewhere behind me to the east there's a small brass trio tooting Christmas carols for the pennies of passing strollers, and these things, reminding me of the season, just make me feel lousy.

But not lousy enough to turn back. I go on, toward Chicago Avenue, and in five minutes I spot Wellington's. It's a small, modest old dive, with lace curtains hanging in the window and a yellow glow coming from inside off dim electric bulbs. I actually speed up my step, and almost get taken out by a streetcar at the corner.

See, I jump off the curb onto the sleek, wet cobblestones without looking either side, and this Chicago Avenue car clips past me so close that I get a nosefull of sparks and my cap goes off me.

Bells are ringing and people are shouting from the car, calling me every name that'd make your mother blush. Me, I just step backwards, and I wait till the streetcar is long past and the crowd around me at the corner has gone on ahead across the street before I stoop to pick up my cap. And then I turn around east towards home.

I've nearly been killed, and I resolve that I'm not going to go from this world an adulterer.

Let Caroline and her lonely soul go on being lonely. I'm not the best husband on this earth and I know I could try a bit harder to be a good father, but I can say for myself at least that I've not violated the sacrament of my marriage to Annie. That's something. Is it not?

So I make this resolution and I straighten my shoulders and set my cap tight on my head and I'm good like this for all of ten or fifteen seconds. But, hell. The truth of the matter is that I *do* have a lonely soul, or maybe just a sick and weak one.

How else to explain myself? I'm born into the Church and raised in a good family, and I still to this day know my catechism backward and forward. I can't plead ignorance. But I know, as I've said, that I've a sickness in my heart, an abnormality. The priests have told me. So maybe the Good Lord forgives me. I'm like a tuberculosis case that coughs; it can't be held against me. Still, I begin the slow shuffle homeward.

But, like a shooting-gallery duck running its course, I change directions again and start back for Wellington's.

Why, oh why? I suppose a lot of things have come together at once. Caroline's a fine-looking girl, of course. And she's got a queer way of phrasing words that interests me — that way she has of making insensible ideas sound sensible. But I've met girls before. Lots of them.

Things have fallen off between Annie and myself. But that's to be expected, really, when a wife is carrying a child in her. It's not the first time I've done without *that*. Maybe it's the hard times. Albert's jazz about cutting expenses. All the news in the papers about the stocks, and the men who own them, crashing. Maybe this entire affair is about nothing more than Horton Moon grabbing himself a little piece of happiness before the whole damn world comes down on my head and I find myself standing on a bread line like Dick Reilly and Stevey Brown and Pat Theile and Junior Dewey and all the rest of them. Seems half the parish have become charity cases.

Or maybe it's the season. The Minnesota nights are cold now, and the Christmas songs are being played, and after the holidays it's nothing ahead but a long, black winter of sadness and hardship, and that's enough to make any sane man tear his clothes off and run mad. I guess that's as good an explanation as any.

But, anyway, I'm not in the mood for explanations. When a man makes a conscious decision to sin against the Holy Roman Catholic Church, he could spend the remaining days of his life explaining that decision or he could spend the remaining days of his life just living. Because it's one or the other. You can't have both. And I've decided on the living.

This time I stop at the Chicago corner and I look both ways, real careful, and I cross the slippery cobblestones as if I'm trying to *count* the damn things through the soles of my boots.

I'm up the stoop and under the dirty awning and my hand is on the door when I pause, for just a few seconds, and take in the sadness of a girl like Caroline "taking her supper" at a shithole like this every Friday night. This pause lasts only a few seconds, of course, because I'm in a state where I cannot pity Caroline and I cannot feel too much the sadness of the low, woodframe chophouse — my mind's gone on ahead of me, like an arrow released from a bow, and I open the door and step out of the cold night and into the hot, smoke- and grease-smelling rooms of Wellington's.

There are a dozen tables, set close together. Every table is occupied. The room is crowded but nobody is talking. At most of the tables, solitary men sit staring down at their flatware. I don't see any single women. There's a few couples, sullen, silent. I catch on right away that this is a sorry crowd. A waiter — no, two waiters — move between the tables, shuffling sideways through narrow gaps between chairs.

The yellow light is bad, and an oil heater close by is making me feel sweaty, and I'm about to say to hell with it and leave when one of the waiters moves and I spot Caroline at a table near the window.

I don't think she sees me, but she does. I mean, she looks up from her bread and her eyes meet mine and then she goes back to her bread like I'm a piece of furniture. Or like I'm a stranger come through the door.

All right, then. Off comes my cap and I make for Caroline's table, when one of the waiters, a big Greek bastard, steps in front of me. He stands like a closed door. A thought comes into my brain about what a laugh it is for this Greek to be guarding his joint like it's the dining room of a downtown hotel. It's a laugh, and I have to smile even though I'm standing there staring into the Greek's tie and, by rights, I should be insulted that he's acting so high on me.

"*Kanna halp-pwew*?" He breathes on me.

Yeah, I want to say. You can *halp* me by getting your fat smelly Greek ass out of my way. But this one isn't even going to get an answer out of me. I just move my head to one side and motion with my hand towards Caroline's table.

The Pride Of The Mediterranean turns toward Caroline and the look she gives him seems to satisfy him just fine, so he steps sideways and lets me go past.

I sit down opposite Caroline.

"Nice place," I say to her.

I know, right away, that this bit of sarcasm is a terrible thing to say. It occurs to me again that this *is* a shithole, and it *is* awful to think of a lonely young girl from out of town taking her supper here regularly — regularly not because this is where she wants to be, but only because maybe once, months ago, she came in here bone-weary at the end of the week, and the room at least was quiet and the Greeks maybe smiled when they dropped the bread on the table in front of her, and she was newly arrived in the big terrible city and she was too tired and scared to look further for someplace else. And almost immediately after I have this thought, I feel all at once very glad that I didn't go back home when I thought I should, back outside on the streetcorner — I'm glad that, for whatever reason, I've made the decision to go ahead with this.

"I'm sorry," I say. "It's a good place, Wellington's."

"Oh," she says. "I like it fine."

"I only thought the Greek was a bit hard."

Caroline smiles at the room over my shoulder. "That's Stavi. He's like that. Don't mind."

"I don't mind. Besides," I say, and I duck my chin down and do that thing with my eyes, like a movie actor, "any place with you in it is the swellest joint in town."

And I see by the look of her that I've had an effect. Though not the effect I'd been going for. That is, she looks pleased. Not swooning with whatever I'd imagined I would set her swooning with, but pleased.

"I'm happy." She looks down at the breadcrust she holds in her hand, blinking at it for a second like she's forgotten what it is. "I'm happy you came."

"Did you think I could stay away?"

"I didn't think anything. That is, I tried not to. But I suppose you could have. Could have stayed away, I mean."

And I could have. Yes. *Did you think I could stay away* was just a line I was handing her. I make a promise to myself now: no more lines. The poor girl deserves better than movie-star eyes and lines. For Christ's sake. If I'm to do this then I'll at least treat her properly.

"Well," I say, and now big Stavi has sidled up alongside the table and my eyes make the climb from his wide hips up his vest buttons and into his dumb dull dark eyes sunk in a flabby gray face. "I've only come for the Hamburg steak. It's all the talk among the finest people."

So I order a chopped beef sandwich. When the Greek leaves us alone I lean my elbows on the table, bending my face in close to Caroline's.

"I need to speak to you about something," I say.

She nods, her eyes wide and her pretty mouth chewing slowly on a small wad of bread.

"Caroline," I say. "I'm a married man."

Her mouth twists sideways. She swallows. "But — how is it that they say it — your wife doesn't understand you?"

I shake my head. "My wife understands me fine."

"But you're not in love with her?"

"No. I *am* in love with her."

"But," Caroline frowns, speaking more slowly. "she doesn't make you happy?"

"She mostly makes me as happy as I'm able to stand."

I'm thinking now, I swear to Christ, about kissing Annie's hand at the supper table. After we'd done our Bergen-and-Snerd act. When I looked up then into Annie's bright, brown eyes, there seemed to be an understanding in them of just how deeply the ache of love pained me at that moment.

Caroline leans her own elbows on the table now and she comes in close to me. "So, what? Why are you here?"

"You asked me to come."

"No, I didn't," she says, which is — I realize — true. "And anyway, that's not what I mean. What are you looking for here? You just looking for an adventure?"

I can't help smiling. "My life is adventure enough."

There's only a few inches between our faces and I can feel the heat coming off her flushed cheeks. Her eyes narrow slightly. "I'm not sure I like playing games, Horton Moon."

"Don't you?" I ask. "But what else is this but a game?"

And, mind you, this is not a line I'm throwing at her. I've resolved to speak straight with her.

Caroline's face changes. The flush is going from her cheeks. "What kind of game is this?" she says.

"A grand game," I say.

"But, you think, harmless?"

"It isn't harmless at all. We're none of us going to come out of it alive."

"I don't want to play."

"No choice, I'm afraid."

Now her elbows are off the table and she straightens in her chair and watches me from far away in her seat. "You're a queer man."

"I am."

"Well." She touches her yellow braid where it's pinned up in a heavy-looking bunch at the back of her neck.

"Well," I say back at her.

I don't like the way she's fading back. One minute she accosts me on the corner in front of the

Bohunk's store with talk of lonesome souls, and the next minute she's playing "you're a queer man, Horton Moon" and saying "well" to me. I don't like this.

"What were *you* looking for?" I ask her.

"I beg your pardon?"

"You heard me, love. What were you looking for? When you came here tonight."

"I always come here," she says, the pink coming up on her throat.

"But you don't always suggest to a man that he come join you. Or do you?"

"Of course not!"

"Then — "

"Okay," she says, a stifled shout.

"Okay, what?"

"Okay," she says, more calmly. She gets all the pieces of herself together. Her lovely mouth tightens into a mean little half-smile. Still lovely. "It's a game. It's a modern game. Me and you. Very modern."

I nod. Where's she going with this?

She says, "I suppose we aren't going to do it like, courtin' and spoonin' and you playing me tunes on a ukulele, and all that old-fashioned nonsense. Fine."

"Caroline," I say, my voice an apology, "I'm only trying to speak honestly to you about this — "

"I said, fine." She crosses her arms over her breasts. "You're married. I'm lonely. Maybe you're lonely, too. Although, I guess," she says, muttering like it's just a thought to herself, "that doesn't really matter."

"I did come here for you."

"Yes. I know." Her eyes are going to some place over my head. Maybe she's looking at Stavi, the Greek.

"And this afternoon," I say, wanting to bring her and her eyes back down to me, "you did say that — when we first met — you sensed something in me. We made some connection. I believe that to be true."

"Okay," she says.

I say, "I want to speak honestly with you. And I want us both to think clearly about what's going to happen. But it is complicated. You can't make it simple."

"Like I said, it's modern."

"Call it that if you like."

"I've got no problem with modern," she says. "It's good."

I tug on my ear. "I don't know if it's good or bad. But I'm here. And you're here. And — and — "

" — and here we are," Caroline says, smiling. It's the real thing now, this smile, her mouth showing big strong white teeth and her eyes taking me in. Taking me in like an opened flume draws in water — pulling, sluicing, sucking. Her arms are uncrossed now, and with one hand she reaches to touch the table in front of her. Just once, for luck.

Seven

On Christmas morning, the grass is showing through the patchy snow on the back lawn. We've had a thaw, and no new snow, and I suppose it's a pisser for the kids to wake up to a Christmas morning like this. Not like in the picture books and the postcards. Anyway, there's sweaters and mittens from Annie's sisters, and a box of candies from my folks. My brother from Chicago has sent a bag of nuts. I've hocked my watch — for less than it's worth — plus two sets of cuff links and a gold-plated tie pin, and I've bought Bridget a china-faced doll and the twins bow-and-arrow sets. Small Richard gets a thick tablet of paper and a box of fifty wax crayons.

I've given Annie a phonograph player. To be paid for in installments. We play a platter of Christmas tunes through the morning, and later, when the kids are off away in their rooms getting dressed for visiting the cousins, I put on a disk of show tunes.

Annie is bent near the tree, scooping crumpled wrap from the floor and smoothing it out between her hands, to be used again. She looks up at me, surprised, when the new music begins playing from the phonograph.

"Horton Moon," she says.

"Himself," I say.

I hold my hand out and she stands upright. Crosses the room to me and the music. She drops her salvaged wrap onto the davenport cushions and then grabs me round the waist, and we pull ourselves together.

She's growing big with the baby, her face getting round and double-chinned, her breasts heavier than normal. Her hands in mine are swollen. She is self-conscious of this change in her body, trying, I feel, to hold her belly slightly back from me. When I work my kisses downward to the fleshy softness of her throat, she turns her face away.

"Ah, Hort," she says.

"What's wrong?"

"I'm big as a house."

"You're lovely as a sultan's palace, is what you are," I say to her. "Open your gates and let me in."

She laughs at this, throwing her head back and grinning up into my face. She kisses me hard, holding onto my head with both her hands.

"You foolish man," she says, when our mouths break apart. "Don't you see? You're already in. You're already in."

And so I am. I take her closer, making her give up holding her belly back, and we don't kiss anymore but only dance. The living room is empty and the colored lightbulbs are shining on the Christmas tree, and Annie and I dance slowly — out of time with the music from the phonograph, which is playing quick and peppy. This dancing out of time bothers me a bit, in a very sneaky way, like the beginning of an itch I know I'll not be able to scratch.

I put my nose in close to Annie's hair and I try to sing, in a soft voice, along with the recording. But this only plays up the difference between the pace of our slow dance and the tune on the phonograph, and so I stop trying to sing into Annie's hair.

I guess we could have gone on dancing like that through the afternoon, Annie worrying about her swelling belly and me worrying over the time, but soon enough the kids come back in, dressed, and then the record ends and the new phonograph player is turned off and covered, and then before long we are all of us shouting and slapping at bottoms and hurrying to get out the door and across town to Annie's sister's place for roomfuls of cousins and eggnog and ham.

The afternoon is gay but things get ugly, late in the evening, when I have to leave. Annie follows me out onto the stoop and has scolding words for me, but I know she'll be okay with the kids. I've left them carfare to get back across to the Powderhorn. I need to go to the Frenchman's to see a man about something, I explain to Annie. Yes, on Christmas night. I'm sorry but it can't wait. And so I leave her there with the children and with her sisters, and I ride the streetcar alone back east.

On the streetcar, the electric heater blowing at my feet makes me feel warm and excited. I've got a belly full of my brother-in-law's eggnog, into which he mixes expensive Kentucky bourbon with a heavy hand. I'm feeling swell. I start to hum and it's a few seconds before I realize I'm humming the dance tune from the phonograph record this morning. A shadow passes across my happy mood. Remembering the way Annie's hair smelled like coffee and pine boughs when we danced in the living room, and remembering the itchy feeling that came over me from dancing off-time, I frown down at the floor of the streetcar. Just now, with Annie on the stoop of her sister's house, her standing there in the cold night telling me not to go, I'd become aware that we were out-of-syncopation in another way. Time was, Annie's scolding me like that would have cut me to the quick — might not have changed my leaving, but it would have soured my mood when I'd gone — but tonight, I could listen to her words like they were a stranger's playing over the radio. It was easiest thing to just walk away from her.

I sigh and I go on humming, being careful to select a new tune. I'm off to Columbus Avenue, to an apartment across the Powderhorn Park from our own place, where I have another, smaller, Christmas celebration awaiting.

Do I know exactly what I'm doing? No. I can't make that claim. I'm making things up as I go along.

I am not running away from my life with Annie. Despite what I say about the odd syncopation between us, I am in love with Annie, and with the life we have together. But Caroline is fresh and clean and new from the country, and she and I have got no history between us, no scars from earlier fights. She waits for me to come to her room in a yellow-brick apartment building on Columbus Avenue, and there I'm going.

It's been easier than I thought it might be. Caroline is nothing if she's not easy. My evenings with her are like time passed without effort. We laugh and talk about small things, and we make a game of exploring one another's bodies in her bed after the lights go out. Nothing to it. And so it should be. With Annie, with my wife, life and loving is a struggle. Not a chore, mind you, but a struggle. I've no complaints about that. It's as it should be. There is no struggle in Caroline. All of it, really, is utterly delightful to me — I can't quite believe how neatly I'm pulling this off. Having my cake and eating it too, so to speak. I have a wife I love and a girl who thrills me. Merry Christmas, indeed. I've never been merrier.

*

The New Year comes and goes and there's no bonus envelope from Albert. First time that's ever happened. Even in my first years with Albert, when the times were worse than now, he always came through with ten or twenty at the close of the year. Don't know what to make of this but, in any case, it's out of my hands.

Two weeks into January, I miss the first payment on Annie's phonograph-record player. I go down to the shop on Lake Street and have a talk with Larry Peat, who owns the place. Larry's a gem and he tells me that just this once it's nothing to worry over.

Sometimes, riding the streetcar to work, I find myself shooting back my cuff to check the time on the wristwatch that's no longer there. Hell of a thing. You can imagine.

But mostly I'm not bothered too much by thoughts of work or of money or lost wristwatches. I've got distractions. The air now is cold and clean and the sky high and bright. My trench-spirit has passed, and I'm not drinking nearly as much as I'd been through the fall. Nights, the stars glint like diamonds over my head as I pass across the Powderhorn from my place toward the apartment where the girl waits for me.

*

Peterson is buying rounds and it's a very good night at the Frenchman's. It's six weeks into the new year and the fellas are happy as pigs in shit, with free drinks coming in, and I'm right there with them.

"What? Another?" I ask Peterson, as Elsen sets me up a third time.

"Why not, Hort? Life is short."

Why not, he says. "Thanks, Peterson," I say. "So. Out with it, now. What was it? You draw the numbers?"

Peterson gives his head a small shake. "I never play the numbers. Games of chance don't interest me."

"No?"

"No. I make my own luck."

"I see," I say. And of course Peterson wants me to ask him just what he means by that. But I'm not even curious. What the hell. He knocked over a jewelers. Or he fenced some stolen opium. I don't give a damn. I drink my beer.

"It's the kind of man I am, Horton," he says. "When things go well for me, things go *very* well. But you're not interested in listening to my ideas. That's fine. No hard feelings. The least I can do is buy you a few drinks."

I nod at the crowded room. "Me and a dozen of my closest friends."

"Whatever," Peterson says. "It's a drop in the bucket."

And, as if to illustrate the point, he tosses a bill onto the bar and waves to Elsen to keep it coming. I stare at the bill. Maybe Peterson really *did* knock over a jewelry store. These capers of his are usually good for one round. Two, if we're lucky. But tonight, Peterson shows no sign of slowing down.

It's almost enough to get my curiosity up.

But I drink off the last of my beer and stand away from the bar, holding my hand up at Peterson when he makes a protesting noise.

"Got to go," I say.

"Annie holding your reins in tight lately?"

"Now, didn't say I had to go *home*, did I?"

Peterson gives me a long look, which I take note of all the while I'm buttoning my jacket and knotting my scarf over my throat.

"You're a man of mystery, Horton Moon," Peterson says.

"I don't aim to be," I say, and I turn to face him. "I just have an engagement to meet a friend. I don't mean any offense to you and your hospitality."

"No offense taken," says Peterson. "Only — "

I'm about to turn and leave. I raise my eyebrows at him.

"Only," he says, "I do wish you'd give a moment. Just to hear me out. I've a proposition to make."

"Go ahead."

"Please," says he, and he motions me to step back to the bar, close to him. So I do.

Peterson lowers his voice. "Horton. You're a good friend and I look out for my good friends. I'd like to help you out."

"I don't need help."

"Oh, for the love of Christ — " Peterson says, sputtering. But he collects himself. "Listen, Horton. I'd like to help us *both* out — okay? See, I've got an idea for a job, but it's a job that requires two men. And there's no man I'd trust on this job as I'd trust you."

I know, by this, Peterson is referring to the way I covered his ass during his dust-up with Big Mike Doyle. This was years ago. Peterson stole a keg of beer from Mike Doyle's block party, and he caught heat for it. Peterson'd had to go into hiding, sleeping in the tulip beds out along Lake Calhoun for a month, and I'd played dumb even when Doyle sent a couple of fellas around to the apartment. Annie had just had the twins then, they were only babies, and she was spooked by Doyle's thugs. It was only a call she made to her Uncle Jack that got Doyle to leave me and Annie alone. Anyway, Mike Doyle eventually got sent down to Stillwater and Peterson was able to return to the Powderhorn.

To me, this is all ancient history. But what the hell. I've a little bit of a beer drunk going.

"What kind of job is it?" I ask Peterson.

"I told you about the vending machines? The Jews and the vending machines?"

I'm growing hot under my woolen scarf. "I think you did, yes."

"These Jews run a syndicate. Hundreds of machines. Thousands of dollars."

"So. We buy a franchise?"

Peterson shakes his head. "We don't buy anything."

*

Caroline meets me at the door to her apartment. It's what they call an efficiency apartment, a single room with a kichenette against one wall. But it's not a sad room — the paint is fresh and the big window on the north wall is clean, and there's a new toilet and bath in an alcove behind the kitchenette.

I like the room best because it's not pretending to be a home. It's not pretending to be anything. Caroline rents it unfurnished, and in the year she's lived here she's placed nothing in the room but an iron bed with a firm mattress, a wobbly bridge table and two mismatched straightbacked chairs. One of the two chairs sits pushed in under the bridge table and the other chair is beside the bed, like a bedside stand, with a bottle and a glass on its seat. Just one glass, as Caroline won't drink.

I step past Caroline into the apartment and I go to the bed and I sit down, kicking off my shoes before swinging my feet up. I reach for the glass.

"Well, hello to you too," Caroline says, coming to me. She starts to loosen my scarf and it's only then that I realize I've not taken off my outside things.

I sit there and I let Caroline take away my scarf and my cap, and she unbuttons my jacket, and I sit more upright while she pulls my left arm out of its sleeve. My right hand still holds the glass.

"You'll have to put that down," she says.

"Good God," I say. I shake my head, as if I'm clearing my thoughts, but my thoughts aren't any clearer. "Sorry, Caroline. Sorry."

"What's happened to you?" she asks.

"Nothing at all. I'm sorry."

"Yes, you're sorry. You said that."

"I'm sorry."

We both smile at this. She takes up the glass, goes to the icebox for ice. Coming back, she pours whiskey from the bottle on the chair and she hands the drink to me.

"Rough day?" she asks.

I shake my head. "No. Only I had a conversation with a friend at the Frenchman's, just on my way over here."

"Bad news?"

"Nothing like that. He just talked about something that's got me distracted. Which is not good. Or it's *very* good — being distracted — depending on how you look at it. Anyway. It's got me in a state."

"Obviously."

"He made a proposition. That's all."

"I see."

Now I look at her and I see for the first time there's something off about her appearance.

"This a new dress?"

"It is."

"I don't like the color on you."

There's a second when hurt shows on her face. But it's only a second, and then she smiles and shrugs. "So, I'll take it off."

"Hold it, kid," I say, touching her hand where it's gone toward the buttons of her dress. "Not tonight."

"You can't stay?"

"I can stay. But keep your dress on." I take a swallow of the whiskey and I smile at Caroline. "Forget what I said. It's a swell color. It makes your skin look so pale. Like Gene Harlow."

She nods. "It's the dress but it's also a new powder I'm wearing. You like it?"

"I like it fine. You look like a million bucks."

"I want you to think I look like a million bucks."

"Well, I do."

"Shall I paint my nails? Paint them red, the color of blood?"

"Sure," I say. I start to relax. This is a game we play together.

"And rouge my lips to match? A dark red?"

"That might be nice," I say.

"You want me to bob my hair?"

"No," I say. "All the girls have bobbed hair now. It's ordinary. It used to be daring but now it's just ordinary. I think it's more daring to leave your hair long, like this."

"Does she have bobbed hair?"

"Who?"

"Annie. Your wife."

I sip my whiskey before answering. "No. I mean, she did. She had it bobbed years ago. But it's sort of grown out now. Let's not talk about that."

"Okay. Let's talk about me. What color dress would you like me in?"

"I told you. This color is swell."

"But, I'm asking. What color would be better?"

I roll my eyes. But this is our game, so I play. "Blue. I like you in blue. Dark blue."

"Indigo."

"Yes, indigo."

"When the spring comes, I'll wear a blue dress with pink flowers pinned in my hair."

"That sounds lovely."

"Will we walk in the park together?"

"Sure. We might."

"You won't be ashamed?"

"Ashamed?"

"Yes. Ashamed." She straightens her shoulders, rising taller beside me on the bed. "It's a fair question. We've been together most every night for a month now and you've never taken me out walking. Except for that first night, when you walked me home from Wellington's."

"It's been very cold."

"That's not it and you know it."

"Well, you know it too," I say sharply. "I'm a married man, Caroline — a husband and father. Don't be foolish."

"I'm not foolish," she protests, but then she kind of deflates and her eyes well up wet. "Oh — maybe I *am* foolish. Of course I am."

"Oh, Caroline," I say. Jesus. Why did I speak to her in that way?

"I don't know anything" she says. She's got control of her face and her eyes are clear. Her voice is steady and flat. "I'm just a dumb girl grown up on a farm in the middle of nowhere."

"Don't say that,' I tell her.

"It's true," she says. She won't meet my eyes now. "I have no idea about anything. I'm sorry. This is not the world I was born into."

"Now," I say, setting my glass down on the chair. "Look at me. Look at me. I've been nothing but an ass since I walked in the door tonight. Look at me. Caroline, you're not a fool. You're a bright girl and a good girl. I'm the fool here."

"You're not," she says, her eyes coming around now.

"I am," I say. "It's a fool who doesn't appreciate the good things he has. I have a girl like you, and all I do is drop by to sit on the bed wearing my coat and cap and speak to you in a coarse way. I'm a fool."

"Stop," she says, moving toward me on the bed. There's an urgency in her, not just in her voice but in the tenseness of the muscles in her arms and shoulders and hips, that reminds me that we don't have all the time in the world, as we never do, and it's not acceptable to waste our moments bickering.

"Stop," she says again, though I've not said a word. She kisses me, her lips closing over my own, hungry and desperate for quiet from all the talk.

*

When I rise to go, an hour later, she stays under the covers in the dark of the small room. I'm quiet while I dress myself, and I wait till my coat and cap are on before I reach for my shoes. But Caroline is not asleep.

"Tomorrow night?" Her voice, from the darkness in the bedclothes, comes to me without a trace of sleepy drawl. She is wide awake and has probably been watching me dress.

"Maybe tomorrow night," I say.

Caroline sniffs. "What was his proposition?" she asks.

"Proposition? You mean — ah. What I said before."

"Yes," she says. "At the Frenchman's. A fellow made a proposition. It put you in a state. You're still in a state."

"I am."

"So?"

I can't say anything at first because I haven't made up my own mind what to make of Peterson's idea. "It's about money," I say to Caroline.

"Money is good."

"Yes it is, Caroline." The room is dark but we can hear the smiles in each other's voices. "Goodnight."

"Goodnight, Horton" she says. "Come back soon."

Eight

The baby is born in the last week in March. The ladies from the parish take up a collection to help pay the hospital bill. The new baby is named Stanley, after one of Annie's cousins, and the pup is strong as a bull ox with a set of lungs in him that can shake the windows when he cries. Easter morning, he's the star of St. Mary's, with every woman in the church cooing over him like he's the first baby they've ever seen. A week later, we have the baptism, and Jack Morrison slips Annie a gift envelope. Later, she shows me that the envelope contains twenty-five crisp, new dollars. After I fall asleep that night, Annie hides the money from me and I never see it again.

*

It's late when I arrive back to the Lake Street office. I've parked the panel van in the lot behind and I hurry up the steps, taking them two at a time and slinging my tool sack off my shoulder as I reach the top. But when I reach the top and when I rush through the office toward the storeroom for to stash the tools and break for the exit, Albert stands up from behind his desk and eyes me with a "hold on, there, Horton" frown. So I hold on there.

But it's a lovely springtime evening and the light is only just now fading in the cold blue sky and I really, really want to be out the door and on my way eastward to the Powderhorn and to Caroline.

I'm taking her out tonight. We'll go to the Chink's on Hiawatha Avenue, to the place we've made "our place," and we'll take our normal table and we'll order our chop suey and beer, and after we eat I'll put a nickel in the juke box and Caroline and I will dance peppy to the jazz, or dance slow to a crooner. And maybe tonight I'll spend the night with her, because I do that now as often as not. It's late in April and the air is rising warm. Only now Albert wants me to hold up.

Albert is not a man who likes to talk. He's only given me this frown three times before — once when I came up short on the register and once when I received a parking ticket in the panel van and once when I told old Glynn to fuck himself. Albert doesn't like to talk and it pains us both when he's forced to talk by conditions such as these, so my face sets to frowning right along with his.

"Albert?" I say.

"I need a word with you, Horton."

"Of course," I say. I go to his desk and he sits down and so I do, too, in the chair across the way.

Glynn and I have been getting on all right and there's been no traffic tickets or accounting errors, and so I'm feeling a bit sweaty as to what this is going to be all about.

"Lovely day," I say, hoping to lose the frowns between the two of us. "Sun was bright and the grass was green on the boulevards. Were you in all day?"

But Albert doesn't even make like he's heard me. He goes on frowning, now not at me but down at the blotter on his desk.

"Horton," he says quietly. "You are my employee. But you are also my friend."

"Yes," I say, my gut sinking. It's never good when somebody tells you you're their friend, is it?

There is a long stretch of quiet now, and then Albert starts up talking very fast. "I don't know the proper way to have a conversation like this and I won't pretend I *do* know. I'll just tell you what I have to tell you. You're a married man, Horton. Married with five babies. Your Annie, bless her, is as good a woman as God made. And you're — " here he pauses for just the quickest intake of breath before, " — you're running around with that fat blond tart. You're behaving like a bastard. And like an idiot."

I'm slapped in the face and I can't respond.

Albert goes on. "You're not an idiot, Horton. I know you well enough to know that. But you're behaving like one. You think you can carry on this way with no consequences. But people notice. People talk. You're a disgrace."

I can feel my color's up in my face. I find I've been holding my breath. I let it out.

"Are you finished?" I ask.

"No, I'm not," Albert says. "You've been with me for five years, and — as I said — you're not just my employee. Somebody needs to talk to you and tell you to stop behaving like a stupid kid. You're ruining your life and you're ruining your family. You may even be ruining the girl."

"Are you finished *now*?"

"I suppose I am," Albert says. He flaps his hands across the desk in my direction. "I imagine you've got something to say. Some explanation or excuse."

"I don't have to explain anything to you. I don't have to make any excuses."

The tone of my voice must surprise Albert. I can see it in his face when he looks up at me from his desk blotter.

"Listen, Albert," I say. "I do good work for you. Six days a week, no complaints. If you've got a point to make about my work habits, make it. If you've got a point to make about my personal life, shove it up your ass."

"Now, Horton. Just a minute."

"Because," I say, "after I drop my tools here at the shop, I'm on my own time. My life then is my business. Not yours."

"You don't need to turn on me, Horton. I'm trying to help you."

"I don't know *what* you're trying to do, but it's got nothing to do with helping me."

Albert's got a face on him now like he's fit to start bawling. He spreads his hands on the desktop and stares at his fingers.

"Hort," he says. "Glynn thinks you've been drinking too much."

"Ah fer the love of —"

"Hort, please. Listen. Glynn may be onto something. Sometimes, when a man gets to drinking too hard, his judgement becomes clouded."

I tap my feet on the floor and stare at Albert. "You people have me all figured out, don't you?"

"Just listen."

"You've all been giving me a lot of thought."

"Well," he says. "We have. Yes. You've got friends who think about you. That's nothing to get cross about."

"I've got friends?" I say, laughing. "No, Albert. No. I've got a date, is what I got." I stand up. "I must be going. If you're finished with me."

"I'm not finished with you."

"Well," says I, feeling all at once like Patrick Henry or like William Powell, "*I'm* through with *you*. I'm a plumber, goddammit. And it seems like what you want here is a kid brother to advise. I'm leaving."

And I go from the room and down the stairs and I hit the sidewalk on Lake Street, too mad still to taste the cold spring air or to notice the pale sky going dark. I walk until I reach the ballpark at Nicollet Avenue, when I notice my shirt is wet from sweating and I realize I have a cigarette burning between my fingers. I can't remember lighting it. I drop the butt on the ground and hop up onto a streetcar, heading east. I find a seat and sit down. If I think about what just happened with Albert, I start to sweat again. Forget about cutting expenses; now Albert's looking at me like a *liability*. And so I don't think about that but think instead about the sounds and the smells of the streetcar — the hum and the bells and the clacking over switches and the fresh charge of electricity and the sweet scent of new rattan on the seats — and about the nice ankles of the colored girl in the seat across the aisle from me.

*

"Peterson," I say. "Let's not talk in loops."

On the stool beside me, Peterson smiles into his cigarette smoke for a few long seconds before responding.

"Loops, Hort?"

"I'm coming at you straight," I say. "So if you'd please to shut up about golf and putting and playing the lie or whatever it is you're saying by way of avoiding the straight talk —"

He laughs. "Okay. Okay, Horton. Let's be straight. No more loops."

"Please," I nod.

"You want to talk about it now?"

"We have already talked about it." I say. "I want more than to talk about it."

Peterson stares up at the bottles on the wall behind Elsen. He sucks on his cigarette and then nudges his glass an inch forward atop the bar, toward Elsen. When Elsen reaches for the glass, Peterson jerks his chin sideways toward mine.

"Couple more, if you would, Mr. Elsen."

He waits till Elsen has serviced us and moved down the bar toward the three Healey brothers. Then Peterson touches the rim of his glass but he doesn't drink.

"It's like this, Horton," he says. "I have an idea. It's not even a plan yet. Only an idea."

"Right. The vending machines."

"Not so fast, there, Horton."

"Not so fast?"

"We're treading into dangerous ground here. We mustn't run ahead." He glances sideways at me and catches the look on my face, which makes him laugh again. "Sorry. I'm going into loops again, aren't I?"

"A bit," I say. "Yes." I drink my beer thirstily, till I've got to come up for air. "Tell me about this idea of yours."

"The Jews are tough sons of bitches. I'll tell you that right off the bat. Don't even listen to my first word till you've accepted that. These bastards don't fuck around."

"I hear."

"They're smart as hell, but the way they've really got ahead is, they're ruthless as the devil. They catch you crossing them and they'll rip the guts out of you and fill your mouth with stones and drop you in the river." Peterson says this and he stares at me hard. "I'm not planning on them catching us."

"Let's talk about your idea."

"Vending machines," he says, "Candy, gum, sodapop. Also jukeboxes."

"It's penny stuff."

"Pennies add up. And — this is the beauty part — the syndicates don't play strictly by the rules. I mean, they don't like bank deposits and accounting to the revenue people. They keep a lot of this stuff off the books, out of sight."

"Easy to do, I guess, with pennies."

"Thousands of pennies. Bags, boxes, crates of pennies."

"Where do they hold it?"

"In warehouses. North side."

"You know any northside Jews?"

"I got a cousin who works in one of the warehouses. He's a gimp — he can't really work with us on this — but he mans the door of the dock, and he's seen it all. Coming and going."

"I think I'd like to meet this cousin of yours."

"That's my idea, yes. I'd like us all three to sit down together and have a nice talk."

"You make arrangements for that, then." I stand up and touch the buttons on my leather windbreaker.

"You're not staying?"

"I've got a date across the park. Spring is bursting over the city and the grass along the boulevards is coming alive green. You just make arrangements with your gimp cousin."

When I leave Peterson at the bar, I feel drunk and happy. Maybe it's from what we've talked about, or maybe it's from what I've said to Albert earlier in the evening, or maybe it's from thinking of

Caroline waiting for me. Or maybe it's just the beer. I can't tell. I don't really care.

When I reach the park I can see the grass on the slope above the lake, and even in the gathering dark I can see that it's a green lawn, growing greener. And though the cooling evening air makes me fasten the buttons of my windbreaker, the green lawn makes me think of the summer that's coming and of all the hot, long days, the good weather heading our way.

*

That night, Caroline and I don't go the Chink's. Caroline is tired from work, she says, too beat to go out dancing. Too beat for anything. I don't care. I feel a little worn out myself, if you really want to know. We can have fun anyway. We can stay in like we do most nights.

Most nights we spend up in Caroline's little efficiency apartment. The days are growing longer now, and so when we sit together on the bed beneath the big window the light from the sky outside fills the room, fading slowly, and we don't turn on the electric lamp that sits on the chair-seat beside us, but only let the evening dark come upon us as it will.

I sip bourbon from a glass Caroline keeps filling, and we tell each other stories.

We still play the same games we did in the beginning, imagining film-star gowns I'd dress her in if I was a millionaire, swapping dreams of fancy downtown restaurants we'd step out in if we could. But we've begun telling each other real-life stories, as well.

My stories are stories I've told before, to other girls, to friends, to Annie. But I get the sense that, when Caroline tells me about herself, she is telling her stories for the first time.

She talks about growing up on the farm. The work was hard, but she mostly doesn't remember the hard work. She tells of the North Dakota winters, when the snow dropped from the sky like from an enormous overturned bowl, falling hard for days until it would stop up the door of the house. She'd had to help her brothers shovel pathways, tunnels almost, through the snowfall to reach the cattle barn across the yard. In the springtime when the snowmelt made the creeks rise fast and cold, she'd run — run just from joy at feeling the sun on her face — through the high grasses that exploded, in brilliant color, with wildflowers. In summer these same grasses would be burned white under the sun, and she'd walk slowly through the prairie, letting the thistles catch and pull on her long dress till the gingham would be torn, because she would be far away, dreaming of broad seas and high mountains from the story books that her mother read to her.

"Tell me about the birds in the rain," I say to her.

"The birds?"

"The chickens. In the summer rain. When it rains so hard."

Caroline smiles. "I've told you that story."

"Tell me again," I say.

"Okay," she says. "When the summer rains come, we all need to round the chickens up and drive them into the barn. Because the rain can come hard, and sometimes it falls so steady and full that it can drown the animals."

Drowned by the rain. Can you imagine a land like that?

Caroline tells me about her father, who is cool and silent but kind-hearted. She tells me about how gentle his hands were when he pulled the thistles from her skirt hems and touched his fingertips, soothing, over the raw scratches the grasses made on the flesh above her summer boots. Caroline tells me about her mother, who is quick-minded, a reader of books, and who seemed often mildly, vaguely dissatisfied with her life in a way that Caroline as a girl could never understand.

Caroline's eyes well and shine with fresh tears whenever she tells a story of her brother Robert, who died from the fever the summer that Caroline was ten years old. Robert was older, and very handsome, and he'd been to Fargo three times.

Caroline laughs when she tells me about her sister Melissa, who cried the first time she saw an automobile, and who still now, at age sixteen, believes that speaking on the telephone can make a person's brain sick with tumors. When she was growing up on the North Dakota farm, Caroline's family did not have a telephone, or an automobile, or a radio, or a gas oven. When Caroline first came to Minneapolis and when she started her job at the Taylor's house on Stevens Avenue, she used to open and close the electric icebox six times a day, just to marvel that the steel racks inside continued to be cold. Her sister Melissa, she guessed, would not trust to eat any food kept in such a modern machine.

Caroline laughs at herself when she tells the story of discovering the Taylor's electric icebox, and when she tells me about how she walked the mile across town to work for the first week because she was afraid to board the loud, sparking, Lake Street streetcar. But I don't laugh along with her. I don't think it's funny. It breaks my heart to think of her that way.

When I tell my own stories, about stealing cigars at nine years old and getting sick from them into the Powderhorn Lake, or about throwing rocks at the cop wagon when they came to take away the Mallick brothers (neighborhood bootleggers), or about Stingo Lear losing the tips of two fingers under the Cedar Avenue streetcar while trying, in his normal clumsy way, to lay pennies for flattening, I can't tell these stories with the same happy relish I'd used to. Now I think of Caroline, coming into this mess from her clean place out on the western plains, coming into the grime of the Twentieth Century from the Nineteenth. I know that last bit sounds funny. She was born into the same age as me, but the miles between the Powderhorn and the prairie stretch for me like an arc of time. She is from another time, one I cannot know. When I think about the way, our first evening together at Wellington's, she called our affair "modern," it pains me. Makes my throat ache to remember it. The more she tells me stories about her life in North Dakota, the more I find myself, afterwards, dreaming dreams about this exotic other world much like young Caroline herself daydreamed of faraway oceans and mountain ranges. Only I've got her.

I've got Caroline here with me, and her North Dakota farm is not a storybook land but a real place. A place that is part of her. As I learn more and more of her stories and see the ways her eyes brighten or her voice catches with laughter when she speaks them, I feel excitement at how, in such a terribly real way, she is bringing this other, foreign world into my own. The time is speeding up, the gap between our two centuries closing.

Maybe I'm putting too much weight onto this. Maybe I'm being carried away by the whiskey that I'm drinking when we're together. Caroline and I are having a time. And it is a good time. But it is only what it is. I am still a married man, with a wife I love.

My Annie is a city girl, built small and hard, run through with muscles like the tendons in a fist; her body seems made for gripping me and taking me up and shaking me till I'm nearly broken with the pleasure of loving her. (Or so I remember it. It's been too long since she and I wrestled ourselves together in this way.) The heat that would rise between Annie and myself, when we were together, could sear like the glow at the tip of a burning stick. Caroline and I, though, are cool together. I am comforted by the plain openness of her. Like the prairie in the stories she tells, her horizons are unobstructed. She is gentle in the dark, and in light the air around her seems cleansed, becoming the wind-whipped, grass-scented air of the west she was born into.

Of course you know, I'm not talking strictly about the physical here. The stories Caroline and I tell to one another, in her bed with the light going from in the window above us, these stories *are* bringing some other, deeper, things into play. I can't deny it. And I can't really explain it, either. Except to admit that, maybe, this is a kind of falling that I've never known before, a kind of falling that has nothing to do with crooner's ballads or Hollywood sound stages strewn with rose petals. This is something else altogether. And, just as you'd think, with a fella like me getting involved in bending time and pulling separate worlds together, it's all more than a little frightening.

Nine

On Sunday mornings like this, when the late-April air is warm already just an hour past sun-up, I feel almost like skipping Mass. It's not like in winter, when the Sunday mornings are dark and the air bitter with hard cold. Then, it doesn't take much thinking to head into the church and sit in the candlelight and incense. But on a morning like this — even with a hangover — I feel good and happy and like I could go out and face the day with or without the priest's blessing.

But thinking like this passes through my head quick as smoke and then I'm back to real life and the kids making noise. Dragging their feet.

"Get a move on," I say to Ralphie, who's playing with his shoelaces.

"Not ready yet," he mumbles.

So I give his pants a kick. Just softly.

Frank looks up from reading Friday's funny papers. "What's the N.R.A.?" he asks.

"Where is your jacket?" I answer him.

"It's the government," Ralphie says to Frank, rising from where he's been sprawled on the floor from my kick. "Like the F.B.I."

"It's not," Bridget says, passing through the kitchen toward the door. "It's charity. The F.B.I. are policemen. The N.R.A. is charity."

"Ray Sellick says only churches are charity," Ralphie says.

"Whatever you call it," Bridget says, "The N.R.A. helps people who need help." The door closes behind her.

"Frank," I say, "where is your jacket?"

"What's it stand for?" he asks me.

"What — your jacket?"

"No!" he says.

"N.R.A.!" Ralphie shouts. "National-Recovery-something."

I scowl down at the two of them. Ganging up on me now. "Frank. Get your jacket on your back or I'll slap you sick. Ralphie. Shut up about the damn N.R.A."

"Horton," Annie sighs, coming up from behind now. "Language, please."

"Daddy said, 'damn'!" small Richard says, his voice rising. And it's a voice that goes right through my hangover. I cringe.

He's holding onto Annie's skirt. Annie's holding baby Stanley, who is sleeping.

"Mama," Ralphie starts in, "what's the *A* in N.R.A. stand for?"

"Association!" Frank says.

"Aggravation!" I say.

"Administration," Annie says. "It's like the government charity."

"Charity!" Frank says, happily. "The government is taking over for the churches!"

"Something like that, yes," I say, and I grab him by the neck and pull him toward the door. I've got his jacket in my other hand. He drops his funny papers on the floor as we go out the door onto the stoop.

The sun out here is nearly hot, and it feels so good I want to stop and light a cigarette. But not till after Mass. Frank wiggles into his jacket and then hops down the stoop where Bridget is waiting, pacing in circles on the edge of the sidewalk. Annie comes out behind me, trailing small Richard. Baby Stanley is sleeping still. Ralphie comes out last.

"Bridget," I call down to her. "Get off the grass. It'll spoil your shoes."

"Please don't shout," Annie says to me.

"Was I shouting?"

"You were. You're going to wake Stanley."

"Then," I say, "you'll not hear another word from me till noon."

"Oh, stop it," she says.

And what's she mean by that tone? I blink at her and she makes a face back at me.

"You're like another child," she says sharply. "Just behave yourself, please."

So that's how it is. I get thick in the throat and I feel my fists balling up. But I open my hands and let them hang loose at my sides. Okay, then. We go on, walking the four blocks to St. Mary's, and I don't speak more than three words — just enough to keep the kids from slaughtering one another on the march.

After Mass it's a quicker walk home, and then Annie sets to frying eggs and bacon at the stove. The twins are in the back yard with small Richard, and Bridget's taken Stanley to the front room, where she's dancing him about to the music on the radio.

"Again you didn't take the Host this morning," Annie says to me through the bacon smoke.

"Yes. That's right."

"Any reasons?"

"Only my own reasons," I say, making the newspaper snap as I hold it open in front of me. It was a long Lent without bacon for me, but now Annie cooks it up once a week, every Sunday. My mouth is wetting from the smell of it frying. So I tell Annie as much.

"*Ach*," she responds to this. *Ach* — not even a word but a sound, an ugly sound.

"What's with you, then?" I ask. I lower the newspaper.

Annie just makes that sound again, but then she brushes, with the back of her hand, at a bit of hair fallen across her forehead. "Horton. You might make Confession."

"Confession?"

"Confession. Speak to the Father. You haven't taken Communion in six weeks."

"You've been keeping count?"

"The children. They do notice, you know. The entire congregation of adults stands and goes to the altar, and you're the only man sits back."

"That's enough of that," I say. And that should do it. I go back to the story I've been reading in the newspaper.

After thirty seconds or so, I speak from behind the paper, shaking my head: "Children discussing the Recovery Administration. It's modern times, ain't it?"

"Horton!" she shouts, dropping the fork on the stove. "Shut up! Have you not heard a word I've said?"

My God. When has Annie ever used such a tone with me?

She leaves the stove and crosses the kitchen to me. "Tell me. How can you live with yourself? How can you? Never mind me. Never mind. But what of the babies? What of Bridget and Frank and Ralphie and Richard? And Stanley? What of them? How can you live with yourself going to the church beside them and you sitting through the Communion because your soul is too filthy for you to rise and take the Host? Have you no shame at all?"

Annie is trembling, I can see, but her voice doesn't give anything away. "Or is it worth all that to you — does that thing mean more to you than your own blood? Does she?"

With that I'm up. I mean to leave straight away but Annie steps in front of me, blocking the door. When I try to shove past her she stays planted, leaning her weight into my shoulder. Well. Say what you will about Horton Moon — I'm a shit and a bastard and a sorry son-of-a-bitch — but I will not strike a woman. So I just stand there and she just stands there. I plunge my hands into my trouser pockets and keep my eyes on the ceiling. Annie is staring at me, trembling, but her eyes are hard and her mouth is set. She won't cry and I won't talk.

"The bacon," I say after a long while, when the greasy smoke in the air starts growing thick and black. "Burning."

"I don't care," she says.

"I'd like to go out for a walk," I say.

Now I see she squeezes her eyes shut, like she's holding back tears. Only when she looks back at me her eyes are dry.

"I'd like to go for a walk, too, Hort. I think I'd like very much to take myself on a long walk."

Annie unties her apron and drops it on the countertop beside the stove and then she takes up her coat from the peg in the hallway and then she goes out the back door. I watch her out the window as she walks past the twins wrestling in the damp grass and she disappears round the corner down the alley. So what the hell now? I turn the gas off under the smoking bacon. I hear the baby crying and when I turn around I see Bridget there coming in from the front room with Stanley getting fussy in her arms.

"Did Mama go out?" Bridget asks.

"She did," I say. And then I let out a curse. I've burned my hand on the fucking skillet.

*

I come to work on Monday morning, same as always, and Albert doesn't say anything more about our conversation on Friday night. He looks a little embarrassed when I walk in the office, and for a minute I get the feeling he's thinking the whole thing was a big mistake and maybe he's even wanting to apologize for butting himself into my affairs. But when I give him a grin and a "good day," he frowns at me with a face like he just took a swallow of bad milk.

"You'll be in the shop today, Horton," he says. "I'll take Tony out with me. We've some calls out west, other side of the lakes. Be out till the end of the day."

He talks over some paperwork with Glynn and pulls on his jacket and picks up his tools. Then he leaves without saying goodbye.

"*He's* in a friendly mood, isn't he?" I say to Glynn.

But Glynn just takes up the paperwork and goes to the big desk in the corner, where he commences studying the forms like they're a lost Gospel. I'm left standing alone to man the telephone. No one calls.

Ten

What an evening, this. Warm air like a woman's breath and the twilight in a big arch overhead going greenish-blue — turquoise is the word. I'm crossing the Powderhorn under the May trees, their branches already heavy with leaves, and under the sky already going turquoise with the dusk. I guess I'm wobbling a little over the pathway. I had a few whiskeys, *several* I suppose you'd say (though only a boy or a bitch counts them) back at the Frenchman's, and I'm now feeling the effects.

Sometimes, and I know you understand what I mean when I say this, sometimes it's kind of not-so-bad to feel loose on your feet and to just let yourself go wobbly. To weave on the pathway, slipping your shoes over the grass occasionally. We're not saints, for Christ's sake. We're only human. And whiskey *does* that to a human. Nothing especially wrong with this. It's nature.

So here I am, weaving a bit and holding my knees kind of stiff so's I don't pitch forward into a drunk run, when I come across Dumb Tim Young. I'm midway across the park, past the lake, when I see Tim. He's standing at the edge of the pathway, holding a rake.

Tim Young and I were in school together. He's one of six brothers. All of them big blonde thick-necked Scandehoovians like Tim. Tim isn't really dumb. He's deliberate, I guess. Slow-talking. But he was never book-smart, and back in school we all took to calling him Dumb Tim and the name stuck, the way some names stick. Poor bastard. Anyway, here he is, in the middle of the Powderhorn standing beside the walkway with a rake.

"Good evening, Tim!" I call out to him. Too loud, I guess.

"Horton," he says back.

I'm about to ask Tim what he's doing standing beside the pathway when it occurs to me that he'd seen me coming toward him, before I saw him, and he's actually stepped off the pathway as I approached. To let me pass.

"I can't help but notice," I say, pointing a finger toward Dumb Tim. "You are holding a rake."

"Yes," he says.

"A rake," I say.

"I work for the Administration. This is my job."

I wave my arm around, taking in all of the beautiful park under the darkening turquoise sky. "But it is night," I say.

"My day is done, yes," Tim says. "I'm only heading back to the pavilion."

"The pavilion!" I say, giving the word special emphasis to let Tim know that I understand everything now. I guess. I mean, it is the whiskey. I'm not now, when I speak, really tightly controlling what gets emphasized and what doesn't.

"How've you been, Hort?"

"Splendid," I say.

"Annie's well?"

"Never better."

"I heard she had trouble with the last baby."

"Nothing," I say, motioning away the thought. "Nothing at all. Doctors now. Miracle workers. Fit as a fiddle."

"Well. That's good news."

"Good news all around."

"Beg pardon?" Dumb Tim shifts his rake.

"News. Good," I say. "Your job. My wife. Everything splendid."

Tim looks like he's thinking about this for a few seconds. "Yes. You're still working?"

"Of course! What do you mean by that?"

"Don't mean anything, Horton. Only, a lot of fellows are out of work. It's the times."

"Sure," I say. "Hard times."

"And I seen you around."

"Around where?" I ask.

"Oh. You know. Here and there. Around."

"I'm a plumber, Tim. I make calls in the neighborhood."

"Sure you do. It's the nature of the job." We're quiet, both of us. If it was later in the season, there'd be crickets and mosquitoes, and we'd hear them in the quiet between us.

"Anyway," Tim says.

"Anyway," I say.

"Good to speak with you, Horton."

"You, too."

"You know," Tim says, "if things do change. If you need any help. This is a good thing."

I'm looking at the rake, which he's raised up.

"The rake?" I ask.

He laughs. "The *job*. The job's a good thing. It's a federal project. Real work. Beats the bread line."

"I'm sure it does, Tim. Thanks for the advice."

"Just in case, I'm saying."

"Sure. I get you. Just in case."

Tim steps off the grass, onto the pathway, and he nods at me as he walks past me, going the opposite direction. "Take it easy, Horton. Best to Annie for me."

"Right," I say, and I start off again, no less stiff-kneed or wobbly, still feeling the whiskey. That

Tim. I make a promise to myself to never call him Dumb Tim again. That's a terrible name to stick a poor bastard with. From the fourth grade, it was. He's not such a bad guy at all, that Tim.

By the time I reach the far end of the park, the sky is dark above me and the lights have come up in the windows of the houses across the street. I was in one of these houses once, years ago. I came with Albert on a call and we were let in the back way, and as I climbed the wide stairway to the upper floor where the trouble was, I'd stopped and stood on a landing, looking out a big clean window at the view of the Powderhorn stretching out like a tablecloth spread on the table of a rich man. To think of living a life like that, with your windows showing nothing but open air and acres of green. It was something to envy, if I was the type. But I wasn't the type to envy, and I'm not still; I'm happy enough with my lot in life — and why shouldn't I be? Tonight I've got a belly full of whiskey sitting nice, and I'm walking in the warm May evening air towards a girl who's waiting for me with heat between her hips.

Beyond the park, I weave and wobble and maybe I let go with bits of a song or two. I'm feeling fine.

But it's a long walk to Caroline's place, and by the time I reach her I'm nearly sober. I let myself in with the key she's given me, and I pass through the narrow hallway, past the tall, silent doorways of the other tenants, slowing when I come to the room of the old Polock who they say hasn't left his room in years. I feel, tonight, an urge to pound on the door and scream, "Come out, you! Be seen! You're a man, for God's sake, not a phantom! This is *life* out here!" But I only slow my steps, letting the floorboards squeak under my weight, and I hope he hears me and I hope that this — this scandal of the caddish lover coming to couple with the young Danish girl at the end of the hall — at least will give some spark to his lonely night.

I go on, burping now and tasting sick in the back of my throat. The happy brown feeling has gone from the whiskey in me and now I'm starting to feel cold and sad. I open Caroline's door and when I enter she is sitting on the bed reading a movie magazine and eating peanuts.

"I expected you earlier," she says, looking up from her magazine, squinting a little as she adjusts her focus.

"The hell," I say. "Like a married frau. You'll be scolding me for tardiness now?"

"Not at all," she says. "I just missed you."

"Sure you did, Sugar."

"I did." She tosses the magazine and stands up from the bed. When she grabs me round the shoulders she squeezes so tightly that I kind of almost lose my balance. We two fall sideways and back against the closed door.

"Well, hell-o," I say into her mouth.

"Ah. Hort," she says, giving me her forehead. "You're — you've been drinking."

"Indeed, I have."

"Okay."

"Sure it's okay. Did I ask you if it wasn't?"

"No, no."

"So give me a kiss."

She does, nicely. It's like the way you imagine the kisses feel in the picture shows, when the pretty girls bend their faces up under the men. Caroline kisses me like the movies.

"Tell me how you missed me," I say.

"I told you."

"I mean. Tell me *how*. The way you missed me."

She takes hold of my hand, the one that's holding onto her breast. "Horton. Wait."

"I'll wait," I say.

"No. Listen. Wait."

So I give my hands a rest and I stop kissing at her. We stand up from leaning on the door and so now we're upright and straight and still close but just holding each other sweet.

"Talk to me," I say to her.

"Come. Sit down."

"Whatever you want." I follow her to the bed and we sit beside each other on the edge of the mattress.

"Horton," she says.

I give her one of my smiles. "I don't like the way you keep saying my name. It's the tone the sisters would take back in school."

She smiles at this, but only in a polite way. There's something going on behind her face.

"It's like this," she says. "I'm carrying a baby."

"You what?"

"A baby."

"You're pregnant?"

"Yes."

"Holy Jesus," I say.

"Yes," she says.

For only a second or two I'm filled with rage. The bitch. She was supposed to keep track of things and make sure this didn't happen. I'm angry. But it's only a second or two, and then it's gone. See, Caroline doesn't cry.

Most girls, in this situation, now they'd brim up with tears and start blubbering and wailing and hugging themselves round the chest. But not

Caroline. She just looks me right in the eyes and this is the thing that makes me let go of all the mad I'm feeling.

I start feeling something else, something I am pretty certain is very wrong.

Right from the start with Caroline, I've tried to keep things straight in my head with regards to her and me and how we fit together. I have what I have with her. I'm clear on that. And I have my marriage, my Annie. The two might seem similar but they aren't — not at all. And, though I've been frightened sometimes by the effect Caroline has had on me, drawing me into strange and dangerous places, I've never for an instant confused what I have with her with what I have with Annie.

Only now, with Caroline sitting beside me on the bed, not crying, telling me she's got my baby in her, I'm beginning to get a feeling I'm not used to feeling with her. Maybe it makes no sense or maybe it makes perfect sense. I'm too close to make the call. But, sensible or not, all of a sudden now I'm looking at Caroline like she's more than what had always been perfectly enough for me before. It's all at once gone past the slow dancing at the Chink's and the Hollywood kissing in the dark, and beyond the low, breathy giggling after we're all sweaty and tired at the end of a night. I'm being swept up, caught up, carried by the force of a powerful torrent, like in her stories of the North Dakota rains. And this, I know, is not right.

I *should* be angry. I should be kicking the walls down and throwing her mattress through the window. I should jump to my feet and run from the room and get away from this whole damn mess. No man would speak a word against me if I did. But instead, my chest has gone soft on me, my shoulders are folding inward, and I'm all thick in the throat when I speak to her.

"Caroline," I say.

"It's a hell of a spot, Horton."

I nod. "It is."

"Any ideas?"

"Oh. Lots of ideas," I say, giving the floor a kind of sad look.

We're both of us quiet for a while and then she lets out a sigh and says, "That's all."

I look up. "That's all?"

"That's all," she says, shrugging and smiling. "Now that it's said, let's not just sit here like a couple of cancer patients."

"No. I suppose — "

"It's a hell of a spot, Horton, but you and me have been in a hell of a spot from the day we met."

"Yes. We have."

Caroline drops one of her hands into the other, on her lap. "There was a boy I knew," she says, "when I was a little girl. During the autumn harvest, his young sister fell into the threshing machine. The next day, the boy came to school, like nothing at all had ever happened."

I watch her. Not quite sure what she's telling me.

"The other kids at school thought it was strange, the way this boy went on with life after his sister's horrible death. But I was interested. I was interested in how he did it. I mean, how his mind worked around it. So I asked him."

"You asked him?"

"Yes," Caroline says. "I just asked him, didn't he feel like falling apart after having seen his sister drop into the machine that way? 'Do we mourn the winter,' he asked me, 'when the springtime comes?' He was a queer boy."

"I'd say 'a queer boy' is being polite."

"But he wasn't crazy," Caroline says. Her clear brow furrows a bit. "Don't you see? There is something to that. The seasons. They come with the turning of the planet. And so does all the rest of life. We can't hold back the winds, or fight the sunrise, or bawl our eyes out over the passing of summer."

"That's how this farm boy saw things."

"Yes."

"Kind of screwy, if you ask me."

"You're entitled to your opinion," Caroline says. "But I've never forgotten this that he told me. Anyway. Can I pour you a drink?"

"Yes," I say, and she stands up and goes to the kitchenette. I watch her ass and try to imagine it's gotten wider. But it's really only the same as always. Just right.

"You look well," I say.

"I've never felt better," she says back to me over her shoulder.

When she comes back with the ice in the glass, she starts to raise the bottle but I take it from her and I pour the drink myself.

"We'll think of something," she says to me softly.

"Sure."

"It's not the end of the world."

"No."

"People have had worse problems."

"Yes."

She closes her eyes and gives her head a small shake. "So. Tell me about *your* day."

"Well, Sugar," I say, after I've taken a good long drink. "Would you really like to hear about it?"

She smiles. "Yes, I would."

"I lost my job," I say.

She makes her smile even bigger, showing me the teeth. She wants to know that I'm joking. "Hort?" she says.

I speak into the chipped ice. "Albert gave me the can. I'm out. Hard times. He had to cut his losses. I'm an expense."

I spend the night with her tonight. We fall in together just holding on and whispering into each other's faces, like we're worn out from a fuck or a hard cry (though we've done neither), and sometime soon after the lights are out I fall asleep. When I wake up after midnight, I'm no longer at all drunk, and I lay awake with my arm held over Caroline's belly. I put my nose in close to her, in a place behind her ear. I know, again, that I'm feeling something that's not right, giving up all my caution, opening up all my gates, putting all my trust in this young girl like she's the wife I already have.

Eleven

When I tell Annie about Albert letting me go, she busts out laughing like a crazy woman. And I do believe, for a moment, she's gone crazy. I worry.

"That's brilliant," she says.

"Annie?" I say.

"Brilliant." And she laughs some more.

We're walking along the lower edge of the Powderhorn, pushing Stanley in the pram. Small Richard is walking beside Annie. The older kids we've just left at the school.

"When it rains, it pours," she says.

"It's not raining now, Mama," small Richard says.

"No," she says to him.

"Annie," I say. "It's nothing to do with me. Albert explained. He says I'm as good as they come and he'll take me back on soon as the times get better."

Annie cocks an eyebrow my way. "Albert said you were as good a man as they come?"

"He said," I tell her, quietly, "I was as good a worker as they come."

This sets her laughing again. Crazy.

"Daddy made a joke?" small Richard asks her.

"No, honey," she says.

"No," I say. "Mama's just not feeling well."

Annie snorts. An ugly sound. I step toward her, taking over pushing on Stanley's pram, and Annie and small Richard fall a few steps behind.

"You're sick, Mama?" I hear him ask her.

"No, honey."

"But Dada said — "

"Never mind."

They're both quiet behind me while we walk. Then Richard whispers, "Have you got laughing sickness?"

"I'm not at all sick," Annie answers him, too sharply.

"Richard," I say. "Come up."

He skips ahead to me. I point at the ducks on the lake and at two dogs chasing circles on the far slope across the water.

"Why did you come home?" Annie says.

I stop pushing the pram and turn. She's dropped a good ten paces back.

"I'm sorry, Annie."

"Why? Why did you bother? Why do you bother coming back to us? Now you're out of work. You're good for nothing. You might as well just stay away when you go."

"Stop, Annie."

"No. I'll speak as I want. You should go away from us to stay now."

"Dada's leaving away?"

I ignore small Richard. "You're talking nonsense," I say to Annie.

"Don't tell me about sense and nonsense," she says. Even on a weekday morning, the Powderhorn draws a crowd, and people are beginning to pause and stare toward the crazy woman.

"Come here, Annie," I say.

"Come here, Mama," Richard calls.

But she holds her ground, alone, separate from Richard and myself and from baby Stanley, in the pram.

"Will you or will you not leave us for good?" she says. I've got to say, it gives me the creeps, the way her voice doesn't sound at all crazy now.

I shake my head at her. "I won't leave my family."

"Hooray!" from small Richard.

"Then," Annie says, taking a step forward, "you'll just continue as you have?"

"Things have changed," I say. "I'll have to find work, somehow. I'll provide. I won't let my family go on the charity rolls."

"You know that's not what I mean."

"Well," I say.

"'Well,' what?" she says.

"Come over here, Annie. Let's not keep on like this."

She walks to me and steps close. "Can you give it up, Horton? Can you stop this? Can you stay home with your family?"

"I won't let you go on the charity rolls."

"That's not what I asked."

"That's enough talk of that."

Her face goes bad, like a broken thing. Not even a false, crazy laughing now. She's pale and looks dying. "Oh, Hort."

"Let's go home, Annie."

"Home!" from small Richard.

"Oh, Hort," she says again.

"I'm sorry, Annie."

"Can't you at least lie to me? Tell me you're through with that? Please, Horton, lie to me about this."

"I won't lie to you anymore," I say.

Richard whacks me on the thigh. "Lying is a sin, isn't it Dada?"

"Shut up, Richard," I say.

And so we walk along the pathway skirting the lake, heading toward home across the park, small Richard and Annie both crying all the way. I keep my eyes down on Stanley, who gurgles and giggles through it all.

*

Andy, Peterson's gimp cousin, frowns at me when I light my cigarette.

"Andy don't like smoke," Peterson says.

"It irritates my sinuses," Andy says.

I drop my cigarette on the floor under the table.

We're in a lunch wagon on Lake Street far east, near the river. It's one of these modern jobs, chromium and linoleum and bright lights, but the waiters still look like last week's newspapers. Under the table, I tap around the floor till I find my cigarette and I step on it.

"What's a sinus?" I ask.

"It's his breathing," Peterson says quickly. "Andy's got a delicate constitution."

"It's the way I was born," Andy says.

"I get it," I say.

"Go on," Peterson says, nodding at Andy to continue what he was saying before I spoiled the atmosphere with my cigarette.

"Tuesdays are when the coinage comes in."

"Why Tuesday?" I ask.

"How the hell should I know, 'why Tuesday?' I'm just saying."

"Okay," Peterson says. "Tuesday."

Andy takes a sip from his cup. Tea. "Anyway. Tuesday the coinage comes in. Late afternoon. The Kikes spend most of the evening with it then. Counting it, I guess. Wednesday morning, a bank truck comes, takes a load. A *small* load."

"They've got to report some of it legit."

"Sure," Andy says. "They send — I dunno — maybe a third of the take into the bank. The rest stays behind."

Peterson leans over the table like he's smelling his eggs. "It's got to be close to three-four grand left there on any given Wednesday."

Andy nods. "But *just* Wednesday. End of day, that gets taken away. After dark. In a regular sedan car."

"To where?" I ask.

Andy shrugs. "Who knows? What am I, a federal agent? I just know what goes on at the warehouse."

"Three-four grand. All day Wednesday," Peterson says.

"Whose warehouse is it, anyway?" I ask.

"Rivkin. Moses Rivkin," Andy says. "Why?"

I look at Peterson. "What do you know about Rivkin?"

Peterson shakes his head. "I told you. The Jews are tough bastards."

"But, I mean," I say. "Is it Rivkin's money? Or is he just letting them use his docks? Is Rivkin the one who gets the sedan full of cash at the end of the day?"

"I don't think so," Andy says. "Rivkin is a young guy. Sweetheart. He took over the warehouse when his pop died. I don't think he's mixed up in the syndicate."

"Well," I say. "Yes he *is* mixed up with the syndicate."

"Yeah. But. He's not a tough guy. He's a sweetheart. I don't wanna do nothing to hurt Rivkin."

"Andy," Peterson says, and I can tell he's never heard this before. "What are you saying?"

"Just that. Rivkin's alright by me. He's a good guy."

"We're talking about knocking over this good guy's warehouse," I say.

"Sure, sure," Andy says. He holds his teacup in both hands and stares from Peterson to me. "But it ain't his money."

"How do you know?"

"Because. The money guys, the big Kikes that come with the coinage, they're different. They all look like cops. They got guns and stuff. Rivkin's just a young guy trying to make a little scratch on the side. That's how I figure it."

I'm thinking I wish Andy the gimp would stop figuring things. That's up to Peterson and me. We just need Andy to give us the picture. Like a photograph. But he's painting us one of those French modernist jobs with swirls and squiggles.

"So," I say. "Big men with guns. They stay all day Wednesday."

"Nope. I see them come with the coinage, I see them go. Then I see them come back next night — same guys — in the sedan car."

"Who stays with the cash during the day?" I ask. "Who's guarding the stuff?"

Andy smiles. "Me."

Peterson smiles, looking at me. "Beauty, huh?"

I just kind of make a sound. I'm thinking.

"What goes on all day?" I ask. "What kind of business does this Rivkin run?"

"Books. Jew books. Bibles and stuff. He doesn't print them but he, you know, distributes them."

"Jews don't use the bible," Peterson says.

Andy makes a face. "Whatever. They're Jew books. Religious books. Prayer books. The Jews use them at church."

"I get it," I say.

"So," Peterson says to me, "see — no reason to have a lot of guards and so forth on the dock of a book warehouse. It would look fishy. So it's just Andy, here."

"On a busy day," Andy says, "six, sometimes seven trucks a day come in. Take a pallet of books. Go. I wave them into position, look over their papers, and salute them when they drive away."

"Who loads the trucks?" I ask.

"Morris and Jake. Nice guys. And the driver usually helps."

"Tell me about Morris and Jake."

"Nice guys."

"Right."

"Morris is big. A little slow. Retarded, maybe. Jake is old."

"They know about the coinage?"

"I dunno. Probably."

"They got guns?"

Andy narrows his eyes. "Come on."

"No," I say. I wiggle out of the deep banquette seat and I stand up. "You find out if Morris and Jake carry guns, and then I'll come on."

Peterson shakes his head at me. "It's a book warehouse, Horton."

"No, it isn't," I say. "It's a bank. You're talking about robbing a Jewish syndicate's bank."

"You're out?" Peterson says.

"I'm not out," I say. Truth is, my heart is pounding and my hands are shaking like I'm on a coffee jag, just from thinking about the money. I'm in way over my head here, talking about men with guns. I don't know anything about guns. But thousands of dollars. Thousands! "I just need more details. Find out who knows what. Who's a sweetheart and who's a gangster. And find out whose money it is."

I'm about to go then, leaving Andy and Peterson, when Peterson grabs hold of my sleeve.

"Hort."

I frown at him.

"The check," he says. "You owe for coffee and a sandwich."

"Right," I say. I find two nickels in my pocket and drop them on the tabletop between Peterson and his gimp cousin. Then I do leave, going out the door and out into the sunlight of Lake Street. I light a cigarette and walk west. Those two nickels were my last. I can't afford the streetcar home. But what really hurts is I can't afford a drink, and I could use one just now. Badly.

Twelve

Being home in the day with Annie is rough. She ignores me as much as she's able, but I'm there and it makes us both feel bad. Evenings, I'm mostly out. After a week at home, I figure out that it's best of I'm not around days, either. The weather's good now, so I go to the Powderhorn and sit by the lake and kick stones at the geese. Sometimes I crawl up onto the lawn and sleep. Albert came through with a few weeks' pay, but he gave the envelope directly to Annie one day when I was out. I made a fuss and Annie threw me a few bucks, which I stashed in the drawer with my socks. I'm making it last. I don't eat during the day and I return to the house in the afternoon and take enough for beers at the Frenchman's.

When the money in the sock drawer runs out, I stop coming home altogether. I sleep at Caroline's. Caroline and I have stopped stepping out.

Caroline feeds me in the evening, when she comes home from work. She cooks me macaroni and wieners in her small kitchenette. She keeps a bottle in her room, too, for me. She's a good girl.

It's like this, for now.

But Peterson and I are getting answers from Andy about the situation at the warehouse. Things there look pretty easy. What's more, with every day I'm spending in the park, and with every night I'm sitting with Caroline in the close air of her room, the risk of taking the Jews' money seems easier and easier for me to live with.

Caroline, meanwhile, is carrying the baby easily. She's not a skinny girl — I've always liked her curves and the solid thickness of her — and now that she's pregnant she doesn't show as much as she might if she were a little thing. She hasn't said a word to the Taylors, the finelys she works for, and she's not planning on saying a word till she absolutely must. There's no question but she'll lose her position as soon as they find out about her.

I've got something in the works, I tell her. You just don't worry. Horton Moon has something on the cooker.

I know you do, she says back to me.

She tells me she never worries for a moment about how things will turn out. I guess I myself catch on to that, from being around her so much. I go hungry all day and I haven't seen my kids for a week, but at night when I lay with Caroline and feel the little round rise of her belly under my hand, I think that everything will be all right. Somehow, somehow.

*

In June, Peterson and I knock over the warehouse. When it all happens it happens like this.

We snatch a Pontiac sedan and drive it up to the north side. Me and Peterson draw kerchiefs over our chins up to our eyes. We climb the steps up to the loading dock and we stand there looking at Andy, the gimp. He's like the guard. Me and Peterson both have our right hands in the pockets of our jackets. Maybe that's all we've got in our pockets. Or maybe we've got guns.

Andy has his hands up in the air over his head. He walks backwards and we follow him, into a room off the dock where two guys — an old man and a fat kid — are sitting at a table drinking tea out of glasses and eating donuts. They look up at us and then they both stand.

The old man reaches into his pocket, and I'm thinking he's going for a gun and I don't like that at all. There wasn't supposed to be any guns. But the old man only pulls a wallet out, and he holds it toward me.

"Take it. It's all I got," he says.

"Pipe down," I say, because that's what James Cagney says in the pictures.

"Where's the money?" Peterson says.

The fat kid doesn't say anything.

"No money," the old man says. "We're books. We got books." He waves his wallet at a pallet of books over by the wall.

"Don't get cute," I say. James Cagney again.

"The coins," Peterson says.

"We better do what they say," Andy says.

"The coins," the old man says, shrugging and turning away. We follow him. We all five of us go through a door and into a smaller room. Then we see the coins.

"We may need some help getting these bags to our car," Peterson says to the old man and to the fat kid and to Andy.

It's not thousands of dollars. It's actually not quite eight hundred. But we get it. Clear. It's ours. Peterson and I split it up evenly. We each tip Andy fifty, and I wind up with three hundred and thirty-six bucks and forty cents. All in dimes and nickels. When Caroline comes home from work that night I'm waiting in her room with a bottle of Champagne wine and three canvas sacks full of coins. She asks me a few questions and I answer her straight. She just smiles and shakes her head, eyeing me in an odd kind of way like I'm a calf born with an extra leg coming out of its ribs. But she doesn't tell me to leave, and she helps me put the coin bags into the bottom of her wardrobe. She even takes a glass of the wine. And now I'm on easy street.

*

It's hot in June but I never go out without my leather windbreaker. My jacket pockets are filled with dimes. I take my first drink at the Frenchman's in the morning at 10:00.

On Friday, I take a bag of coins to the bank on Chicago Avenue and change it to paper bills. Then I go to Annie and hand her one hundred dollars. Annie stares at the cash and she doesn't say a word for a few long moments.

"Where'd this come from?" she finally asks.

"Does it matter?" I say.

She starts to say something else but bites down into the words before they come fully out. "No," she says instead. "It doesn't matter."

We're standing at the back entrance to the apartment, and Annie's not making a move to let me in the door. Taking the money from me, she steps backwards and begins to close the door.

"I'd like to come by on Sunday," I say.

She shakes her head and pushes the door closed.

"I need to see my children," I say at the door.

No response.

I think of knocking, and I raise my fist to do so, but instead I only spread my palm open on the wood frame of the closed door. Anyway. I've done what I've come for. Annie has the cash. Enough to keep her and the kids for a good while. I don't really need any more than knowing that. I step backwards off the stoop and cross the small back lot to the alley.

I might head back to the Frenchman's, but I've already had enough to drink. It's not even noon. A hot day like this, the drink doesn't sit right in me when I walk in the sun. I decide to go to the park and find some shade. There's a willow beside the lake that I'm thinking of, where a fellow can take a nap down out of the sight of the good citizens strolling on the pathway.

Tim Young is poking at the edge of a flowerbed when I pass, and he looks up from his work to call my name. I stop and walk over the lawn to where Tim is working beside a little Negro.

"Hot day," Tim says.

I nod. "The hottest yet."

"You on a call?" he asks.

"A call?"

"Work."

"Ah. No," I say. "I'm through with that."

"You with Albert, yes?"

"I'm through with that," I say again.

"You're not working?"

I jingle the dimes in my pocket. "I keep busy."

"Good for you."

I squint at the park and the lake and the flowerbed. "How's this?"

"Hard work. Honest."

"Don't overestimate the worth of honest work," I say. We both laugh. The little Negro laughs, too, looking up from his hoeing.

"But this is a fine bunch of men," Tim says. He shrugs one shoulder toward the colored kid.

"That's great," I say.

"A good team. We're here for you, too, Horton. If you need. We're all going through these times together and so there's no sense in not pulling together."

"Right," I say.

"The days of the rugged individual are passed. It's a new era, now."

"Sure," I say. "I get you."

"The working man who provides his labor will be given his due."

I'm wondering why Tim is starting up like this when I suddenly catch on that Tim has got religion. Not religion, of course, but that new thing that everybody's catching — socialism or whatever they want to call it. Franklin Roosevelt and that crowd. Count me out.

"Well, Tim," I say. "You keep up the good work. We all hang together or we hang separately, eh? Myself, I'm off to hang a capitalist. String all the bastards up, that's what I say."

Tim just gives me a queer look. "You take care of yourself, Horton."

"Will do. Will do." I turn and walk back to the pathway and make for the lake.

Strange times. Dumb Tim has gone Red on us. Well, maybe that's not so strange. The lefties always seem to be either the dumbest ten percent or the smartest. The in-between, the fellas like myself, we're left to fend our own way. And I'm fending okay, I says to myself, getting hold of a fistful of coinage inside my jacket pocket. I get a sudden memory of two bums I saw from the Lake Street streetcar last year. A kid and an old man. Now there's a pair who *should* be storming the banks — put off without enough change between them to ride the car. But I remember the old guy didn't look the least bit bothered by things. I guess even those two fended for themselves okay, in their own way.

But I can't spend the morning contemplating the state of the republic. The heat is playing my head like an injun tom-tom drum. Had a few beers in the morning and the fizz has all gone out of me and left me feeling sticky inside. A nap in the shade of the big willow sounds like just the thing to settle my head and clean out my insides. Sleep cure.

But now: "Horton Moon," the voice says, calling me from behind, and the sound of it makes me go cold up my back.

Father Pat.

I stop on the pathway. I can hear my heels grinding down into the gravel as I turn toward him. There he is. He's a short man — shorter than me. Heavy through the middle. Wire-framed spectacles giving him a kind of doctor-ish look, but otherwise the man could pass for a bad-tempered butcher in a Roman collar.

"Good day, Father Pat," I say. My throat's gone dry.

"Horton," he says, walking right at me. But he stops, at a respectful distance, and we two stand facing one another. "What is this?" he asks, demanding an answer.

"What's *what*, Father?"

"All this idiocy. You know just what I'm talking about."

"Annie and me," I say. "We've been having a bad time."

"Take care of it," he says. If he weren't a priest, I think right now he'd take a swipe at me.

I look down at his hands. "Father?"

"Take care of it. End this idiocy."

I shake my head and make a sad kind of half-smile, like there's more to it all than he understands and I only wish I had a lifetime or two to spare, to explain it all. "I wish it were as simple as that," I say.

"Don't give me that horseshit," he says.

"Father?"

"Stop the act, Horton."

"There's no act, Father."

"There's a problem. *You're* the problem. I want the problem fixed."

"It's a complicated situation, Father."

He's breathing hard and heavy. "Take *care* of it Horton."

"Oh," I say. "Just like that?" He's not carrying on like a priest and so I'm starting to feel like I don't have to talk to him like one.

But he doesn't blink. "Yes," he says. "Just like that. Take care of it."

"Father Pat," I say. "Listen to me."

"Okay. I'm listening."

"Annie and me are having difficulties."

"Annie's only difficulty *is* you."

"Fine. Put it how you want. But anyway. I know you're a priest and you've got to watch out for people, and I'm not going to tell you that this is none of your business and that it's between a man and his wife to sort their difficulties out. I'm not going to tell you that."

"Good."

"I'm not going to tell you that there are aspects of this situation you can't know, that you can have *no idea* of. I'm not going to tell you that."

Father Pat takes a step in closer to me. "You listen to me, Horton Moon. You've got a wife and five small children at home. If you're a man, you'll accept all that that means. Don't talk to me about *aspects*. I know about your little Protestant whore."

The blood drums in my head and the light is going black around me. "Oh, you do, eh?"

"I do," he says. "You disgust me. But my feelings don't matter here. What matters is your behavior. And your behavior has got to change. Immediately."

Oh, Father. Don't take on a man when he's sick. I'm sick with the heat and the drink and I'm not completely myself. And him talking at me like this, using language like this, is just twisting me in a way I'm too brittle to be twisted. I take a step backwards and Father Pat takes a step forwards, so that the whole thing is being played out like a fistfight, and this only adds to my feeling like a man who needs to lash out for his own defense.

"Father," I say. "You're a *priest*." I say that last word in a really awful way, like a university Communist would pronounce it, or like a Protestant whore would. I shake my head slowly and stare right into his steel-rimmed spectacles. "You don't know nothing. You really don't. I'm sorry for you."

Father Pat is standing there sweating and breathing hard, a fat man in the sun wearing a black suit of clothes. I leave him, turning my back on him and walking away down the path, toward the lake where my big willow is waiting for me to spread out in its shade.

When I reach the spot, I go off the path and hurry down the hill, slipping a bit in the goose shit on the grass, and by the time I drop myself into the grass I'm feeling hotter and sicker than ever.

Even the grass feels hot under me. It's in the shade, and it's been in the shade since early morning, but it's not cool and it's damp, like the ground itself has been sweating. Hell.

I can't sleep and so I just lie there with my eyes closed. I listen to the sounds of the water sploshing against the mud bank below me and to the soft happy voices in the park, and to the hum of motorcars rattling through the streets that run out from the squared greenery of the Powderhorn like dirty spokes on a wheel.

*

Audrey Markus is a plain, slight girl, skinny in all the wrong places, and she's taken up with Caroline as a kind of self-appointed guardian angel. See, Audrey is a cook's helper at the Taylor's house, she works with Caroline there, but she fancies herself someday becoming a midwife and she's decided that she'll practice her craft on Caroline — Caroline being in no position to go looking for a *real* midwife.

Weeks ago, I took one look at the situation and I read it that Audrey was one of them that's running to be elected to sainthood. Audrey is a sharp-eyed girl, always sizing things up like she's judging a close prizefight, and I sussed out that Audrey saw a young girl in trouble, mixed up with a married man, so Audrey was set to take Caroline under her wing.

But the deal is more complicated than that. Audrey is not such a bad girl after all, and I like her fine. She *is* serious, and she is always making judgements on people, but she also has a quick tongue and she likes a drink. Which is always a good thing. I understand that a girl needs a friend — especially a girl in a mix-up, like Caroline. And as girlfriends go, Audrey is better than most.

She's been spending lots of time at the little apartment with Caroline and myself, and on hot nights we all three step out to the popcorn wagon on 38th Street. I buy the girls ice creams and sodas there, or we stop at our old place, the Chink's on

Hiawatha Avenue, and we drink cold beer and steer the electric fan onto our booth.

Tonight is hot and thick, but at sundown the rain comes sweeping over the bowl of the Powderhorn, where Caroline and Audrey and I are smoking cigarettes under an oak, and the rain drives us back to the apartment. Inside, we drop ourselves into chairs, our rain-wet clothes mucking onto our bodies like plasterer's rags, and Caroline sets to work with the ice pick. It is too hot even for electric light, so we three sit in the dark and when the small window fan is turned on, its rising *homm* drowns away the hiss of night rain outside.

"Thanks, kid," Audrey says to Caroline, who's brought her a highball of chipped ice and gin.

"Here's how," I say, raising my own glass. Cold gin.

Caroline is drinking root beer from a bottle. "Here's hoping the rain puts an end to this heat wave."

"I like it hot all right," I say.

"You're not carrying a baby in you," Audrey says.

I look toward Caroline. "Is it bad in the heat?"

"Ah. You know. Not too bad."

"Next week is July already," Audrey says. "You'll be showing soon."

"I'm showing now," Caroline says.

"But I mean. So's others would notice."

I think about Annie and the way she carried our babies. Annie is small and slim, and the babies always made her puff up, stout like a fireplug, within the first months. Jesus. To think of Annie at a time like this. But I can't help myself. She is still here, always, just alongside or behind or above my conscious thoughts, like a fingerprint on a windowpane.

I drink. "By 'others' you mean the Taylors?"

"Yeah," Caroline says. "The time'll come. I've accepted it."

"They won't have it. You'll be sent out without notice."

"I've accepted it."

"We'll be all right." I say to Audrey.

"Yes," she says. "Of course. The five-and-dime king. Frank Woolworth himself."

Both girls laugh.

"We'll be all right," I say again.

"Till the nickels run out," Audrey says.

"Nothing's running out," I say.

"The whole damn country is running out," she says.

"Not the country I live in."

"Which country is that?"

"Horton's own. I make my own way."

Audrey snorts. The ice sings in her highball when she motions with it to indicate Caroline. "So I've seen."

"Go chase your tail," I say to her.

"Go chase your own tail," Audrey says, giggling.

"I'll chase whomever's tail I wish."

"Oh, you."

"Both of you, stop," Caroline says lazily. She's settled herself on the bed and her head is resting on the pillows. She speaks toward the hot dark of the ceiling. "We will be okay, won't we Hort?" she says.

"Sure," I say.

"You'll find work?"

"Sure," I say.

"I mean, real work."

Audrey drinks, her ice clacking.

"We'll get by fine," I say.

"I'm sorry I started up," Audrey says now. "This sort of talk is making me blue. Let's not sweat thinking about tomorrow or the next day. It's a lovely night tonight."

"I'll drink to that," I say.

Caroline stretches herself atop the mattress. "Lovely."

"Cooler already, I think," Audrey says.

"Definitely," I say.

"The heat wave is broken."

"Tomorrow will be cool and dry."

"Clear skies. No haze."

"The sun will shine but it will not burn," I say.

"The birds will sing but they will not shit," Audrey says.

"Fairies and elves will flit about on the Powderhorn," I say.

"Prosperity is just around the corner," Audrey says.

And we all three of us have a good hard laugh at that.

Caroline turns on the radio set I bought her and we listen to dance music and Caroline makes more drinks. Audrey and I drink until the gin is gone and then I run down to the saloon at the end of the block for cartons of beer. When I get back to the apartment, Caroline has fallen asleep and Audrey is listening to a radio preacher deliver a hell-and-damnation sermon. I stop in the doorway before I enter the apartment.

"Turn that off," I say.

Audrey looks up, blinking into the light that's coming in the open door from the hallway behind me. She smiles at me.

"Funny," she says. "I wasn't even listening to it. I mean, to what he was saying. I just love the radio."

"Well," I say. "Turn it off now."

She does, fumbling at the knobs with her drunk hands. The radio goes dead and I close the door. It's all dark in the room now.

"Let's turn a light on," I say.

"I want to let the kid sleep."

"She'll sleep with the light on," I say.

"You don't know."

"I know," I say. I snap on the lamp closest to me, a floorlamp along the wall just inside the doorway.

On the bed, Caroline makes a face and rolls sideways away from the light. But she stays sleeping.

"You got any more smokes?" Audrey asks.

I toss her the pack. Just to watch how she can't catch it.

"Thanks," she says, bending to pick up the cigarettes from the floor.

"Beer?" I ask.

"Sure."

"Stopped raining."

"Good," she says.

I open the two cardboard quarts of beer and pass one to Audrey. It's gone warm but it's strong beer.

"How long till Caroline starts to show?" I ask.

"You mean till she gets the can from the Taylors?"

"Yeah. How long?"

"Another month. Maybe."

Audrey's sitting injun-style on the floor, an unlit cigarette between her fingers. I fish out a box of matches from my shirt, strike a light, and bend down to her.

"Thanks," she says, blowing smoke. "You really worried?"

"I suppose I am. Yes."

She shrugs. "She's a big girl. Sometimes big girls can carry it better. She might not show proper for another two months. Maybe longer. I can't tell."

I nod at this. I drink my beer. "And then?"

"Then?"

"After she gets the can and she's really showing it."

"What about it?" Audrey says.

"Well. What'll we do?"

Audrey smiles at me but it's not just a drunk smile.

"What *we'll* do," she says, "is we'll take care of the girl."

Thirteen

I'm in the Powderhorn early, like I mean to be most mornings, so that I can see the kids walking, skirting along the east side on their way to the summer program the parish nuns have organized. This morning I want to raise my hand and wave to them, just like I want to every morning, but I don't. Instead — just like always — I sit still on my bench and I watch them there two hundred yards distant, young Bridget and Frankie and Ralphie and small Richard, hopping on and off the curb and jostling one another. I'm their father, for Christ's sake. But still. It would be queer, them seeing me here in the park in the morning. I can't imagine what Annie has told them. But I'm sure she hasn't told them I'm living across the park with a girl I knocked up pregnant.

Anyway. There they are and there they go.

I've bought myself a new glass-lined Thermos jug and I've got coffee and I've got cigarettes, and it's a cool bright morning in the park, and you can't really ask for more than that. I pour out another cup from the jug and then I screw the cap back on and place the jug on the slats of the bench beside me.

There's Peterson. Hell of a thing, to see him out this early in the A.M. But look here. He's out for a purpose. He's coming toward me. I watch him crossing the Powderhorn, making a bee-line to me and ignoring the pathways — he slogs through the wet grass and he steps over the plantings that Tim Young and his crew have prettied the place up with.

Now he's kicking through a mess of tulips and he's upon me.

"Horton," he says. Breathing hard, as is understandable.

"What's under your bonnet?" I ask him. "You look to be running a steeplechase race."

Peterson's eyes are not quite right. Has he been drinking this early? No.

"Horton," he says, making his voice steady. "It's Andy."

"Andy?" I say. This isn't good.

"Andy," Peterson says. "They got him."

"What do you mean?"

"Andy. Andy's dead. The Jews got him."

"Mother of Jesus."

Peterson nods at me. "The Jews got him," he says again.

"What happened?"

"He — Andy — they found him last night. Late. His body was in the park below Minnehaha Falls. Piano wire 'round his throat."

"How do you know who did it?" I ask.

"I know. Okay? The way it was done."

"Okay," I say. Of course. "So what?"

"So I think they know what the situation is."

I get a sick taste from the back of my tongue. "Us?"

"I dunno. Maybe. Probably."

"You think Andy talked?"

"I think. I dunno. But I'm thinking, yes. I'm thinking, they know everything."

"So," I say. Only I have know idea what comes after this "so."

"Get out of town, Hort," Peterson says.

"Where to?" I ask.

"Anywhere. I'm leaving now myself. I won't tell you where."

I just shake my head at Peterson. "No. I can't go away right now. We just have to give them back their coinage — what's left."

"It ain't that way, Hort," Peterson says low.

"How do you mean?"

"The way they did Andy. It's not about getting their money back. It's about making a statement."

"Statement?"

"A message, like. They see it as we made them look bad. It's an appearance of disrespect. These people are big on appearances."

"So we beat it. We split up," I say, kind of just thinking it out loud to myself.

Peterson nods. "Yes. We've gotta blow town. And we shouldn't be together in case ... you know."

"Sure," I say quickly. Mother of Jesus. I can't leave town. Even with all this hitting me now, I can think clearly enough to know that. I'll lay low. But I can't leave. Can I?

Peterson holds his hand out at me and it takes me a second or two before I realize he means to shake hands. I don't think Peterson and I have ever shook hands in the years we've known one another. But I shake his hand.

"Good luck, Horton."

"Thanks, Pete."

He chews on his lips a bit. "Give it a while. Maybe six months. A year. It'll probably be okay after that."

"Yeah," I say. My voice, I can hear, is dry and dead.

"I'm sorry, Horton. I know this is hell. You with a family and all."

"Yeah."

"But there's really no choice."

"Sure. We've got to get out."

"You'd better keep your farewells vague."

"Hmm?"

"Myself, I'm not telling my old lady a thing. This afternoon I'm going out for cigarettes. She'll put things together from there."

I nod. "I see."

"It's a mess. Fewer people get dirty, the better for everyone."

"I get you."

"S'long, Horton."

"Goodbye Peterson," I say.

I watch him go off. He stays to the pathways this time, though he's walking with an odd hurried step and he keeps turning his head this way and that, like to scan the streets at the edges of the park. He passes the lake and goes up the hill toward the north end of the green.

That sick on my tongue has not left. Fucking shit. I knew it was never just a lark, I knew we were playing for real stakes here, but it's always hell when it blows up in your face like this. Andy dead. Strangled with piano wire. That's professional service. That's "do it clean and do it right." Of course Andy talked. If they nailed Andy, they had to know all the rest, too.

Caroline is at the finelys. At the Taylor's house. I can't say goodbye to her. I could, I suppose, wait until tonight, when she's off work. But that's madness. These guys aren't going to just sit around and wait before they make the next move. Bam bam bam — that's the way I'd do it if I was these people. I've got to get out this morning, without saying anything to Caroline. Maybe a note.

But I'm not one to write notes. I'll probably muck it up if I try. Best thing may be to just go and let her think I've left her in the lurch with the baby coming.

But just thinking on this line gets me all wet in the eyes and choked-up. Blessed Jesus. I'd *never* leave Caroline in the lurch. I'm a bastard but I'm not that bad. Besides, there's more keeping me here with her than just a sense of responsibility. But I've got to leave her, for her own safety.

I feel a little better now, thinking about this. It's a kind of noble thing I do, walking away from happiness to save a woman from harm. She won't know this, but I feel a little better. A little. I try to make like a character in a play or in a picture. Noble guy doing a far better thing now than he's ever done, like what's-his-name, long-nosed guy, putting up a bluff to hide his true heart. But of course, getting past it all, I'm only Horton Moon. So I can't stand up and stride away like Ronald Coleman, but instead I just slump there on the bench in the Powderhorn and I stare at the morning light glinting off the lake and I finger the lid of my Thermos jug and I wait for something to come down from heaven and change my whole life so I won't have to go through with this now.

Because, of course, running out now is not just running out on Caroline. There is Annie, too. I've left her, but I haven't completely abandoned her. So how can I now? Especially if she may be in some danger, if Rivkin's people come around to the house looking for me, I can't just leg it out of town on a boxcar and leave Annie to that.

The truth of what's happening to me eventually, after a few minutes, stirs me from the bench. I realize that I've got to move and so I move. I'm not clear on where to go, but I know I've got to go. Just the moving seems to be enough. Better than not moving, I mean.

I walk and I'm watching across the park toward the pathway where I'd seen the children, when it suddenly hits me hard. I saw them, but they didn't see me. I was here, but I was invisible. I pick up my pace, stepping more lightly over the pathway. I've got an idea. I *don't* have to leave town. I *don't* have to go away from the women I love. I can disappear, right here in the city.

I walk down toward the water but then I turn and head uphill to the far end of the park, and I leave the Powderhorn and cross in the direction of 17th Avenue, to Annie.

She's got the back door open and I see her through the screen door, standing in the kitchen behind an ironing board. I climb the stoop and stand there for half a minute, just watching in at her. She's humming a song, a popular ballad that people are all singing these days. Annie hasn't a singing voice, and even her humming is off. This touches me, and I pause with my hand on the knob of the screen door and smile at her and her flat voice and at her dark damp hair falling out of its bounds. A few lank strands have dropped across her cheek. The hair frames her eyes, downcast, and I notice how young she still looks, after all this. I take my hand off the knob and touch the doorframe with my knuckles.

Annie jumps, almost dropping the iron.

"Mother of God! You frightened me!"

"Very sorry," I say.

She watches me and I watch her and I see her face change through a half-dozen moods, fear and relief and near-happiness and puzzlement — it makes me think of when I turn the big tuning knob on Caroline's radio set and the stronger signals fight through the static — and then Annie settles on an expression of quiet anger.

"What are you doing here?" she asks.

I almost say that I've come to say goodbye, but I stop myself.

"I've only come to say hello."

Annie shakes her head quickly. "Go away."

"Annie. Please."

"No. I can't see you."

"You don't even have to let me in. I'll stand out here."

This seems to do the trick. She looks down at the ironing board and she puts the electric iron down on its stand, and I can see that she's not going to come round and slam the door on my face.

"What is it you want?" she asks.

"I want nothing. I only want to say hello."

"You've said that."

"Yes. I have. But I don't want to leave yet."

She gives me a hard look. "You stole that money."

"What are you talking about?" I say, feeling my gut flutter up like a spooked bird.

"The money you brought here last week. You stole it."

"What do you know about it?"

"I know you didn't come by it honest."

"I came by it. That's all. And now you came by it. Don't worry anything more about it than that."

Annie juts her chin out and tilts her head back, tossing the loose hair off her face. "What have you got yourself into now?"

"Nothing that matters to you."

"I suppose that's true. It no longer matters to me."

It hurts me how quiet it is between us now. "I saw the priest," I say. "Father Pat."

"He came around here, too," she says. "He's a fat ass."

I have to smile. "He is."

Annie stares at me smiling. Her face gets harder. "Horton," she says. "You've really no business here, do you?"

I try to think up something to say but I can't. "Not really, no."

She's standing very still behind her ironing board. Her hands hang loosely at her sides. "So go away," she says. "Please. It slashes into me like a knife, seeing you. Do you understand that? Do you?"

"Annie," I say.

"Or don't you? Don't you understand anything, you stupid man?"

"I am a stupid man. Yes," I say. "I'm not a bad man, but I fear I'm stupid. I've made mistakes. Wanting to hurt no one, I've made mistakes that have resulted in — in — "

"Oh," she says. "Shut up. Just shut the hell up."

"I'm only trying to — "

"Shut up." Her voice is soft, calm and certain. "Shut up and go away."

I nod. "I'll go away now."

"You've bought yourself a clear conscience. The money will keep us. You can go live your new life."

I swallow. "I don't have a new life. I've only the one. The same old life. But I've got to live it. I need to do that."

"Yes." From where I stand, I can see a muscle move in her forehead and it looks like her face is about to lose its cold hard anger, but Annie holds on.

"I do love you, Annie," I say.

She looks away from me, to the wall.

"Annie," I say, "I don't expect you to make sense of this, but I do love you. I do. But my heart, my soul, is flawed. It's not like a normal man's. I am led in directions I cannot control."

Annie looks to be holding her breath.

"I'll go," I say. "I only wanted to see you again. To say something. I don't know what. There's really nothing I *can* say. I don't know the language to speak the things inside me. And talking ordinary words, like this, only makes me see how far I am from knowing how to speak the truth. I'm sorry. I'm sorry."

Annie raises one hand as if the limb is made of stone.

"I'm sorry, Annie."

"Go," she says.

"Yes," I say. "I won't come back."

And when I reach the alley at the back of the yard I can hear, through the opened windows of the kitchen, the release of Annie's tears. They come out in sobs that break as shouts. It makes me go cold between the shoulder-blades to hear her falling apart in the cool darkness of the kitchen out of my sight.

I'll go, all right. I'm leaving Annie, and God be with her and protect her from knowing the truth. By that I mean the truth about the money, which she doesn't need to know, especially now, but also I mean the truth about my heart.

Because, if it wounds her like a gash from a knife to see me again, then how much more might it pain her to know how deeply I am in love with her still? Not denying all that has gone on with Caroline, I am more in love with Annie than ever. I am overcome. I am physically affected by having stood so near her again. What do I make of that? Can a man love two women at once, like this? Has it ever been so? Am I the first, a new link in the chain in what modern thinkers might call the *evolution* of romantic love? Or am I just a freak? Perhaps so. I am sick and a sinner, and I am not proud. Anyway. However I try to explain my heart to myself, it is a heart that has done damage.

I've cut my Annie near dead, and when Caroline finds me gone she'll likely be destroyed as well. Better if neither of them had ever met me. But what the hell. They have, the both of them, and all I can do now is try to limit the hurt.

I *did* behave better than I might have, with Annie. I resisted the urge — very strong it was, too — to throw myself on my knees before Annie and hold my arms around her hips and bury my face in her. No. Instead, I played it close to my chest and ducked out without giving anything away.

If Annie hates me now, so much the better. I'll leave her alone and in a few months her anger will soften into something else easier to live with. Same with Caroline, I suppose. She can hate me, but maybe she'll go ahead and have a life with the new baby, maybe return to her North Dakota farm and let the kid grow up with his grandparents in the clean cold air of the prairie. Neither Annie nor Caroline need to know how much I love them, how I'd never leave *either* of them, really, if these times and circumstances hadn't forced me. That is my own hell to live with, but it needn't be theirs.

At a diner on Lake Street, I sit in a booth and order coffee and I ask the coffee man for a piece of paper and a pencil. I write a note.

Dear ~~Uncle~~ Jack,

I need to go. I am leaving town all alone. Please take care of Annie for me. By this I do not mean money but just take care of her. She has money all ready. There is a ~~sitchuation~~ problem. I have brought this on. It has nothing to do with A. There are men who want to hurt me but its important that these men do not hurt her. You being a man with power and pull, please do what you can to keep her safe out of this problem. Thank you very much.

Your ~~neee~~ Annie's husband,

Horton Moon

That bit about leaving town, a lie to Jack, might be of some help down the line. I'm hoping that my specifying "alone" will keep Jack Morrison or anybody else from sniffing around Caroline, looking for me. Anyway, there's no real connection to me, as far as the north-siders know, in Caroline. She'll be safe from this at least. I fold the note over three times and stand up from the booth.

I cross the street to the Democratic Party headquarters and I go into the reception room on the ground floor. Here's Jimmy Lemke, sitting behind a big oak desk. I hand him the note.

"Please be sure Jack Morrison gets this," I say.

Lemke takes the note and puts it down on the desk in front of him.

"It's important," I say.

Lemke nods. "Jack Morrison is an important man."

"It's a personal note," I say. "Family matter."

Lemke just nods again. But now he takes up the note and slips it into the pocket of his suit jacket.

"Thanks, Jimmy," I say, and I leave.

I walk to Caroline's place, where I collect two small bags of dimes and nickels plus a fistful of bills I'd changed at the bank — singles and fives, a wad the size of a pack of Camels. I leave dear Caroline with the rest, more than enough coinage to get her back to North Dakota, or to live on here for another few months. I stand for a minute or two in the middle of the small, bright room. I think about writing another note. But putting words on paper to Jack Morrison is nothing like trying to write the truth to Caroline. So no note. Still, seems hell to go from her without even anything like the few, clumsy words I left my Annie with. Maybe Caroline will understand what I'm feeling without me having to explain. Yes, I tell myself, that's the way it will be. Like when I used to leave her in bed, going from her room at the end of a night together, and I'd smile at her and it'd be enough; she'd fill in all the unsaid words. I take off my soft cap and drop it on Caroline's bed, leaving her with only that of me. And then I head out.

Fourteen

To reach the Gateway, I ride the streetcar downtown and all the way through the good part that's clean and bright as a Sunday afternoon, past the department stores and past the white-lit soda fountains with their plate-glass fronts, and past the high limestone office towers where men hurry in and out carrying briefcases and wearing new snap-brim hats, through to the end of the line. Here, the falls of St. Anthony sound from behind the grain towers — the land drops away behind the towers, down to the river. This neighborhood here near the riverfront is nothing but dirty old buildings of black brick and blocked windows, their sidewalk storefronts loud with half-working electric beer advertisements and hand-painted signs pushing haircuts and day work and rooms to let.

The first thing you pick up on, looking out at this place from the slowing streetcar, is that the men here aren't moving. Nobody's going anywhere. There's nothing but men leaning against the black brick, and groups of men standing on corners talking in loud voices, and men asleep in the middle of the day sprawled on the benches around the fountain in the Gateway Park.

I hop off the car and walk west along Washington Avenue, stepping around the men who won't move out of my way, and I walk to the park. It's not a real park, not like the Powderhorn. The Gateway is just a square of pavement and scrawny trees, with a public toilet house made to look like a Greek temple on one end and a big stone fountain bubbling in the middle, laid out in the space where

Hennepin Avenue comes into the city from the river bridge and runs up against the foot of Nicollet Avenue. The automobile traffic moving past on either side makes the square loud and foul-smelling. The breeze off the river seems taken up by the heat of the day before it reaches the Gateway Park.

I find a bench away from the fountain, where I'm mostly to myself, and I sit down and light a cigarette and try to take in where I'm at.

The Gateway. I used to come down here with my old man when I was a kid, visiting some uncle of his who lived in one of the flop hotels. I try not to think about my dad too much, and mostly I'm able not to, but this place is bringing back memories. The Gateway used to scare the hell out of me then, when I was a kid. It was the same then as now, lots of dead-looking men standing around, and when we'd go up to my dad's uncle's room and when the two of them would sit on the bed and share a bottle without using glasses, I'd stand at the window to avoid looking at them drinking. I'd listen to my dad and his uncle talking, in low voices at first, growing louder as the liquor went down. Out the window, there was an alleyway. The pavement down there was littered with broken wine bottles and piles of shit. Human shit, I guess. I'd watch cockroaches racing up and down the bricks and sometimes, when my dad and the old uncle were slow drinking, I had to stand there for a long time and so I'd make a game out of trying to see which of the bugs was fastest. I could see the end of the alley where it opened up onto the sun-bright street, and I'd watch out at the men on the street, smoking and laughing and kicking stones into the gutters, and something about the way none of them was heading anywhere scared the hell out of me.

It doesn't scare me now. I look around and none of these characters looks so different from me and the people I know back in the Powderhorn. That's the times, of course. In the old days, the Gateway was filled with old lumbermen and Swede day laborers, all of them out of work because they were too old or too dumb or too lazy. Now, I look around and it's fellas just like me, young and healthy and quick, but with no work on account of the times. I guess some of them come down here on their way to the rail yards, where they'll hop a freight looking for better places. Others will shuffle over to the employment agencies once a day and hope for ten hours' work. Others, maybe, are like me, and they're here just wanting to be lost to people who are looking to find them.

It's an easy place to be lost, I think. I'm counting on it.

I smoke down my butt and then I stand from the bench and cross to a row of the dirty-brick buildings that have signs propped up in their cloudy windows, advertising rooms.

Inside the rooming house, the man behind the counter is a sleepy mulatto with something ugly growing out of his face. Like a wart or a cyst or something. I try not to look at the thing.

"Need a room," I tell him.

"Got a cage," he says back at me.

"A cage?"

He nods. Looks even more sleepy than before. "Got a cage," he says, stifling a yawn. "Got safe cages. Ten by ten, clean bed, chicken wire over the top. Only you got the key. Safe cages."

"You don't have regular rooms?"

"This here's a cage house," he says. "You a millionaire, you best head over to the Pick-Nicollet Hotel."

"I'm just looking for a room," I say. I don't bother trying not to stare at the thing growing out of his face.

He shifts in his chair and his eyes snap open. His voice doesn't sound sleepy anymore. "So," he says. "You a man of means."

I don't like the way he says this. Like he's sized me up all at once and he's got me figured out.

"I haven't any means," I say. It feels like hell saying it, but I've got to play things close to my chest.

"So what you need is a cage," he says, getting sleepy again.

"Sure," I say. "A cage sounds about right for me. Can I take a look?"

The mulatto stands up and comes around the desk. He's taller than he looked sitting down. He's taller than me. He goes up the stairs and I go after him, following.

As we rise, the air gets thicker. At the top of the stairs it's hot and dark, and it stinks like sweat and vomit and piss. Down a long hallway, there are 25-watt bulbs glowing on cords from the high ceiling. It takes me a few seconds to adjust my eyes and to see that this isn't really a hallway. Maybe this was a regular hotel once, but someone's come in and knocked away all the walls and now the whole floor is open, only this passageway is formed in the space between two rows of compartments pieced together side-to-side. I follow the tall mulatto down this line to one of the compartments halfway to the end. It's a cage.

Ten feet by maybe eight feet. There's plywood for walls. The front is a gate of chicken wire, and there's chicken wire over the top, dropped down about two feet from the tin ceiling of the room. Through the chicken-wire gate, I can see a narrow bed with a thin mattress. There's a low table in there, too, with a bucket on it. I think I know what the bucket is for.

"Where's the toilet?" I ask the mulatto.

Without speaking, he raises his hand and points one of his long, thin fingers down to the end of the line of cages, where I see a closed door in a real wall. In the gloom, I make out the figures of two men standing against the wall outside the closed door, waiting.

What the hell. I'm trying to disappear. I guess this is about as invisible as you can get. I turn around. In the cage opposite, there's a window, but it's painted over and seems sealed shut. The mulatto desk clerk makes an impatient noise in his throat and I turn back around to face him.

"So," he says. "I know it's not the Ritz Hotel. But we ain't in Mayfair, are we?"

"No," I say. Now I'm lower than him and it makes looking up at that thing growing out of his face even worse. I look instead at the bed behind the chicken wire. "How much?"

"Dollar a week," he says. "First week in *advance*."

I'm feeling a little sick from the air in the place. I pinch my nostrils shut. I slide the toe of my shoe over the floor, pushing up a little ridge of greasy-looking dust. This isn't a place to disappear, for Christ's sake. This is a place where men come to die. I smile up at the mulatto. "Well, Captain," I say. “I hope you won’t mind, but I think I’ll pass. Thanks for your time, though.”

He just shrugs and walks me back downstairs. No hard feelings. I leave that place and go across the square to one of the bigger rooming houses along Washington Avenue. I find a room for eight dollars a week, paid up front, and it suits me just fine. There’s a window that’s not painted shut, a decent bed, a washstand in the corner and a clean bathroom in the hall with a proper shower. I’m living the life of Riley.

At sundown I walk the avenue.

The blinking lights are coming up in the signage and the crowd seems a different sort than in the day. There are couples now, and men moving quickly from one bar to the next. They’re like tourists, I guess, come downtown to slum in the Gateway for an evening. I walk for five or ten minutes, up Washington Avenue away from the Gateway Park and then back again, but these bars all give me a bad feeling. Inside, there are jukeboxes playing loud — tinny-sounding, fast-paced jazz — and gangs of men and women laughing too much.

After a while I turn off the main drag and find a small place half a block away. It’s a quite saloon with no jukebox and no crowd. Just a few calm-looking fellas minding their own business, nursing drinks. I go in and stand against the bar, and the bartender comes over soon enough.

“Beer and a bump of rye,” I say to him.

He’s quiet, and quick with the drink. Just what a man looks for in a bartender.

*

I've drunk too much. It's to be understood. I'm in a strange place, in stranger circumstances. And I'm carrying more money than I'm used to. Nobody talks to me in the saloon, and so I just drink and order another, over and over till after midnight. I get back to the rooming house all right, and I find my door up at the top of the stairs. I fall onto the bed and sleep through till morning with my shoes on.

I feel like hell when I wake at noon. I guess it's not the best whiskey, this that they serve down here. I need to throw up in my chamber pot. I try to lie down again but my head aches and the room feels too hot now. I go to the bathroom in the hall and splash cold water over my head. I go out for a walk.

There's a lunch wagon near the train depot and I sit in a booth and drink coffee. But the sun shining in the big plate-glass window is bouncing hard off the chromium plate of the sugar jar and the salt shakers and the flatware, and it's doing my head no favors. I pay for my coffee and leave. It's time for me to start my life in the Gateway.

Fifteen

The Union City Mission rises up over the Gateway like some kind of modern cathedral; modern it is, square and sharp, though looking a little gone to seed — with the pointing crumbling from its brickwork and its windows cracked and sagging in their frames, the Union City is showing, I guess, how modern things age. I don't pay too much mind to the dark walls rising up over me as I pass along the sidewalk to the main entrance of the Union City. I'm on my way to a meal.

The whole point of this is that I'm to blend in to the scenery down here. I've got to become the kind of guy that people look at him and don't see anything. That's the idea. So, even though I can afford a plate of macaroni and a chop at one of the counters up the way on Hennepin Avenue, I've decided to stick to the Gateway and take a turn on the soupline. What the hell. It's only till the heat passes over the Powderhorn.

I've already walked around the block a few times, and then around some of the other blocks. I walk past the saloons without slowing down. I've decided maybe I was too free with the coinage last night, and so I'm determined to play things a little closer to my chest from now on. But it's a bitch to try to kill time in a new neighborhood without spending any money. We're near the river here, near the falls, and if things worked according to plan this neighborhood would be fresh with cool breezes wafting off the falling waters. But nothing seems to work according to plan down here on the Gateway. The air is hot and still and there're flies buzzing over the slop spilled in the gutters. Drunks have puked and pissed on the curbs, and nobody seems to be rushing forward to clean it up. It turns my stomach at first, but after a few blocks of walking I'm grown used to it. I walk in the heat and I can't help but think that Caroline has woken from the night without me and knows I'm gone now. This thought just throbs through my hangover and makes me feel worse than ever. Anyway, I've decided now to go to the Union City, the biggest of the missions in the district, to sit for a minute or two out of the sun and the bad sidewalk air.

At the Union City, the door is locked, which seems a hell of a thing for a mission. Spotting a slump-shouldered jerk inside leaning on a broom, I rap my knuckles against the glass. He shakes his head at me. I don't give up at that. I tap the glass again and signal for him to come over. He does.

The jerk — he's a curly-haired jerk, maybe my age, wearing glasses — fiddles with the lock and then pushes the door open just enough to stick his chin out at me. "Closed."

"I know it's closed," I say. "But when's it open?"

"Supper line opens at six."

It's just three now. "Hey, friend," I say to the jerk. "How's about you throw me a piece of bread?"

He makes a face at me. "Can't help you."

He starts to close the door, but I've got the toe of my shoe in like a Fuller Brush man. "Hang on," I say.

The jerk looks a little scared behind his eyeglasses.

"Listen," I offer, trying calm him a bit, "what about if a fella wants to come in and say a prayer?"

"You can pray in the park."

"Or meet with the priest?"

"No priests here, Paddy."

He says this last bit friendly. He even smiles at me.

"So," I say, "whaddayagot, ministers? — so if I want to meet with a minister and confess my fallings. Say, I'm seeking redemption — "

"Come back for the six o'clock," the jerk says. He says it like it's the end of the conversation, and I guess I understand that clear enough. I remove my shoe from the doorway. The jerk nods at me, just to show there's no hard feelings on his part, and then he closes the door and sets the lock.

So I walk away and across the street to the park. I sit down at the first bench I see, but it's at the edge of a crowd that's gathered, listening to some guy talking. The guy is standing atop one of the benches a few feet away, and the men gathered around him look to be listening not because he's an especially interesting speaker but just because there's nothing else for them to do on a hot afternoon. The speaker is a Swede Commie going on in a bad accent about property and class. I always like the sing-songy sounds of a Swede accent, no matter what garbage is being said, but just now the crowd gathered seems to be making more heat in the afternoon, and so I get up from my bench and move further away, looking for shade and quiet.

I go across the street, away from the park, and I find a big swipe of sidewalk shaded by a three-story flophouse. There's a newspaper shop and an employment agency on the ground floor, and I see a couple of fellas sitting on the sidewalk down the way from the employment agency storefront, their backs against a blank brick wall. Nobody's bothering them there. I make my way over.

"Hey," I say. It's an old man and a young kid.

They both look up at me. They look frightened. It seems I'm scaring everybody today. But I recognize these two characters. They were on Lake Street last summer. Maybe I saw the two of them somewhere else, too.

"Okay if I join you?" I ask.

The kid shakes his head. The old man says, "Suit yourself."

I sit down and the old man coughs, covering over his mouth with a small, delicate-looking hand. He's like a gentleman. Though worn from rough living. I figure he's maybe sixty, with a three-day beard, his face lean and sunburned and underfed, his white hair greasy. The kid is sixteen, handsome, with a dirty face. Maybe he's a Mexican or an Italian. When I sit down on the cement beside them, they both shuffle slightly sideways, away. Seeming spooked again.

"Hot day," I say. I'm trying to sound friendly. I don't want to scare anybody at all.

The kid grunts and the old man sighs.

"It is," the old man agrees.

"Hell of a thing," I say, just talking out loud at the both of them, "but you know, I just tried getting into the Union City and the bastard at the door told me to come back for the six o'clock supper. I about asked him if I needed to sign a reservations book."

The old man smiles politely at this, but the kid doesn't react at all. Maybe he doesn't speak English. His clothes are too large on him and his big nervous eyes avoid mine. He's barely a shaver. He touches with his dirty hands up the back of his head where some barber butchered him high and tight.

"You been to the Union City?" I ask the old man.

"Yes," he says.

"Is it worth the wait?"

"The food is edible, yes," he says. "And there's a fella works there who is a good sort."

I wait, giving him a chance to say something else. But I guess that's all I'm getting from him. I don't know: Maybe everybody down here on the Gateway is jumpy and suspicious. Maybe, if I want to blend in, I should stop trying to be so goddamned friendly. I dig out my smokes, and I'm lighting a cigarette when I notice the old man staring at me like I just pulled a steak sandwich out of my breast pocket. I take the pack out again and shake it toward him.

He reaches out that delicate hand of his and takes one of the cigarettes — carefully, like he thinks I'm going to change my mind and pull the deck away from him any second. I guess a pack of cigarettes really is something strange around here. I did see some of the Gateway Square bums scrounging for butts under the park benches.

"Thank you," the old man says.

"Cheers," I say. I offer the kid a smoke but he shakes his head no.

I light the old man's cigarette and I think maybe, now that we've got that between us, he'll open up and give me a piece of conversation. Funny how, when you're alone for a day or two, you can get hungry for talk just like a person gets hungry for food. But the old man just smokes without talking.

After a long while, after he's almost through the cigarette, the old man says, "You're very kind."

This embarrasses me. You know. What the hell? I only gave the man a cigarette. I shrug and smile.

I decide to try again for conversation. "You got a place to flop down here?"

"No," the old man says. "We're just passing through."

This, I guess, is pretty obvious, really. They've both got rucksacks on the cement beside them. "Traveling together?" I say. "Where to?"

The boy tenses. I get that even from where I'm sitting. But the old man only blows out his lungsmoke slowly. "Just traveling," he says. He touches his rucksack with his left hand. "I'm an artist. I sketch. I paint pictures of the things we see on the road."

"You on the rails?"

"Sometimes. On the hoof when we need to be."

"Where'd you start out?"

But the old man doesn't answer this. I look at the kid's face and now I'm pretty sure he does speak English, or at least understands the English I'm speaking. He's staring straight ahead, away from me, but it seems he's working very hard at it.

Then I all of a sudden get the idea. I look at the boy's face more closely. Is he even sixteen? Maybe younger. Round cheeks, with a little rash of pimples near the jawline. Big Wop eyes and a too-large, blubbery-looking mouth. Christ.

"If I may ask," I say, lowering my voice. I motion between the old man and the kid. "What's your relation?"

"None," the old man says, and "I'm his nephew," the kid says. The dark eyes of the kid grow blacker. He glares down at the sidewalk, wipes at his nose. "We ain't blood-related," he says.

So he does speak English, and without an accent. But his voice is odd, its tone forced deep, a boy trying to pass for a man. Maybe the boy's fourteen.

I look away from the two of them. "I get it," I say.

I'm an adult. I know the score. Still. I start feeling a little dirty, just sitting beside them on the ground. What did I expect? I'm down here on the Gateway with the cockroaches and the rats and the bedbugs.

"Sprague," the old man says. I turn back to him. He's got his hand out, like he wants to shake. "Name's Edmund Sprague."

I look at his hand and then I look at the kid beside him. The kid is again running his dirty fingers over his dark, close-clipped hair, staring down at nothing on the sidewalk in front of him. I look back at Sprague and then, I guess just because I really am feeling lonely and like I'm missing conversation — *any* conversation, even in the company of a pervert — I take the old man's hand and shake it.

"Tom Powers," I say. That's Cagney's character from *Public Enemy*. "But don't try too hard remembering that. You know what I mean?"

"I think so," Sprague says. "This here's Ben. But don't try too hard remembering us, either."

I nod. "I've got the shortest memory in Minneapolis."

"We appreciate that."

I get a good long look into this Sprague fellow's face and he seems to me a pretty decent sort. Even if he's a filthy sodomite, he's playing it pretty straight with me. I like that.

"You new in town?" Sprague asks me.

"Yeah," I say. "Let's say that. I'm new in town."

He gives a quick nod, understanding. "Right. Well, the Union City is good for what it is. It draws a crowd, though. There's some smaller missions east of here, off the square, where the folks'll actually look you in the eye, and where you can sit over your meal longer than five minutes without someone shoving you out the door."

"I don't mind a crowd," I say. "I can eat fast. And I don't need anybody looking me in the eye."

Sprague stares at me. Now he seems to be trying to get a good long look into *my* face, trying to read what sort of fellow *I* am. I guess I pass muster, because a muscle twitches in Sprague's narrow, sun-reddened cheek, and under the white bristle of his beard something like a smile shows itself.

"Me and Ben," Sprague says, "we eat every meal at the Union City."

"I get it," I say.

"If we ever see you there sometime," he says, "I hope you won't mind if we don't join you. Ben and I move mostly on our own."

"I bet you do," I say. Then, just to take the edge off the nasty crack, I say, "I guess I also move mostly on my own."

This brings out a full-blown grin from Sprague. Taking his cue from the old man, Ben turns to me, and the kid gives me a smile, too. His wide, blubbery lips curl up in the corners and his black, wet-looking eyes change, narrowing, their long lashes closing in on each other. It makes me squirm a little, the way this pansy-boy looks at me now, though I can't really say why.

Sprague and Ben and me sit there against the wall and smoke through half a pack of cigarettes, though none of us says much of anything else. I've given up trying to make normal conversation. Oddest thing is, I start to feeling pretty comfortable with these silent queers — the two of them are the type of fellas you can sit beside without speaking and have a perfectly fine time. But then a half-memory flashes behind my eyes and all at once a kind of wild idea comes over me.

I tap my heels against the sidewalk. "You two aren't really just passing through, are you?"

Sprague smiles. "And you're not really new in town. What of it?"

"Well," I say, "I saw the two of you on the Lake Street streetcar line last summer."

Sprague's smile lessens a little. "I thought you said you had the shortest memory in Minneapolis."

"I do, I do," I say. "Forget the streetcar. Only listen: last fall, I had a bad drunk and fell asleep in the park. Powderhorn Park. South side of town. I probably would have froze except somebody covered me. I just now had this idea that — "

"No decent man could pass a fellow in that state," Sprague says.

"No?" I ask.

"No."

"Come on, Ed," the kid says. He pulls on the sleeve of Sprague's shirt as he's getting up. Sprague stands, too.

"Was it you two?" I ask. "Because I have memories, but they're all messed up from the drink."

Ben stops tugging on his sleeve and Sprague looks down at me with those weirdly calm eyes of his. "Does it matter who it was that helped you?"

"Well," I say. "I'd like to thank the man. Or men."

"I doubt that's necessary," Sprague says.

"I'm a fella who believes in paying debts owed."

"You don't owe me and Ben a thing."

"Don't I?" I touch my shirt pocket, where I've got a couple of bills folded up. "Listen," I say. "Let me throw you a buck. I can spare it — don't ask how or why — and I think you two could use it."

"We don't need any money," Sprague says. "We get along all right."

"That so?" I say. I take a look at the kid, who has moved off a couple of steps away, his face turned toward the Gateway fountain across the street. I drop my voice, quiet. "Take it for the kid. Give him a night in a decent flop. Or a shower, at least."

"No," the kid says. He comes around back beside Sprague. "I'm with Ed. We don't need money. We do all right on our own."

"You've given us cigarettes," Sprague says. "And now, you'll forget about ever having seen us. That's thanks enough."

Looking into Sprague's eyes, I see now why I remembered him in the first place, why out of a hundred bums I've seen on the streets, he stayed in my memory. It's those eyes — the way they looked so calm when the Lake Street conductor turned him and Ben off the car, and the way they look so calm now, like everything is just fine and all any of us has to do is just play along nice.

"Okay," I say to him. I understand clearly enough why a pair like this would want to keep a low profile. "You've got it."

Sprague drops his chin down, a kind of bow, and then he and Ben leave me. I watch them walk across the street and into the square, but then I remember what I've agreed to, and so I stop watching where they're walking. I don't see where Sprague and Ben go. They just disappear into the crowd of tired-looking men who are not moving much. They just disappear.

Sixteen

The food at the Union City mission is free. I guess that's all you can say for it. But I'm hungrier than I knew, and the watery soup goes down fast. It's about like Sprague said, just five minutes or so before the staff starts moving among the tables, collecting the plates. I see that some of the other fellas at my table are shoving bread into their pockets and so I do, too.

I don't rush out with the crowd and I'm one of the last sitting. A big bastard with orange hair, one of the mission staff, starts yelling at me to move on. I won't even be bothered to look at him, but I stand up and begin moving toward the exit door behind the others.

"Say, friend — did you speak to the minister?"

I turn around to see who's talking at me now and I see the jerk. The curly-haired, glasses-wearing jerk from earlier in the afternoon, who wouldn't open up the door for me.

"No," I say. "I didn't see the minister. I decided my soul was about right just as it is."

The jerk smiles at this. "Good for you."

I don't quite understand what he means by that, and I don't quite understand why he's following me out the door instead of staying behind and clearing the tables with the rest of the staff. I nod my head back toward the eating room.

"Don't you have work to do?" I ask him.

"Nah," he says. "My shift is done. I mop up in the afternoons. This here's the evening shift."

"It's quite an operation they run here, isn't it?"

"It's something, all right."

We come out of the mission onto the sidewalk. This time of summer, the sun is still high in the evening. Even from here, I can hear the voice of the orange-haired bastard inside, shouting at somebody. I look at the jerk, squinting into the sun.

"Tell me something," I say. "How come everybody's such a son-of-a-bitch in there? Ain't you folks supposed to be doing God's work?"

The jerk laughs at this. "I'm doing my own work. I push a broom and get paid thirty cents an hour for it. Not a bad gig."

He pulls out a pack of cigarettes and offers me one. I take it.

"My name's Dave," the jerk says. "Dave Levin."

I've got the cigarette between my fingers and I hold it right there. "Levin," I say. "That a Jewish name?"

He shrugs. "I suppose it is."

"Well," I say. "There's no supposin' about it. Are you Jewish?"

"I ain't nothing, pal. I'm an atheist."

"What? You don't believe in God?" I say. "But you work in a mission."

"I told you. It's a gig. A job." He lights his cigarette and holds the match out to me.

I stick the cigarette between my lips and take the light he offers.

"But, okay," Levin says. "I guess you might call me a do-gooder. I kind of feel like I'm helping out some, down here. You know what I mean. My fellow man or whatnot. But don't worry, I'm not going to give you a lecture about class struggles or workers' movements or anything like that."

"Good," I say.

Levin touches the wire frame of his eyeglasses and bends his head a little forward. "Anyway. I didn't catch your name."

"I didn't offer it."

"I see." He looks a little embarrassed.

"Tom Powers," I say. Cagney again. "I'm just a guy on the soup line."

Levin shakes his head at this. "Don't let the times crush you, friend. You're still a man, whatever your circumstances."

"Okay, Levin," I say. "You've done your good deed for the day. Gave me a nice little pep talk. I feel like a new man. Think I'll go join the W.P.A. with the rest of my fellow-mans."

He just laughs at this. Maybe he's not such a jerk, really.

"I like your attitude," Levin says.

"Have I got an attitude?"

"Yeah," he says. "You're a wise-guy. I think you've gotta be, living down in these parts. Lose that attitude and you've lost the whole game."

"Who said I was playing a game?"

I thank him for the smoke and I say goodnight to him. I start walking back in the direction of my room. My hangover is just now leveling off, and I'm tired as hell. No drinking tonight. I just want to go to sleep.

*

I spend a week at the Washington Avenue rooming house. I never drink like I did my first night down here. I've placed limits on myself. A few beers in the afternoon is all. In the morning I have coffee at the wagon across from the rail depot. Then I normally sit in the Gateway Park and read a newspaper or stare at the pigeons. If it rains, I duck into the big waiting room of the Great Northern station and sit. I go around to the Union City mission for the noon meal, and I usually see Levin there.

We make small talk. Throw a few lines back and forth at one another. I'm a bit jumpy around him at first. But I feel him out, kind of coming at the subject from the side, about what kind of Jew he is and who he knows. He's come just recently from the east, from somewhere in Indiana, and he doesn't have any relatives — or any connections at all — here in Minneapolis. I begin to relax around him. He tries introducing me to some of the other men at the tables. I don't think Levin gets it that I'm not interested in having a social life down here.

Levin is, like he said, a do-gooder. I guess he really is an atheist, and he laughs along with the rest of us at the Methodist preachers who sermonize before the soup is served in the mission. Levin is an atheist but he's not a Communist. He pokes fun at the Reds same as he laughs at the Methodists. He's educated — he tells me he dropped his studies at the university just a year shy of graduating with a bachelor's diploma — but he doesn't put on airs. I don't quite know what Levin is. But Levin looks out for the men in the mission.

"Stay away from the rail jungle down the tracks near the water," he'll say. "Bad folks."

Or, "There's a barber college on Tenth Street gives haircuts free Wednesdays."

Levin tells me, "Cop named Ryan — big blonde — avoid him. He makes trouble."

And, "There's a news vendor over on Marquette who'll hand out free cigarettes. One or two at a go."

"If you want," Levin says to me one day, "you can pick up an hour of work in the market, loading trucks. Ask the drivers."

The fact is, I'm spending the money I've got fast. Can't imagine how. I eat a meal a day at the mission, and go to the cheap diners for the rest. The landlord wants another week's rent on my room now, and so there goes another handful of bills. I could use some income.

So the next day, before his shift starts, Levin walks me over to the market district and he points out to me which drivers will hire free men to help load their trucks — got to avoid the Red drivers, see, who only use the organized packers. Levin brings me over to a driver named Schneider, a fat-necked Kraut with a smile full of gold teeth, and Levin introduces us. The morning next, I get up extra early and head over to the market to find some work.

Schneider takes me on.

"My daddy taught me to never mix with them Commie union fellas," Schneider says. He talks to me while I unload crates of strawberries from his truck, that gold-toothed smile of his flashing all the while. He's a happy son of a bitch. Besides never mixing with Commies, he says his daddy also taught him to always keep himself clean. And his daddy taught him to never drink anything stronger than milk. Schneider puts a lot of stock in his daddy's wisdom, and he likes to spread it around.

"My daddy taught me, treat a man fair," Schneider says when the truck is unloaded, paying me two bits for an hour's work. More than fair. I like Schneider.

"You back tomorrow?" I ask Schneider.

"Nope," he says. "But Monday, Wednesday, Friday. Look for Schneider."

"I will," I say.

I walk out of the market heading for First Avenue, back toward the Gateway. As I pass the docks, some of the truck loaders from the union give me bad looks. But most of them ignore me. It's a hot summer morning, coming up on noon, and men are tired from the morning's lifting and nobody wants to make trouble for a poor slob scrounging up a few nickels. If these men give me any thought at all, they likely just pity me — another man out of work and out of home, living down among the invisible in a rented room on the Gateway.

*

Another week passes and I'm running out of money. Monday, I sleep through my chance to work for Schneider in the morning market. Tuesday, I arrive early and haul boxes of lettuce for three hours, for a Polock who then pays me twenty cents for the morning. Wednesday morning, I get to the market late and two other men are already working Schneider's truck. I can't find anyone else who'll take me on. Thursday and Friday, I sleep in again, sick from cheap rye and too much beer. Levin's taken to lecturing me about the drink, and so things have fallen off between us. He's directing his do-gooding and advice to other men who, I guess, seem to hold more promise.

I sit on my bed up in my room and I lay all my coinage and bills out over the blanket. I count it twice, three times. It's running out. I never had a head for money — at home, Annie always took care of this kind of thing — but now, for the first time in my life, I try to make up what they call a budget. A plan. I calculate what I'm spending and how it jibes with what I've got laid out on the bed in front of me. When the rent comes due, I leave my Washington Avenue room. I cross the Gateway to the cage house on the square.

The bored mulatto desk clerk with the ugly growth on his face walks me up the stairs again to an empty cage, one in a line. I take out some coins and hand them over right there. The desk clerk fishes in his vest pocket for a key, which he hands over to me. Now that he's got my money, he seems to brighten a bit.

"Welcome to the Aldrich Arms," he says. "Stay a week or stay a month. No eating in the cage. Drink if you need to, but no food. It brings out the rats."

"I got it," I say.

"My name is Mr. Charles, by the way."

He holds out his hand to shake but I don't feel much like shaking hands.

"Hello, Mr. Charles," I say. "My name is nobody's business."

If he's insulted by my not shaking his hand, he doesn't show it. He grins at me, which makes the ugly thing on his face twitch upwards.

"You're a mystery man, eh? We get a few of those from time to time."

"No mystery about me," I say to Charles. "You clear on that? Nothing mysterious about me at all. I'm just nothing. As far as you're concerned, I'm like a bug on these walls. I'm nothing."

His grin fades and the big wart-thing slumps downward.

"Okay, Mr. Stranger," Charles says, squeezing my dollar in his fist. "Whatever you say. Though you'll find soon enough that *everybody* here on the row is nothing. No need to make special requests from the management on that front."

He seems pleased with his joke, and he goes away laughing. He laughs all the way down the stairs. He stops laughing once he's down back behind his desk on the ground floor. I turn to my cage and stick the key into the padlock. I open the door and step inside.

*

I ride the streetcar late at night. I can't afford to drink in the saloons now, and so I'm mostly sober. I can't sleep in the heat of the cage. I walk around the blocks or sit in the square till the cops chase us all out at midnight. After midnight, I ride the streetcar.

Sometimes I take the line that runs out to the Lakes on the west end of town, and I ride the rear platform and catch the breeze from Lake Harriet. Sometimes I hop off and walk down to the grassy edge of Lake of the Isles, and I can fall asleep for an hour or two until I wake up with the light, my body stiff and bitten red by the mosquitoes and horseflies. I catch the car back downtown as soon as I'm able. A solitary man, unshaven and in unclean clothes, I'm too easily noticed in this neighborhood of bluestone walks and well-tended lawns, once the morning people come out.

One night, long after midnight, I ride the Portland Avenue car out to my neighborhood, out to the Powderhorn. I'm alone in the car except for a couple of bleary-eyed college boys, who are having an earnest conversation about atoms, and a hospital intern who's fallen asleep in his white labcoat. I climb off the car at Lake Street, which is near deserted at this hour but for the moths clattering against the overhead streetlamps, and I walk quickly up the block away from the light.

First I walk past Caroline's apartment building on Columbus. I'm not sure why. Her window faces back, away from the street, and all I see here is the concrete stoop I've rushed up a hundred times, on a hundred different evenings. Maybe I'm hoping I'll see something, anything, that will tell me she is still there. That she hasn't quit the city and gone back to North Dakota. I know I'll never find her again if she leaves. I guess I want also for the apartment building to tell me that Caroline is safe — that nobody, looking for me, has made the connection between her and me. But the squat, yellow-colored building is telling me no secrets. Its windows are dark, its bricks as dumb as the stones of Egypt.

I skirt the park and walk to 34th Street, not hurrying as much as I was before, and go up 17th Avenue to the house where my family is sleeping. It's a humble old thing, this house. Clapboard, from the nineties. The landlord painted it the summer before last, but it still looks like it's drooping with age. The maple in the front yard is full and heavy with summer. I stand across the street and two lots down, feeling like I need this distance, and this angle, for safety. I make my eyes go to the upper windows first, to the Brinks' flat. I think of the old lady there, probably in her silly, old-fashioned night-cap, and the old man snoring loud enough to be heard in the rooms below.

When I let my eyes turn to the lower floor, I see that the windows of my home are thrown open in the heat, and this to me closes up the distance I've arranged for myself, here across the street; I know that the sounds of the singing crickets and the June beetles slapping against the screens are reaching the people asleep inside. I am sharing the air with them, taking deep breaths of the same 4:00 AM damp. I watch the windows. I see the twins' bedroom, with a paper cut-out of a Buck Rogers missile taped on the window glass. In Bridget's window the nightlight is on, breaking the dark behind the screen with the slightest yellow glow from its spot near the floor. And from my place across the street I can see the window at the side of the house, back, the bedroom Annie and I shared, where I know she is just now lost in her deep, unreachable way — a sleep I always envied — in the warm air dense with Stanley's talcum-y baby scent and with the occasional dream-whimperings of small Richard (climbed in beside Annie an hour ago), and with the even, untroubled risings and fallings of their breath in sleep.

I walk away. At the end of the block, passing beneath the streetlamp, I take a cigarette from my pack. My hands shake, and I burn through three matches before I manage to get the cigarette lit. The smoke tastes like salt-fish and it stings in my nose. I drop the cigarette away and walk with my hands shoved down into my pockets.

I make my way to the Powderhorn Park, but when I stand at the edge and look out over the slope to the lake, I see far across the way a single dark sedan cruising slowly. It's the first car I've seen moving in the neighborhood in fifteen minutes. I decide then to walk fast back to Lake Street, for the downtown streetcar.

At the Park Avenue corner, Lake Street is bare and quiet and I step back out of the streetlamp light, into the shadow cast by the awning of a shuttered dentist's office. I stand still and wait for the downtown car.

A minute later, a cross-town streetcar approaches, gliding up through the predawn silence, heading east. The car stops for the traffic light on the street just in front of me. Out of sight, I watch the streetcar while it waits, humming with electricity. By the light cast from the bulbs in the car's ceiling, I can see that it is empty but for the driver, standing in the front over his lever. But no. Someone far back, in the rear seat. Two someones — a couple. Mother of Christ. It's the two queers from down on the Gateway, fallen asleep into one another's arms. Well, actually, it's the old man, Sprague, who's fallen sideways, asleep. The kid, Ben, is wide awake and staring straight ahead toward the driver's back. Sprague is dropped over, his mouth agape beneath his silver beard, looking dead as Christ down from the cross. Ben holds him round the shoulders. While I'm watching them, Sprague's mouth twitches and his chest heaves, and I see Ben tighten his grip round the old man.

The light changes and the streetcar rattles and hums more loudly and then glides forward away. I stand in my place in the dark and stare at the rear of the car as it goes away down Lake Street. So that's the state of things. The sodomites are passing the night together in their own kind of love, while I am left alone, waiting for a streetcar to take me away from my people, back down to my cage in the Gateway. I light a cigarette, being careful to hold it in the cup of my hand, shielding its glow in the dark, and I wait. It's another ten minutes before the downtown car arrives.

Seventeen

July in Minneapolis comes on just like the weather in one of those Saturday Evening Post romance stories set on a Georgia plantation. The air hangs on you. It kind of sticks in your mouth when you breathe. But I'm not taking naps on the veranda while the Darkies sing in the magnolia bushes, and this July air is wearing my body down.

I'm not eating well. I've lost weight, and I'm not a heavy man to start. Three of my teeth have come out, loosed in a pounding I took down in the hobo jungle one night. I know Levin the do-gooder said to steer away from the jungle down at the riverfront, but it's a society open to any who'll play by the rules, and it's down there in the jungle that a man without money can get drunk if he knows how. The head man in the jungle sends me for firewood or scrap tin to use for shelter, and when I come through, he pays me with a share of a bottle of wine. He looks out for me, too, if the wine makes me mean and a fight starts. But the other night, the head man wasn't around, and I got beat badly.

The hearing in one of my ears seems to be going on me, and I've a cough I can't shake. I think maybe I caught something from sleeping up in the bad air of the cage house.

My money's all gone. It's spent. But I've grown used to living without. I panhandle for the dollar a week I pay for the cage. I eat all my meals at the mission now. Every once in a while, I make it down to the market early enough to pick up work with Schneider or one of the other drivers, unloading fruit trucks. I'm grown used to this.

I don't drink every day any more. My empty pockets are my own personal Temperance League. Maybe once a week, if things went the right way for me and I wasn't feeling too miserable, I'd make my way down to the river and into a hobo bottle gang. But I think I'm through with the bottle gang, after the other night. Anyway, I don't like the way the drink makes my brain lose its focus, because in the life I'm living I need to focus. Mostly I'm just trying to stay alive.

I can't quit the Gateway. Believe me, I've considered it. It's a bad time, this, but whenever the thought of quitting comes upon me I remind myself again of that one lone sedan I saw cruising the edge of the Powderhorn Park at 4:00 AM.

Levin collars me one morning as I'm leaving the Union City. "Hold up there, Powers," he says.

I stop. Maybe he'll give me a cigarette. "Hello, Levin."

"I heard you ran into some trouble down at the water."

"You heard this where?"

"From a friend of yours."

"I haven't got any friends."

"An older gentleman. He sketches. Does drawings."

This has got me stumped. Then it occurs to me. "Sprague? The old queer?"

"Queer?" Levin asks.

"Never mind," I say, shaking my head. "He travels with a kid."

"That's the one. The two of them come and go."

"Do they?" I say. My curiosity is up. How did Sprague know about my run-in down at the water? And when he and the kid go from the Gateway, where do they go to? I decide to let it drop. I feel bad enough for having let slip that "queer" reference.

"He told me," Levin says, "that he thought you were hurting."

"No more than anyone else," I say.

Levin looks like he wants to say something else about this business, but he seems to change his mind. His hand in his pants pocket, he jingles a ring of keys.

"You getting any work?" he asks.

"You know," I say. "When I'm able."

"Well," Levin says. "Are you able now?"

*

Levin has a car. When his shift ends at the Union City that afternoon, he goes around to pick up the car and then he drives it to the First Avenue corner where I've agreed to meet him.

Levin's car is a big Chrysler, five years old but nice. I guess Levin comes from money. It makes sense. People from money always seem to have the time to work in soup kitchens and do good deeds.

Levin's good deed today is that he's driving me over to his girl's house to paint her living room. I don't know if this good deed is a good idea or not. But the sound of getting out of the Gateway for a few hours appeals to me.

"She'll pay you two dollars for the afternoon," Levin says to me, though I get the feeling this whole ride isn't really so much about me making another dollar.

Levin wants to talk.

"You'll like my girl," he says. "Dolores, her name is."

We're driving on the parkway with all the windows down. I'm letting the wind hit me across the face and it feels like the most wonderful thing in the world. "Dolores. It's a swell name," I say.

"She's a swell girl." He looks sideways at me. "She's a Catholic."

"Is she?" I say.

"You got a problem with that?"

"Me? No."

"Why not?"

This makes me turn from my window. "Why don't I have a problem with you dating a Catholic girl?"

"Yes," Levin says. He touches his eyeglasses. "See, some folks do have a problem with it."

"Which folks? Her folks?"

"Her father, yes," Levin says.

I smile at him. "Is the father's problem with you being a Jew or you being an atheist?"

Levin smiles, too. "I haven't really brought up the atheism with the old man."

I turn back to the open window and just let the wind hit me some more. The big Chrysler is a powerful thing. We're doing forty, easy, and there's no strain sounding in the engine.

"She an Irish girl?" I ask.

Levin shakes his head. "French. Her father is French."

"Ah," I say. I laugh into the wind. "Who the hell knows how the Frogs think."

Levin just wrings the steering wheel between his two hands. He doesn't really want to laugh about this. "But you're Catholic," he says.

"Yeah?"

"And you're a pretty sharp guy."

"I am," I say.

"Too sharp to get caught up in some of the business you're messing with downtown," he says. "But never mind that."

"I'll never mind, all right."

"Anyway,' Levin says. "I thought you might know something about — about how I could talk to Dolores's father."

"I don't know nothing," I say. "But I like your car."

*

Levin's girl, Dolores, lives with her father in a pretty little stuccoed bungalow — one of those jobs from about ten years ago, done up to look like an English cottage, with the leaded glass panes in the windows and the timbered eaves — across the river in St. Paul. The father's not home. He owns a framing store on Snelling Avenue and he works the store till after dark. So it's just the three of us, sitting around together in the small, clean house surrounded by lilac bushes and hydrangeas and birdsong.

There's no work to be done in the living room. Not that Levin was misleading me. But Dolores has forgotten to buy dropcloths and masking tape, so it doesn't make sense to start messing things up. She's got nothing but a bucket of blue oil paint and a two-inch brush. We all have a laugh. No work. Instead, we three sit down in the kitchen and Dolores makes a pitcher of iced lemonade.

I like the looks of Dolores. She's skinnier than I want a girl to be, but she has a marvelous mouth and eyes the color of the lemonade icecubes. Her hair is remarkable, dark red and put up high on her head in an old-fashioned way. It looks like it would reach to her knees if she'd let it down. She doesn't do her face up with makeup, and this makes her look younger than she is. I mean, I can see that she's no kid. I think she's older than Levin. I could begin to wonder what a girl this age is doing still living at home with her father, but I let it go. I'm having a good time.

We sit at the table in the kitchen and the two of them do most of the talking. They're having a conversation about some book they've both read — the name means nothing to me — and they're arguing over the characters and the plot-line like they're discussing a radio comedy. Dolores has got brains, like Levin. I don't mind. I'd forgotten how the sound of a woman's voice can change a room. I think about a solarium I passed through once in some finely's house, a room filled with rubber plants and tropical ferns – how the air was richer there, so lousy with oxygen that it made you move quicker just to get a sniff of it. I look out the kitchen window and listen to Dolores's voice, talking.

It's a kick to see Levin changed, too. Down at the mission, he's all about giving advice and watching after men. Maybe he acts a little more on top of things, a little more street-wise, than he is. Here, now, he's softened up. I can see that he's smart as hell, and clever with words, in a way that he tries to mask in his place downtown. He's not putting up any fronts here. It's always something to watch a man around the girl he's in love with. All the masks go out the window. Dolores calls him "Davey," which only adds to the picture of her being older than him.

They go on talking, every once in a while nodding my direction or lifting their eyebrows at me like they expect me to agree or disagree with whatever it is they're saying about this book of theirs.

I catch on that Dolores doesn't seem too bothered by sharing her table with me, a strange man in unpressed clothes and an unshaved face. I think maybe Levin brings around mission cases to her place all the time. That must be it. But then they finish up with their novel-talk and Dolores turns her attention to me.

"So," she says. "You're the first of Davey's friends from downtown that I've ever met."

"Am I?" I say. I look at Levin. He's just staring into his lemonade.

"Have you been on the row long?" she asks me.

The row? Sounds funny, slang like that coming out her marvelous mouth. Maybe that's how intellectual types talk. I shrug my shoulders at Dolores.

"You know," I say. "It's a temporary situation."

"It seems sometimes," she says, "that you men down there have simply dropped off the face of the Earth."

"Yeah," I say. "That's the general idea, for some of us."

"But we're not letting you fellows be forgotten," Levin pipes in, suddenly taking on his Union City manner again.

"I appreciate that, friend," I say to Levin.

Dolores laughs. She seems to get that I'm poking fun at Levin. I don't think Levin gets it.

I take Dolores in. "So," I say. "Dave tells me you're a Catholic."

"Well," she says. "In a manner of speaking. I'm kind of fallen away from the Church."

"I get it," I say. "I'm a little fallen away myself."

"When I met Mr. Powers here," Levin says now, "he was looking for a priest. Looking to confess."

"Is that so?" Dolores asks me. Her ice-colored eyes aren't laughing anymore.

"Ah, you know," I say. "I was giving him a line. Trying to get into the —"

"Relax, Powers," Levin says. "I was just teasing you."

I look at Levin. His eyes are shining behind his glasses and his funny, fleshy mouth is curled up into a grin I've never seen on him before. He's teasing me. I can't remember the last time somebody teased me. The whole game of it gets me laughing, and I laugh so hard I start in coughing. I can't stop coughing.

"Take a drink," Dolores says.

I drink the lemonade but it takes me a few more minutes before I'm recovered. Dolores and Levin, once they're satisfied that I'm not going to die on them there at the kitchen table, have begun a conversation about some play. They didn't see the play performed, from what I gather, but they read the script of the thing in a book. It seems a hell of a play, by the way the two of them get caught up in their discussion of it. I let them go, but I'm beginning to feel a little restless. There are some books on the enamel-topped table, pushed off away to the far end, and I reach to take one off the top of the stack.

I turn it over in my hand and it's got just one word embossed on its cover. Swinburne. I'm thinking it's some kind of book of jokes. But I open it, and it's just poems. I start to read one of the poems near the middle of the book and it's not bad. I kind of get lost in the reading and I don't even notice that Dolores and Levin have stopped their talking.

"It's wonderful, isn't it?" Dolores asks me, after a while.

I kind of jump, looking up from the book. Levin has stood up and gone to the screen door of the kitchen, where he's facing out at the neat little back yard. Dolores is lighting a cigarette, narrowing her eyes at the book in my hand. "It's alright, I guess," I say. "I don't know anything about poetry."

"Me neither," she says. "Davey recommended him to me. I'm trying to understand it."

"What's to understand?" I ask her. "Seems pretty straightforward to me."

"Well," she says. "On one level, yes. But I'm working on reading into it to the next levels."

"I get you," I say. Some people have too much time on their hands. I signal for one of her cigarettes and she hands me the pack.

"Davey and I are going to step out into the yard," Dolores says to me. "Relax. Help yourself to more lemonade."

"I will," I say. "Thanks."

The two of them go out and I read a few more pages of the Swinburne book. Then I shuffle through some of the other books on the table. French novels and German plays. There's a biography of some Admiral from the last century. It gives me a bit of a headache just reading the covers of these books. I stand up from the table.

I go to the door and look out at Dolores and Levin. They're off under a weeping cherry tree, just talking. Dolores is standing with her hands on her hips and her face dropped down toward the shaded ground. She's smiling at whatever Levin is telling her. He's picking in a nervous way at the branch closest to him, shredding the leaves between his fingers, and he's swinging his hips a little side to side. He's like a kid around her. Looks like he's pouring out the secrets of his heart. Or maybe he's just analyzing one of the deeper levels of some European poem. Can't really tell. Is Levin pitching woo or turning over the folds of her brain? The damndest thing is, I think they'd both be equally happy whether it was one or the other.

They're a couple, all right. I guess I'm no idiot myself. I did okay in school. I mean, when I took the time to be there. Anyway, I graduated, with a high school diploma. That's something.

I stand at the kitchen door and smoke, blowing rings that break apart through the screening. I never cared much for intellectuals. I never wanted to know more than what's right in front of me. But now, watching Dolores and Levin out in the yard under the weeping cherry, I wish I could read some book or attend some lecture just so I'd understand why seeing the two of them this way makes me feel so goddamned happy.

I all of a sudden feel strange, watching out at Levin and his girl this way. I can't hear what they're saying, but I should stop looking. Let them be. I turn back to the kitchen and cross to the table, where I sit down and pour myself another glass of lemonade from the pitcher. I finish my cigarette and take another from the pack Dolores has left. I don't bother trying to read any of the rest of the books.

*

Levin drives just as fast coming back into Minneapolis as he did on his way out to see Dolores. I like a man who drives fast. Funny, I wouldn't have pegged Levin for a leadfoot. But we're slipping over Selby Avenue like a rocket shot through the atmosphere.

Levin seems gloomy. I guess from just having said goodbye to his girl. He's glaring out at the road ahead of the Chrysler's long hood.

"She's a lovely girl," I say to him.

His face doesn't change. "You think so?"

"Yeah. Too bad about the religion, though."

He kind of blows out some air between his lips. "Too bad is right."

"But it's only the father, right?" I say. "Dolores seems happy as hell around you."

"She does, doesn't she?" he says, smiling a little now.

"Yeah," I say. I look out at the trees as they tick past us. I don't say anything else for a while. Then, I say, "Levin. Let me ask you something."

"Shoot," he says.

"Why'd you bring me out here?"

"I told you. The painting."

"No, you told me it was about me being Catholic, like Dolores."

He taps his thumbs against the steering wheel. "I don't know. I just thought you might be able to talk to her."

"You and her were doing enough talking without me. Besides — like I say — it's not Dolores who needs talking to. It's her old man."

"I know. I know."

"It seems to me," I say, getting my wind now, "that you and your girl have a good thing going. Maybe you don't have the whole world all laid out in front of you — most of us don't — but you've got a pretty nice situation, for what it is. Have fun with it." I can see by the look on his face that he doesn't like being lectured to. But he's not arguing against me.

"You're right, of course," he says.

"Sure I'm right," I say. "What did you think, that I'd come out here and teach you the secret Catholic handshake, or clue you in on some bit of forgotten Church catechism that offers a loophole for godless Jews marrying Catholic girls?"

Levin laughs softly at this. "Maybe I didn't expect you to say anything," he says. He presses his foot onto the accelerator, passing a slow-moving newspaper van. He smiles. "Maybe I just wanted to show off."

"Show off?"

It hits me then that Levin really doesn't have any friends. I'm it. Kind of sad, but I'm touched. Every fellow needs to show off his girl.

Levin is grinning now. "She's a swell girl isn't she?"

"Sure she is."

"She's the brightest thing I've ever known. She reads four languages. She's a genius."

"Yeah, yeah," I say. "A genius." Like I know anything about genius. "She's got nice hair."

"Her hair, yes." Levin does that thing I'd seen him do before, wringing the steering wheel between his fists. "She's been growing it out for nine years."

"What's nine years?" I ask. "She was sick?"

"Sick, yeah," he says. "You could say that." He starts up laughing, like he's got some private joke playing inside his head. "I forgot to tell you, Powers. Dolores is a nun."

He shoots me a quick look sideways. "An ex-nun, of course."

He laughs some more, and I let him laugh. I don't get that it's that funny.

Levin shakes his head at the hood of the Chrysler. "Not bad enough that I take a tumble for a *shiksa*. I had to fall in love with a nun."

"What's a *shiksa*?" I ask. But Levin doesn't answer me.

After a short while, his laugh kind of runs out of gas. The private joke has played itself out inside Levin's head, and nothing's funny any more. He's making that face again, glaring through the windshield at the oncoming traffic.

We drive, fast, across the bridge onto Lake Street, then toward downtown. It's late when Levin drops me off in the Gateway, though still light. It'll be light for another two hours. I wave at Levin as he lurches away in his big Chrysler, heading from here for I don't know where. I walk over to the fountain and stare down into the rust-smelling water splashing over the dirty marble basin. Then I walk away to a bench downwind and I sit down. A mist comes off the fountain, feeling cool, and it washes over me until after sundown.

Eighteen

Schneider, the happy Kraut driver from the market, has not showed in a week. Some trouble with his vehicle, somebody said. I miss Schneider.

I've been going to the market most every morning. Broke now. Can't afford to drink at all, and the summer heat makes the cage hotel unbearable, and so nothing is keeping me from being awake and out at sunrise. I've been unloading berries and greens for whoever will take me on, but the most I can pick up is twenty or thirty cents a morning.

Levin is always good for cigarettes. The other day, I asked him for some change to buy a real meal away from the mission, and he cut me dead. I looked at him and he looked at me and I guess we were both thinking the same thing — that I'd ridden in that big Chrysler of his and I'd seen the life he lives with that girl, and he and I both know that he can spare a few bits for a man sick and broke and hungry on the row. But he wouldn't give me a thing. He started playing out some line about friendship and money and independence, but I wasn't hearing any of it. Things are pretty cold between Levin and myself now. To hell with him. Him and his stolen Bride of Christ. This morning, walking back from the market, I find myself scanning the sidewalk for smokeable butts.

I'm as low as I can go. My health is no good and I guess my mind will start to go on me next. Already, I know I'm too jumpy, and racked by dark fears. Passing a drug store on Marquette Avenue the other morning, I spotted one of those posters the

St. Paul millionaire puts up, offering reward money for his missing servant-girl. If Mr. Steven Linen can cover downtown with these posters, maybe the northside gang can, too, in their own way. Maybe they're offering a "substantial reward" for what they're looking to find. Maybe they're wise to how a man like me might try to disappear down here among the hard cases.

I've taken to staying in my cage during daylight. At night, when I go out, I keep moving. I don't sit in the square. I just walk and walk. I see a slow-moving car and I quickly change direction. I don't like anybody looking me in the face — I break out panting and sweating like a marathon dancer.

But I won't let my mind go on me. I can't keep up this way. I need to get out of the cage, get myself a clean room. I need to eat normal food. Maybe I even need to get good and drunk. I need money.

I walk east, across Hennepin Avenue and past the big department stores. With the fifteen cents I've earned from unloading asparagus this morning, I hop the streetcar for the Powderhorn.

*

"Daddy?"

"Hello, Ralphie," I say. "Where's Mama?"

He's standing in the front yard. I'm standing a few feet below him, down the grade on the sidewalk.

"Daddy?" he says again. He looks a little stupid in the face. My heart is speeding and my back feels sweaty. My voice shakes a little when I talk.

"Is Mama in the house?" I ask.

He begins to cry. I step forward and move past him without saying anything else. I walk around back and climb the stoop and open the kitchen door.

There's nobody inside. I can hear somebody moving in the living room up toward the front and so I go there.

It's only Bridget.

"Hello, Bridget," I say. "Where's Mama gone to?" Bridget laughs and says daddy daddy daddy over and over again but she doesn't tell me where Annie's gone to.

"I need to talk with Mama," I say to Bridget. I've got both my hands on her shoulders, trying to hold her still. She just laughs some more.

"You smell funny, Daddy," she says.

I let go of her shoulders and step backwards.

"I'm sorry," Bridget says. She laughs but her eyes are filling up with tears. She's just seven years old but these aren't baby's tears. "I didn't mean that, Daddy," she says.

I leave her there in the living room and I go into the bedroom. I stand in the middle of the room, at the foot of the bed, and I turn around in a circle. I realize that I have no idea where to begin looking for the money. Annie learned years ago to hide money from me. She's very good at it.

I sit down on the bed and shout out toward Bridget in the living room. "I need to speak with Mama!"

Bridget comes into the bedroom now. That is, she stands in the doorway, hesitating, just like always. It's my bedroom, after all.

"She's not home," Bridget says.

Sitting on the edge of the bed, I turn my face to Bridget. "Where is she?"

"With Aunt Cath. Shopping."

"Shopping?"

"You know. At the grocer's. They left a half hour ago."

I try to make my breath come slow. I'm sitting down but my heart is still pounding. It seems the pulse in my neck is making my head wobble. Taking careful breaths like this makes something catch in my chest and I have a coughing fit.

Bridget stands very still, in the doorway, and she watches me. When the coughing passes, I turn myself on the bed full around to her.

"How've you been, girl?"

"Just fine," she says.

I look down at my broken shoes. "I've been away."

"Yes," Bridget says.

"I'll have to leave again," I say.

Bridget doesn't move and she doesn't say anything for a long while. "I wish you didn't have to," she says then.

"It can't be helped," I say. "There are troubles."

"With Mama."

"No," I say. "Not with Mama. There's something else. I can't stay here."

"Ever?"

My neck throbs again and I have to fight to keep my head still. "No," I say. "Not forever. Just for a while."

"You'll come back," Bridget says.

"I'll try," I say. "After the trouble passes."

"Is it the men in the fancy suits?"

"Is what the men in the fancy suits?"

"The trouble."

I stop looking at my shoes. I hold my hand out and wave Bridget into the room. "Tell me about these men."

"They come around," she says. She doesn't leave her place in the doorway. "They ask Mama things.

Frankie said they were G-men but Mama said they weren't policemen. She thinks they were bad men."

"Are you afraid of them?"

"Yes," she says. "A little."

"Don't be," I say. "They won't hurt you. They're not bad men. They only want to talk to Daddy about something. I don't want to talk to them, so I'm avoiding them."

"They try to be nice to us," Bridget says. "One of the men gave Richard a candy bar. A whole chocolate bar, just for himself."

"I see."

"Richard was sick," Bridget says. "From the chocolate bar. He ate it all very quickly and then he threw up."

"I'm sorry for that."

"He should have shared the chocolate with the rest of us."

"Yes, I suppose so." I wish Bridget would come into the room. I want her to come to me. But she did say that I smell. I look at my hand, turning it over. My nails have black under them and my knuckles are dust-colored and scraped.

"Daddy?" she says.

"Yes?"

"Show me a coin trick."

"I haven't any coins," I say.

"I'm sorry," she says, like she's done something wrong, a girl asking her Daddy to show her a trick.

My whole upper body throbs now. Neck, shoulders, back. I'm utterly beat, exhausted, like when I've just finished hauling melons off one of the marketplace trucks. At the same time I'm feeling this in my body, a shock goes through my brain as I realize — like for the first time, all at once — what I am doing here. Annie could walk in at any moment.

I don't want to be here when she comes home. I'm remembering now what she said about me cutting through her like a sharp knife.

"Bridget," I say quickly. "The money. The grocery money. Do you know where Mama keeps it?"

"She has it with her. She and Aunt Cath — "

"I mean the rest of it," I say. My voice, despite my trying to control it, is shaking. "The other money. When Mama takes money for the groceries, where does she get it?"

"I don't know, Daddy," Bridget says. "I don't know." Her face seems to be going, twisting into a frightened little pink ball. I don't want to scare her.

"That's okay," I say. "That's okay, Bridget."

Neither of us says anything more about that. The empty apartment is silent except for a ticking noise on the wall outside. "When I go," I say to Bridget, "if the men ever come around again, promise me you won't say that I've been here."

"I won't tell on you, Daddy," she says, her face clearing now and becoming brave. "I'd never tell on you."

"Good girl," I say. "And promise me you won't tell Mama I've been here, either, won't you?"

She doesn't say anything. There's that *tick* against the outside wall.

"Bridget," I say. I try to make my voice hard, like a father to his young daughter, but it's no good. "Never mind," I say.

"She cries," Bridget says.

"Who?"

"Mama. She cries."

"When the men come around?"

"No," Bridget says. "Just other times. Sometimes, she cries."

"Do you cry?"

She starts to answer but doesn't. She swallows and shakes her head. "No, Daddy."

"That's a good girl," I say. A tapping sound, a *tick*, on the wall outside the bedroom window.

I turn to the window and stare at the sunlight on the curtains. "What's that sound?" I say. I can't imagine standing up. It seems it would require more strength than I have just now. The weariness has crept downward, into the bones of my legs. "Bridget," I say. "Please go to the window and look out. What's that sound?"

She comes into the bedroom and crosses in front of my place on the bed. She stands at the window and looks out.

"Ralphie is throwing stones at the house."

"Is he?"

"Yes. Should I scold him?"

"No, Bridget."

"He may break a window."

"Let him be," I say. I hear Ralphie's voice outside now, shouting.

"Ralphie said a bad word, Daddy."

"Let him be, Bridget."

I stand up, with immense effort, but Bridget doesn't turn from the window. I start toward the door.

"Goodbye, Daddy," she says.

"You're a good girl, Bridget," I say back at her.

I go out the back way, through the kitchen, and I stumble stiff-legged across the grass toward the alleyway. I want to run but my body is too beat to run. So I only move as fast as I am able, away.

Nineteen

Downtown, July seeps wetly into August, pounding down on the Gateway like a damp rag dropped onto asphalt. I'm staying in my cage days and walking nights. More then even before. One night I walk out as far as Lake Street, on the west side near Lyndale Avenue — it is three in the morning and I take a piss against the brickwork on the sidewalk beneath Albert's shop — and then I walk all the way back again to the Gateway. Sometimes I go to the Union City mission for a meal, but mostly I don't come out from my cage till the mission is closed. I get most of my food down in the hobo jungle.

I can't drink anymore. It's the strangest thing. Something has gone bad in my stomach. A gulp of wine makes me vomit. But, late at night in the dark, I collect firewood in the jungle and get paid in beans and bread. It doesn't take much to fill me. I'm left alone in the jungle, moving around sleeping bodies, mostly ignored by the men who are still awake in the hot dark. At sunrise, I climb back up the sandy slope to the Gateway, to my place on the second floor of the cage house.

One night, I walk out to the Basilica across from Loring Park and then I find I am too tired to make the walk back. I don't have car fare and there are no automobiles passing at that hour to hitch with. So I lie on the stone steps of the Basilica and sleep until I am kicked awake, just before dawn, by the caretaker.

Walking back toward the river through the rising morning heat on Hennepin Avenue, I need to stop and rest three times. I'm leaning against the wall outside a shuttered pinball parlor, rubbing at my thighs to work out a cramp, when I find myself staring dumbly into the sketched face on a handbill pasted on the bricks. The image is of an unremarkable Spic girl, and I try to distract myself from the leg-cramp pain by wondering who in the hell took the time to draw such a picture in the first place.

"Dream on, friend," a voice off to my left says.

I turn. It's a Hennepin Avenue sharpie in a cheap, flashy suit. "No paycheck there, I'm afraid."

"Beg pardon," I say. My voice comes out like I'm spitting up clods of sawdust.

The sharpie grins and jabs his cigarette toward the wall behind me. "Dreaming of the reward? Sorry. But the word 'round here is that the girl blew town. Place got too hot. No longer in the vicinity."

I can't even make sense of what he's saying. I stare at him while he takes a set of keys out and opens up the shutters. I guess he runs the pinball room. I ask him for a cigarette and he gives. After he's lit my fag, he goes on in and I stand up away from the wall. I see now that the picture I'd been studying, of the Spic-looking girl, is a tattered and sun-bleached "Wanted" poster for the runaway St. Paul servant girl.

I move off, shuffling stiffly along Hennepin. Too hot. The whole damn world is too hot in daylight. I'm sweating wet and feeling faint-headed by the time I reach the Gateway. I promise myself to never again walk so far at night.

So lately, I've been sticking to the hobo jungle. Closer to my bed up in the cage. One night late under a moonless sky, I'm off away from the main jungle, upriver at the spot where the barges take on and unload gravel and sand for ballast. This is a place of high, powdery lime-sand dunes and shifting surfaces underfoot. The night sky overhead is washed out in the pinkish light shining from a lamp post above the night-watchman's booth. At night like this, when the air is cooler, I move more easily. My body aches less. I've come poking around for scrap lumber or old bits of barge rope, but there's none to be had tonight. I'm taking a piss against the side of a dune, all alone there in the shadows out of the pink nightlight, and I guess I speak out loud as I let go, the way any man might when he's taking a piss. *Sweet relief*, I says to myself. Then I hear a voice behind me that makes me about jump out of my pants.

"Sweet relief," the lady's voice says.

"Beg pardon," I manage to squeak out, once I've recovered and shaken the loose piss from myself.

"Sweet relief," she says again, as I, buttoning my trousers, turn from the dune to face her.

I've been out here for an hour and my eyes are used to the bad light. I can see her clearly. She's an old thing. Forty if she's a day. But she's nobody's mother. Even in this light, I can make out her dirty clothes and her worn walking boots, but her face is painted up like it's Saturday night. She's standing there with her hands on her hips and her chest pushed out toward the August sky. She's got a nice pair on her, I can see.

"Well," I say. "Who're you?"

"I'm Edith," she says. "Who are you?"

"Oh, I'm just nobody."

"Hello, Nobody," she says.

"Hello, Edith," I say.

"A man needs relief," she says.

"No doubt about it," I say, coming over the sand toward where she's standing.

She lifts her chin up and looks at me from under her eyelids. "For *real* sweet relief, a man needs a woman."

"You're not telling me anything I don't know, Edith."

The pinkish light from the lamp post beyond the dunes is lighting her. She's old but she's got a nice pair. Her face, under all the paint, is no good for me. It's one of those Russian-looking faces, narrow and mean. Her hair is awful — a bird's nest, dyed boot-polish black — and her hips are bony and her hands look unclean. But she's got a nice pair of tits.

"You look like you could use some relief yourself," I say to her. My hand is shaking like with a bad-gin hangover when I reach out for one of her breasts. But Edith steps backwards away.

She smiles a narrow little smile at me. "This ain't about what I need. It's about what you need. And before anything else, *you need* to show me two dollars."

"Two dollars?"

"Two dollars," she says.

"Well, Edith," I say to her. "We've a problem now. You see, I haven't got two dollars."

"I don't believe you're telling the truth."

"I am," I say.

Her skinny Russian face clouds over. The smile is gone now. "I know you," she says. "I seen you over in the jungle. You ain't no hobo. Ain't no penniless tramp."

This I've got to laugh at.

"Edith. That's exactly what I am."

She frowns and stares down into the sand between us. She chews at her lower lip, leaving rouge on her teeth. She looks back up at me. "You ain't got two dollars?"

I shake my head. "I haven't got a cent."

"Son of a bitch," she mutters. Though I don't take it personal.

"Times are hard," I tell her.

"For you and me both, brother," she says.

I watch her draw a cigarette from a marbleized plastic case that she's taken from her handbag. "Can I bum a smoke?" I ask.

She hands me a smoke and a box of matches and I light our two cigarettes. The flare from the match hurts my eyes.

"I appreciate the kindness, love," I say to Edith, handing her back the matchbox.

"Sure. I got nothing but kindness," she says.

"Like I say. Thanks."

We smoke, and we both look up into the pink-colored haze, searching in vain for stars.

"So," I say to Edith. "You on the road?"

She takes some time blowing out smoke. "No. I got a place with my sister, Nordeast. I just come by the river to take in the air."

"I hear you," I say. It's quiet as hell here. The sand and the gravel kind of suck up all the sound.

"Still," I say. "I don't imagine there's a lot of — y'know — *air* to be had. I mean, these folks are just broke and beat."

"You'd be surprised," she says.

"I been around this rail camp most of the summer," I say. "If any of these fellas had two dollars, they wouldn't be on the road."

"Says you," she says. "A man picks up change. Panhandling. Stealing milk bottles. Whatever. He needs food, he goes to the missions. He needs drink, or pussy, he spends the change."

I turn the cigarette over in my hand. Horton Moon is a man who's never needed to pay for it, and

I'm unused to whore talk. Makes me kind of squirmy, to hear a lady use such language.

"Okay, okay," I say to her. "I see your point. Anyway. I haven't got it one way or another."

And maybe I'm glad I don't. By that I mean maybe it's just as well I don't have two dollars, because, if I did, I'd only be banging on her ass instead of having a conversation, which, really, is much more what I need just now. The conversation, I mean. Even if she does use language like that.

"And what did you mean," I ask her, "by that business you said before, anyway? About you seeing me back at the jungle and me being no tramp?"

"Just that," she says. "I seen you. I was down with a fella yesterday night and I seen you walking off away from the fires. You don't carry yourself like the rest of them. You don't look like you belong."

I nod. "I ain't like the rest of these sorry bastards. Mine is only a temporary condition."

Her mean Russian face gets a little softer. "I bet you was a big-time businessman in real life. Before the times."

"The times?" I say, not understanding at first. "Oh. Right — the times."

"On the radio, Mr. Roosevelt calls it a Depression."

"Well," I say, grinning at my cigarette. "I've got my own personal depression. But, yeah, I was a businessman. I owned my own plumbing shop. Actually, two shops. One on the north side and one on the south side."

"Ain't that something?" she says.

"Well ..."

I shake my cigarette out toward the shadows in the sandpit. Why am I lying to her? Christ sake.

She's the first person I've spoken with in weeks. Why not just speak straight?

"Hey," I say. "You want to sit?"

We go to a sand pile away from where I was pissing and we both settle back into the soft slope.

"Listen, Edith," I say. "I'm no big-shot businessman. I don't know why I lied about that. I'm just a guy. Fact is, I was barely making it back home before I got a lucky break. And then *that* blew up in my face. That's why I left. Now I'm just living in a cage hotel above a shoeshine parlor on the square."

She looks off away. "I don't mind lies. They're always more interesting than the truth."

I laugh a little. "So I'll lie. You wanna hear about my war record?"

But she's not laughing.

"Do you like the pictures?" she asks me.

"I like them all right, sure."

"I love the pictures," she says. "They're beautiful."

"Sure. Beautiful people. Greta Garbo. Fred Astaire."

"It's all lies."

"What, the pictures?"

"All lies. But they're so beautiful. I love them."

I look at her from the corner of my eye and I take up a fistful of the coarse sand and raise my left hand, letting the sand run out between my knuckles.

"You wanna know what's a kicker?" I say. "I bet you if you could get inside the brain of some California film star right this very minute and see what they're dreaming about, chances are they'd be wishing they was sitting in the warm sand by the shore of the Mississippi on a summer night, watching the sky. Just like we are here."

"You think that's true?"

"Sure?" I say. "Why not?"

Her chin moves slightly. "It's a load of shit."

"I'm just saying. People always want what they haven't got. You never know."

"*I* know," she says.

I suck the last bit of life out of my cigarette and I flick the butt away. "You do, huh?"

"I do," she says. "It's a load of shit. Life's a load of shit. All that's beautiful is the lies people make up."

She's jammed out her cigarette into the sand and I sit there next to her, being quiet, and I wait till she takes the cigarette case out again from her handbag before I make a motion with my hand for another smoke myself. She hands the case to me this time.

"So, that's what you do?" I ask, drawing out two cigarettes. "You take your two-three bucks and you go to the pictures?"

She shakes her head. "I need money for food. I gotta feed my sister and her kid. My sister's blind. She can't get relief 'cuz we was born in Prague. She's not even a citizen. Me, I married an American guy when I was sixteen, so I'm legal. But my sister."

When she flicks her eyes up at mine to signal thanks for my lighting her cigarette, I see — in the hot, white light of the match — a hatred that makes me shudder. It's not really directed at me but it's there nonetheless. It makes me pull up short. I say this, and you understand that I've just spent weeks on the row, in the Gateway, surrounded by the eyes of strangers filled with nothing but degrees of misery and sadness. But this thing in Edith's eyes makes me shudder to see it. Though not in a bad way. It's *life* that's in that hate. She's got a spark in her that I haven't seen in anybody since I left the Powderhorn. It's like a breath of air to a drowning man. I'm not sure I can explain why. Maybe because hate, rage, is the only reasonable thing to feel in times like these. Nobody else seems to get it. The morons back in the Gateway square, Sprague the old queer, the tramps I see in the jungle. Even some of the idiots back in the Powderhorn, Tim Young and his like, they're all of them either smiling through the hard times or moaning sad with self-pity. By rights we should all be boiling over with the urge to kill, like this Edith here.

"I come round here to get money for food," she says. "Then I go to the pictures, sure. I'd go mad if I didn't."

I settle back against the sand and let out a stream of smoke into the pink air above us.

"So, Edith," I say. "Who's your favorite?"

She's looking off into the black shadows but she answers without hesitation. "Gary Cooper."

"Ah. He's good," I say. "Me, I like Cagney."

Edith is quiet. There's a silence between us, and it's not till after nearly a minute has passed that I notice she's not even smoking her cigarette. She's like frozen in the sand beside me. I don't think she's thinking about the movies anymore.

"Edith?" I say.

"Yes?" she says. Her voice seems changed.

"Are you okay?"

Now she raises her cigarette to her lips and takes a drag.

"You do look a little like him."

"Like who?"

"Cagney."

"So I've been told," I say.

She takes another quick drag. "What's your name?" she asks.

Now, why is she asking me this? "Call me Tom Powers," I say.

"That was Cagney," she says, sending smoke out of her nose. "In *Public Enemy*."

"Good catch."

"What's your real name?"

"Never mind my real name."

"Is it Moon?"

My stomach spasms upwards, leaping up into my Adam's apple. I lean forward, sitting up from the cool sand.

"What'd you say?"

"Is your name Moon?" she asks. Her voice is calm as hell. "It is, ain't it? You're him. You're the little Mick the suits come round asking after."

Twenty

I try to stand up but my feet slip out from under me in the loose sand.

Edith is on her feet, fast. I've never seen a whore move so quick. She's thrown away her cigarette and her hand goes into her handbag. When it comes out, I see she's holding a blade.

"Edith," I say.

"Don't try anything slick," she says. She raises the blade in her right hand. "I know how to use this."

The light from the watchman's lamp post is behind her now. I can't see what her face is doing.

"Put the knife away," I say. "I'm not going to hurt you."

"They said there was a reward," she says.

I try not to move at all. "Do you know who those men are, looking for me?" I ask her.

"I got a pretty good idea, yeah," she says.

She steps backwards. Even if I could get up and make for her, she's opening up the ground between us to give herself room enough to strike.

"Edith, please," I say. "Me and you, we're a couple of human beings. I believe that you're a good human being."

"Sure," she says. "I got a heart of gold. I also got a blind sister with a kid. The men said there was a reward."

"Do you know what will happen to me?"

"I don't care," she says.

"Forget the reward," I say. "Please. Give me a break."

"Shut up, Moon."

"No," I say. "I can't shut up. Listen. I've got a family. I've got five kids. A wife."

I notice something softening in her posture. But she holds the knife steady.

"Your sister's kid," I say quickly. "How old is he?"

She sniffs. "She. Little girl. Just turned four."

"Ah," I say. "My Richard is four. What about that? You see? Look at me. I'm a father. A decent man."

She shakes her head. Her face is still in shadows, but I can hear a change in her voice now. "Sure. A decent man with a price on his head."

"A mix-up," I say. "A mistake. I was just trying to help my family out, just trying to put food on the table. Shoes on the babies' feet. You understand. I got mixed up with some bad people. But my intentions — "

The knife lowers slowly. "Save it, Moon."

"You understand?" I say. The knife-hand is at her side now, but the blade is still pointed toward me.

"I don't understand nothing," she says. "I gotta think."

"Yes. Think about it."

"It might be a lot of money, the reward," she says. "I ain't a dope, you know."

"I don't think you're a dope, Edith."

"I gotta go," she says. "Don't move. You stay right there. Don't try to follow after me. I ain't afraid to use this thing."

"I understand."

She backs away another ten feet and then she turns and goes out between two piles of sand. She's gone.

I stand up. I look down at the cigarette between my fingers. I lift it and take a deep pull, filling my lungs. Then I move away in the opposite direction from where Edith has gone, and I scramble up the side of a sand pile, going slow, slipping backwards, then down the other side and up and over another, then another. I climb over the heaps, away toward the lights of the city up the hill. Beyond the black forms of the skyline, I can see that the sky in the east is already going red with the morning to come.

*

Levin has pulled the early shift at the Union City, and it's him — I breathe a prayer of thanks to Jesus — that comes to the door to answer my pounding. He looks annoyed until he makes out my face in the predawn shadows on the other side of the glass, and then he smiles in a kind of condescending way.

"Powers," he says, swinging the door open to me, "you know the routine. First meal isn't till — "

He stops talking, I guess from taking in the look in my eyes.

"What is it?" he asks.

"I'm in trouble," I say.

"Come in."

Levin locks the door behind us and hurries away down the vestibule hallway, waving for me to follow. He leads me down a way I've never been, away from the eating room, and at the end of the dark hallway we bump through a set of swinging doors into the big kitchen. The lights are on bright here, and the place is loud with a dozen or so colored kids and Indians, spraying water into pots and slamming pans back and forth at one another. Nobody looks twice at me and Levin.

Levin goes over to a big copper coffee urn and pulls two cups of hot joe. He hands one to me and I hold the cup up under my nose — my hands don't shake — and I breathe. I sip at the coffee, carefully.

After he's given me some time to let the coffee do its work, Levin asks me, "You've been down at the tramps' jungle again, haven't you?"

"No," I say. "I mean — yes, I have — but that's not what this is all about."

"Cops?" he asks.

"No."

It's not that I don't want to tell Levin everything. But, just now, all I can do is taste the coffee. It seems about the best damn coffee I've ever tasted. Levin gives me a look, squinting at me from behind his glasses.

"Come on," he says. "I'm really supposed to be upstairs now, mopping. What's this all about, Powers?"

I look up from my coffee. "Sorry," I say. "My name's not really Powers."

"Yeah?"

"Yeah."

"So, to start, how about telling me your real name."

"Moon," I say. "My name is Horton Moon."

Levin just keeps squinting at me in that same way, but then his face changes. His eyebrows slowly go up and his mouth, frowning, tightens up a little.

"Moon," he says. "That's the name they used, I think."

All the taste goes out of the coffee. "Somebody asked after me?"

"Yeah. Couple of guys."

"What did you say?"

"I told them I know about every man comes through here, and I don't know any Moon. They described you pretty well, though. I guess I kind of knew it was you they were asking for."

"When was this?"

"Yesterday," he says. Then he taps his chin with his fingertips. "No, day before. Who are they?"

"They're just guys," I say. "Bad guys. From the north side." I look down into the black at the bottom of my coffee cup.

"What, exactly, is the trouble you have with them?"

I shake my head. "The less you know the better."

"Okay," he says. "How bad is it though?"

I look him in the eye. "They're going to kill me."

The color in Levin's face goes. Just like that, while I'm looking at it. He's gone the color of carp's belly.

"The truth is," I say to him, "they're Jews."

"Meaning what?"

"They're your people."

"I don't have people," Levin says quickly. He touches at his eyeglass frames, the way I've noticed he does when he says something he's not quite comfortable saying. "Or, if I do, my people are the fellas that come around the mission here. Just folks like you."

Hearing this, something comes over me and I feel like I may be sick. I don't know why. It's a hell of a nice thing for a man to say, but the way it hits me makes my stomach go over funny.

I swallow down the vomit-y taste in my throat. "Thank you, Levin," I say.

He starts up pacing, crossing back and forth our little corner of the bustling, brightly lit kitchen.

"Okay," he says. His normal color is coming back, and just moving seems to slip his brain into gear. "Have you got family?"

"On the south side. But I can't go back there."

"Anybody else?"

"No. Not really."

He pauses in his pacing, gripping his coffee mug at chest-height. "You can't stay here."

"No, I can't" I say. "I know that. There's somebody seen me just now. She's telling the Yids."

Levin flinches a bit at this last word, which makes me feel lousy. Then he starts up pacing again.

"Why did you come here?"

"I didn't know where else to go. I thought you could help me."

"I'd like to try."

I watch Levin going back and forth. I look over at a colored kid breaking eggs into a steel bowl the size of a bathtub. The fact of the matter is, crossing through the dust of the sand pit on my way here, my reeling brain had grasped itself onto memory-scents of clean air and hydrangea bushes.

"How about your girl's?" I ask. "Dolores has got that nice quiet spot out in St. Paul where I could —"

"Are you mad?" Levin asks, spinning on the tile floor toward me. "No! No! Don't even think like that. What's the matter with you? Who the hell do you think you are, anyway?"

"I'm your people," I say.

Levin scowls down into his coffee. He takes a gulp of it and looks like he's going to gag. He steps over to a big sink and empties his mug down the drain.

"I'm sorry," he says, coming back to me.

"No," I say. "You're right. It was a bad idea."

"But you've got to get out of town."

"I think so, yes."

"You really don't have any other family, anywhere else?"

"None," I say. "They're all out around the Powderhorn, and that's no good."

"Okay," he says. The sound of his voice and the look on his face show that he's made some kind of decision. I have no idea what he's decided, but I feel a little better already.

Levin grabs a big waxed bakery sack and begins stuffing bread into it. He takes one of the breadloaves, splits it open with his thumbs, and goes to a pan of scrambled eggs set on the warming shelf above an oversized gas stove. With a wooden spoon, he scoops eggs into the split loaf.

"You'll need to take some food with you," he says, coming back and dropping the hot egg sandwich into the sack with the other loaves. "You're leaving town, Mr. Powers."

I smile at him. "It's Moon."

"Not yet it's not," Levin says. "You've still got four or five hours' work to do down at the market before Schneider takes you with him in his truck."

*

Levin skips out of the mission and walks me west to the market district. Schneider already has two young toughs hauling melons off his truck, but Levin takes Schneider aside and has a few words with him.

"What? Again?" I hear Schneider say. He laughs. "I should start punching tickets."

The two kids are dismissed. I climb up onto the truckbed and start lifting off the crates. Levin stands there and watches for a few seconds, half-turns to leave, then turns back to me on the truck.

"Goodbye, Mr. Powers," he says.

I lower the crate I've got. "S'long Levin," I say. "I owe you."

"I don't believe in those kind of debts."

"Tough shit," I say. "Because I do. I won't forget you."

"Well," he says. "I promise I *will* forget you."

We both kind of grin at that. Levin doesn't leave and I don't pick up the next crate. I don't think either of us really wants to say goodbye.

"Levin," I say, "tell me something."

"Shoot."

"What's your angle?"

"My angle?"

"Yeah," I say. "You're an atheist, right? So there's no heaven waiting at the end of the line."

"That's right."

"So why bother? Why bother with a fella like me, or with any of those clowns down at the mission?"

Levin's face gets serious and he touches his eyeglasses. "I suppose," he says, "it all comes down to what you say, about there being no heaven at the end of the line. No other world, nothing afterwards. To me, that only makes it more important to do things properly here, now. It's logical."

"But you're not exactly creating a Paradise on earth."

"No," he says. "I leave chasing paradise to the Reds. I don't think I could stand the disappointment."

I decide to let it drop. Levin says it's logical. His is the mind of an intellectual, and there's no percentage in me trying to read sense into that. I look out over the crowd in the market. The light is coming up full now, casting long shadows over the market and setting the skyline beyond First Avenue in silhouette.

"What was that," I ask Levin, "that Schneider said about 'again'? Have you put other men out of town like this?"

Now Levin does turn away. Over his shoulder, as he's walking away, he says, "You're not the only man in Minneapolis with secrets, Mr. Powers. Now get to work."

I watch Levin go away across the cobblestone plaza of the market, and I take up the crate of melons at my feet. The other packers on the other trucks are faces I don't know. I notice again the looks the unionized men give me from the loading docks. My brain is beginning to go places I don't like. But after a half hour of work, the ache rising in my wasted muscles chases away all my thinking. The morning passes quickly, and when the truckbed is clear I drop myself down onto the ground beside Schneider. He gives me a kerchief soaked in cold water to wipe the sweat away from my face and neck.

"Fair pay for an honest morning's labor," Schneider says cheerfully, holding out some coins to me.

"You don't have to pay me today, Mr. Schneider," I say. "A ride out of town is enough."

"Don't be a ninny," he says. He motions at me with the money in his fist. I hold out my hand and he drops three bits into my palm. "A man needs money, wherever he goes."

"True enough," I say.

"And there's this," Schneider says. He takes a folded ten-dollar bill from his pocket, hands it to me.

"It's from Levin. He said to give it to you after he was gone."

I fold the bill over again and pocket it, along with the coins.

"Levin's an odd bird," I say.

"He helps people," Schneider says. His lips close up over his gold teeth. "You're right. That's an oddity in this world. So. Where will you be going, anyway?" Schneider asks, as I follow him around toward the cab of the truck.

"Wherever you're going," I say.

"I'm going west. But only to just past Mankato. If I were a young man like yourself, I would continue westward."

"Yeah?"

"Yes. That's where a man can *live*. My daddy taught me that a man thrives best in a free place. Open plains. No cities, no crowds."

"Sounds about right for me," I say. Though the truth is, I'm right now feeling a little unsettled about leaving Minneapolis. Leaving Minneapolis for the first time in my life. I cough into the wet kerchief. "Will I see red Indians and cowboys?"

Schneider laughs at this, his gold teeth shining again in the late morning. "You might. You just might."

He's still kind of chuckling over this as he moves Levin's bakery sack full of bread off the passenger seat and onto the floorboard, to make room for me. I climb up into the cab.

"Tell you what," Schneider says, starting up the truck. "You head out west and you find yourself some wild Injuns to tame. Get yourself a big white hat like in the cowboy pictures!"

He's laughing like hell at this as he maneuvers the truck out of its place. He stops laughing about it and he frowns with nervous concentration as we move out of the narrow westside streets that lead from downtown, and we're speeding up on the highway at the city limits before he speaks again.

"It was my daddy taught me to drive a truck," he says.

I settle into my seat and I'm ready for an afternoon of "my daddy taught me"s, but, in fact, Schneider never says another word to me for the next six hours. I fall asleep ten miles out of Minneapolis.

Twenty-one

Schneider leaves me in the town just beyond his farm. It's a homely little town, with nothing much to it but a gasoline station and a grain elevator and a handful of small, low buildings, including a clapboard general store with a lunch counter in the back. In the general store, I sit on a stool at the counter and order a hamburger and a bowl of onion soup. There are rooms to rent above the apothecary next door, and I take one with a bath. I soak in a hot tub till the water goes cool, and then I sleep through the night and well into the next morning.

In the morning, over coffee and fried eggs at the counter, I ask the counterman about how I might find work in the area.

"Strawberries," he says.

The counterman gives me directions, and I find my way to a farm two miles out of town, where the fields are swarming over with men and women and kids stooped over the berry plants. I ask the man in charge about work and he hands me a basket. I start picking. I never go back to the little town.

*

Two weeks later, I'm still at the berry farm. I sleep nights in the bunkhouse with the other pickers. I'm not making any friends. The work is exhausting, and I fall into bed as soon as I reach the bunkhouse. The other pickers know one another from other farms. I hear them talk about harvests they've worked, and they swap rumors about where the next job lies. They're Holy Rollers of some kid, and they pray and sing in the evening before the lights go out.

We're in the fields till dusk, every day, except Sunday. Sunday, the pickers sit around in the grass under a big elm and somebody reads aloud from the Bible. Then there's more singing and clapping and praying. I'll have none of it. I spend Sunday in the bunkhouse, smoking cigarettes that I've bought from the foreman.

The air in the fields and the hard work are good for me. My body is growing stronger, and my cough is lessened. My arms and face are brown from the sun.

One night, lying on my bunk before the lights have been turned off, I hear someone coming across the room toward me. I sit up.

"You on to Bierdsdorf's?" a runty little man with a black moustache is asking me.

"Beg pardon?"

"Bierdsdorf's farm," he says. "Melons. Ten miles west of here. You heading on there?"

"Well," I say, "I don't know. I haven't thought about it."

"You'd better start thinking about it," he says, grinning. "Berries is all up and out by tomorrow noon. Then we're done here."

"Done?"

He nods. "No more berries, no more work."

For days, I'd been working mindlessly, conscious only of the sun and the earth and the basket on my hip. It had never occurred to me that the work would end. But of course. We've picked all the berries there are.

"Bierdsdorf pays fair," the runt says. "More than here — but then, it's melons."

"Sure," I say. "Melons."

"If you're on to Bierdsdorf's," he says, "you can hitch with us. Bunch of us is riding out tomorrow evening."

I look at the runt. "You say it's west of here?"

*

I stick with the Holy Rollers. Who knows what they think of me? I don't pray with them, but I don't talk much at all. They're friendly to me in their way. Nobody's trying to convert me, but we share water and food, and when the picking ends on one farm they take me with them, in their overloaded Ford, on to the next job.

With the Rollers, I pick melons at Bierdsdorf's, then peaches at the orchard of a Japanese, then greens in the Red River Valley. We're moving west, staying for a week or two at each farm. We sleep in bunkhouses or tents or dry barns. Late August and September in southwestern Minnesota are hot and dry, without the hard rains I'd heard about in Caroline's stories of North Dakota. We work steady.

I'm paid only pennies a day but I don't mind. I don't need money much. My food and bed are provided six days a week, and every Sunday I leave the Holy Rollers, hitch a ride into whatever passes for a town nearby, and spend what money I've got on cigarettes and bacon sandwiches. Anything I don't spend, I carry back with me and keep in a sock beneath my bunk roll, along with what's left of Levin's sawbuck.

I've grown used to the work, and I'm not as tired as I was when I first came west. My body is lean, but hard and sun-browned and healthy. My thinking is clear. I don't know if the way I lost my stomach for drink back in the Gateway has passed;

there is no liquor among the Holy Rollers, and on my Sundays in town the blue laws in these parts keep the saloons closed up tight.

In late September, the pickers begin talking about heading to the south. The big grain farms around here don't hire our kind — there are local crews that specialize in the harvesting and threshing — and so the Rollers will go south for the winter citrus harvests. But I'm not interested in the south.

We part ways, on a Sunday when I don't go to town but stay with them for an afternoon of hymn-singing and foot-stomping. I play along, mouthing the words to the holy songs, nodding in agreement while the women recite the Bible verses. The next morning, they drive away in their Ford truck and I wave them off from the side of the asphalt road.

I head north up the Red River Valley.

For a week, I stay in a railroad town, where I spend the remains of the money I've saved from my time picking. I sleep in a hotel bed and have my clothes laundered by a Chinaman. I dine every day on ground steak and potatoes. I wash down my meals with hot coffee and with fresh, tart apple cider from the local presses. One night I even order a beer, but it isn't good beer and it does nothing for me but leave my tongue feeling thick and my teeth feeling sticky. When all my money is spent, I leave the town.

I hitch rides north. I find myself in a rail yard and I hop a freight. But the boxcars here are crowded with people — men and women, families even — and I find that I travel more comfortably alone. I leave the trains and walk west.

Funny, how much easier it is to be broke when you're away from the city. True, there are no folks around to panhandle, but the warm September air and the sunshine and the trees along the road make it all seem like a lark. I'm out for a walk in the country. When I come upon a farm, I go to the house and ask for water. More times than not, the lady in the house will give me a meal of boiled eggs and coffee, or at least a few slices of bread. In exchange, I split firewood, or carry water buckets into the house from the well. Once, I was given two blankets to take with me, for the cooling nights. When the rains come I sleep in horse barns or beneath bridges. The people out here don't seem to find me unusual.

I'm not sure where I'm heading. I'm not sure where I am. I have a kind of picture in my head of the place where Minnesota meets North Dakota. A change has come over my thinking — a change I like — and I'm able to walk the western Minnesota farm country without a destination in mind. From picking through the long days with the Holy Rollers, I've learned to move without thinking too much about what I'm doing, content to know only that I'm moving forward. It somehow feels right just now for me to live this way.

Moving without thinking of where I'm moving toward, I find other thoughts come to me most clearly. I think of Caroline, of the weight of her in my arms, of the plains she'd laid out for me in stories told in the gathering dark. I'm approaching this story-place now; the high prairie lies ahead, just beyond my western horizon. I frown to think of Caroline back in Minneapolis alone. Heavy with the baby now, she's lost her job, I guess, and the money I left her must be running out. I tell myself she has Audrey there with her, and I tell myself Caroline can always return to her parents' farm. Still, I feel the big pale sky grow heavy over me while I walk.

I walk and other thoughts come upon me, thoughts of Annie, of her work-swollen hands and of her dark hair grown too long now to be in style; I can remember her bobbed and slender, fast-moving, quick with a laugh. But I know these are memories of Annie from long ago. She's not that girl any longer. Years have passed beneath us – not many years, but years that matter. Annie and I, together, have felt these years slipping by underfoot.

Once, last winter in the first week of March, a freak thaw came over the city all at once. In the morning our breath clouded and the milk-horses steamed, but by mid-afternoon the wind blew warm as May and the high sun was melting the gutter-ice into ankle-deep lakes in the streets. When I walked home from the streetcar in the evening after work, my winter shoes were destroyed, the cold water soaking them through to my socks. I stopped on the back stoop and peeled off my shoes, then hopped into the kitchen of our flat. Even after sundown the air was pleasantly warm, and I left the heavy outer door ajar as I'd found it. I stepped softly on stockinged feet into the kitchen, expecting to find Annie there cooking. But she wasn't there.

I walked through the dining room and through the parlor, and still there was no sign of Annie or the kids. I heard voices up at the front of the apartment, in the bedrooms, and so I crept toward them. I don't know why I *crept*, but by now I knew that they hadn't heard me come in, and I felt like an intruder in my own place, and I decided to go along with this game.

I followed the voices to the twins' bedroom, and there I found Annie and the boys. I stood back, in the shadows cast by the electric wall sconces in the hallway, and I watched through the doorway into the room at them.

Ralphie and Frankie were sitting on opposite sides of the small room, on the floor. Ralphie was turning over some bits of balsa wood in his hand and Frankie was reading a kind of pamphlet, directions to a model they were building.

Also on the floor, sitting close to Frankie, there was Annie. She was heavy with the baby then. Her belly was round and, with her legs tucked under her on the floor like that, her bottom flared out straining against the fabric of her dress. It was a dress I didn't recognize, a simple thing of dark-green corduroy. I supposed she'd made it herself, now that she was this late in her pregnancy and none of her other clothes fit.

Her dark hair was loose and streaks of silver grew out from the side part. I'd never noticed these gray hairs before. She was only twenty-five years old. I felt stirrings coming up in me, the way they came without calling at odd bits like this: silver hairs in a young woman's dark hair.

But I stood in the shadows and watched, and the stirrings changed into something else. Something deeper and broader. I watched Annie's face, watched her mouth when it smiled at something Frankie said, and I watched her hands, small and square, reaching to help Ralphie with the model parts. When she spoke to the boys, Annie's voice didn't have the hard edge I'd grown used to hearing in it. She spoke instead in the soft, hopeful tones I remembered from when she and I were young.

It was, there in the twins' bedroom, like I looked at Annie and I could see in one moment both my past with her and my future. She seemed to me, all at the same time, as fresh as a girl and as wise and as calm as a woman twice my age.

I stepped forward then, out of the shadow, and I stood in the lighted doorway of the room. Annie turned her face up to me. The face she'd been presenting to the boys lingered in her smile, but the smile fell quickly when she saw that it was me.

I'd been drinking hard then for weeks, moving farther and farther away from her. And by then I guess there wasn't much hiding what I'd started with Caroline. Whenever Annie had tried to pull me back to her — kissing me with her hot, hunger-fever mouth, or even just trying to get a laugh out of me, with a joke — it had felt threatening to me. I'd only moved deeper into the drink, farther away. Annie was a strong woman but she'd grown tired of chasing after me, chasing after me though I was always within arm's reach. This is what I saw in her face now.

It killed me to see her face change like this. I hated her then for the way she turned herself off to me. And I hated myself for having brought us both to this. The hate I felt must have showed on my own face, as Annie turned from me and spoke to the boys harshly, telling them to collect their things and wash up for supper. Daddy's home.

She struggled to rise from her place on the floor, and when I came forward to give her my hand she only shook her head and braced herself on the edge of the dresser. I was close to her now, my hand still held out to her, and I wanted terribly to take hold of her and pull her in against to me. I wanted to grip her in the old way, wanted to hum a dance tune into her hair, wanted to feel the familiar, dangerous heat rising between us. That, I somehow thought, would burn away all the hate between us, and make everything bad that was in our lives then magically go away from us. I wanted to do this but I did not.

Who can say why these things happen this way? Why is it that when we want something so badly — something as simple as a touch, an embrace — we are unable to just take it? I can't say. I haven't figured it out. I don't even try. I only let the memory play itself out, again and again, along with other recollections both painful and happy, and I just keep walking.

There are lakes out here in the west, lakes that in summer I suppose are used by the people from the towns nearby, for bass fishing and rowing and swimming. Now, in fall, the lakes lie glassy and cool, seen only by the cows that sometime come down over the grass to the shore, and by me passing. I never stop when I come upon one of these country lakes. Their emptied sand beaches and silent, unmown picnic lawns make me sad. I walk past and I let my thoughts and my memories come to me, like water lapping quietly onto one of those gently sloping lake beaches. No curling, breaking ocean-waves of recognition. No sudden crashes of understanding. I'm not looking for these. I walk and my course is not set, and that's fine with me. I'm only happy to be moving forward.

But I'm passing into another country, north, and the farms are less well-kept here, and farther apart. The black flies swarm and bite, raising ugly red welts on my sun-burned arms. When I pass through towns in this country, the people are unfriendly. One afternoon in one of these towns, pausing to rest on the wooden walk in front of a drygoods store, I'm bothered by a trio of men. They wear American Legion ribbons and they tell me to be on the next boxcar leaving town.

"I'm not riding the rails," I say.

"You are this afternoon," one of the men says.

Just to be sure of things, these men walk behind me across town and out to the railyard, and they wait with me till the next freight stops to take water. When I climb onto the boxcar, I look out at them and I see that they are staying, watching to be sure I don't jump off. We stare at each other until the train picks up speed and the railyard disappears from sight behind.

The trains are crowded, and seeing the traveling families only reminds me of Annie and the kids, and this makes me feel like hell. And the old timers, the hoboes, remind me of the jungle back in Minneapolis, and this makes me feel lousy, too. I hop off next chance I get, and I walk away from the rail lines.

One day in October, I'm somewhere in western Minnesota where the farmhouses are a mile apart and the folks who live in them are cold and stupid as stones. I've walked a day now away from the trains and I'm half-starved and sick in the heart. I approach a house — a wind-battered, grey, slanting thing — and I give a knock at the door. A fat man comes into the doorway.

He shakes his head before I can ask him anything.

"Nothing," he says. "Go 'way."

"I was only," I say, feeling defeated, "only going to ask you for a drink of water."

The fat man looks me over like he's thinking of *refusing* me the water. But then he leaves for inside and comes back shortly with a tin cup. "Well's in back. Leave the cup when you're done," he says.

There is a well in back of the house, beside a chicken yard. I draw the water and drink. The day is hot. Hot especially for October. The water is good in my dry throat, but my belly is empty and complaining. Off away in the distance I can see a bunch of trees where it seems this big flat farmland finally ends. Maybe a river or a lake or something. I turn toward the grey house but there's no sign of life in any of the dusty windows. I look at the chicken yard.

Ten minutes later, I'm walking on the road that slopes downward away from the grey farmhouse into the forest. The trees are starting to change their leaves, bits of gold and red showing in the thick growth, and I'm in a fine mood. I like the changing of the leaves. I've left the fat farmer's tin cup beside his well. I've taken two of his chickens. Snapped their necks and ran with 'em.

I drop down into the valley and I'm passing through some trees shading the road, and it feels so good to be out of the hot October sun, and now I can hear water splashing behind the trees from a creek or a river or some such, and so I decide then and there to have myself a picnic breakfast.

I step off the road and duck through some brush and then I'm into the woods proper. I sniff around and kick at the trees till I find a kind of footpath, and I follow this in the direction of the falling water sounds.

The closer I get the louder it gets, and by the time I'm upon it, maybe two hundred yards in from the road, I could jump up and down in the dry pine needles and not be heard coming; it is a waterfall, a pretty thing, ten feet high, spilling a little forest creek down into a wide, still pool. The woods are grown thick here, and it's a private little place. I see them before they see me.

Here's Sprague, the old man from the Gateway. He's slouching against a rock, facing me but not looking up from the bound pad he's got on his lap. He's sketching something with a stubby pencil. Why he's facing away from the falls, I can't say — it seems to me, *that's* your picture, right there. Lovely.

Now I see young Ben, behind Sprague and across the pool, in the water. Bathing himself. Kind of ruins the picture to me. He's got hold of soap somewheres and he's lathering himself up like a maniac. Little peaks of the suds flicking off him and washing away from the falling water, drifting slowly across the still surface.

Ben's under the falls and then he dives. He comes up ten feet closer to the bank, rinsed off. He stands. The water's not so deep here. Only up to his knees. I see him. Naked as the day of creation.

Ben sees me and drops down. Trying to get under water. Now I look at Sprague and see that he's seen me, too. Sprague is staring at me. I'm staring at Ben in the water. Ben looks scared.

I step over the rocky ground toward Sprague. For the love of Christ, I can't think of a word to say. I stare at Ben. Maybe I'm thinking the whole picture might change on me, only it's real life and pictures don't change like that in real life. It is what it is. And what it is is Ben is a girl.

Twenty-two

Sprague makes no move to stand. He's got the sketchpad on his lap and he holds the pencil poised above the paper, like he's about to finish the line he's been drawing.

"Tom Powers," Sprague says to me.

"Himself," I say.

I still can't take my eyes off Ben. He, or *she* I guess I have to say, is sitting low in the brown water. Not moving.

With neither of them moving and Sprague just sitting there with his back to the pool, I get a sort of crazy idea that maybe Sprague doesn't know what's going on.

"Ben," I say to Sprague, "is a girl."

He nods. "Yes. Benedetta is her name."

"It's a secret?" I say.

"Not any more," he says.

"I'm sorry," I say, though I don't know why.

Sprague moves the sketchpad off his lap and shifts himself, from one rock to the next. He makes a motion for me to sit down beside him.

I'm still staring at Ben.

"Mr. Powers," Sprague says. "If you will grant the young lady an ounce of privacy, she will rise from the water and join us. Please."

With the end of his pencil, he taps the rock beside him.

So I go and sit beside him. While Ben gets herself out of the water and clothed, I listen to the sounds of her. The water is churning up around her as she stands. The water's dripping off her now, and I hear the rustling of her trousers and shirt. She's stepping into her worn-soled boots. I'm listening. I can't help myself.

She comes around and sits on the ground on the other side of Sprague from me.

Now I stare at her again.

The face all makes sense now. It bothered me as a boy because it made no sense, but now it makes sense. Big Wop eyes, black and deep. Big Wop mouth. Makes you think of things, a big full mouth like that. Her skin is bad, with pimples and rough spots, but it's not enough to spoil her face. It's a good face. The haircut she had when I saw her last is grown out, looking a bit shaggy round the ears and, just now, slicked back wet off her face. It could be awful, but it's not. Not on her.

And I'm remembering, thinking about how I saw her shoulders and her shining breasts and her long belly and the curve of her hips where the poolwater fell from the black fur between her legs.

"Mr. Powers," Sprague says softly.

But I'm lost. Remembering her body and taking in her face.

"Mr. Powers," Sprague says again, not so softly. "You are staring."

"I am," I say. "And who wouldn't be staring?"

"I understand," Sprague says. "But now you've stared enough. Stop it."

"What's that?" I ask.

"Stop staring," Sprague says, and now for the first time ever his gentleman-y softness is gone. His face has gone hard and he's talking to me like an angry schoolteacher, or like a cop.

I stop staring at Ben. I stare at Sprague.

"It's rude to stare like that," he says to me. "It makes a woman uncomfortable."

"Yes," I say. "I get it."

He keeps giving me that hard look and, I swear, I really *do* get it, and I feel kind of awful for having stared at Ben, and for having seen her naked in the water before.

Now Sprague's nose twitches. "What's the story behind those chickens?" he asks me.

I look down at the dead things I've brought. "Yes. Chickens. I ciped them from a bastard farmer."

I smile at Sprague and I smile, quickly, at Ben. "Would you like some lunch?" I ask them.

I light a fire and Ben plucks the birds. Sprague whittles up a pair of spits and we three have a feast of roasted chicken. While we eat, I hear their story. Sprague tells me.

*

Benedetta grew up poor as sand on a small pig farm in Mendota. Six brothers and she was the only girl. The brothers were older than her and they treated her like dirt. She worked slavishly for them. Cooking them spaghetti and doing their washing. When she was fourteen, she ran off with a big handsome half-breed injun named Joe Branch.

Joe Branch sold moonshine and he drove a new Chevrolet. He bought Benedetta dresses and he brought her home with him, to a house in the Bohemian Flats down under the Washington Avenue bridge. She stayed. She liked working for just one man instead of a whole pack, and life seemed easy. But Joe Branch the moonshiner drank almost as much as he sold, and he was a mean drunk. He'd beat the hell out of Ben. He once locked her in a closet for three days, just because she walked into a room when he was counting money.

Mostly he just beat on her for no reason at all. He was big anyway, and he could have smacked her around easily with his fists, but he preferred whipping her with his belt or with lengths of rope.

It finally got so bad that Ben left. She went back to her brothers' farm. Joe Branch came after her with a shotgun. He shot one of her brothers in the knee and then grabbed Ben and took her back home with him. He cracked her head with the butt-end of the gun and whipped her till she passed out. She decided never to run away from Joe Branch again.

Joe Branch had a moonshine customer named Steven Linen. Linen was a big man in St. Paul — owned a chain of gasoline stations and lived in a big mansion on Summit Avenue. Steven Linen was a millionaire a couple times over. He bought liquor from Joe Branch not so much because it was good liquor, but because he liked the idea of associating with a Bohemian-Flats, half-breed moonshiner. Linen would throw big parties, and he always came round beforehand to see Joe Branch about the refreshments. Well, Steven Linen took one look at Benedetta — she was a beauty then, with long black curls — and he fell hard.

Linen started coming around more often, throwing money down for booze, but mostly he came just to see Benedetta. He was by one afternoon when Joe Branch had spent much of the morning beating on Ben, and the sight of her all bruised up and bleeding made Linen blanch pale.

Steven Linen wasn't a stupid man, and so he didn't confront Joe Branch. He placed his usual order for six cases of hooch to be delivered, and then he left. But he returned the next day. He'd brought a leather satchel with him, and he told Branch that they needed to speak privately. Linen didn't even look at Ben. She left the room and the two men sat at the table and spoke in low voices; Ben couldn't make out the conversation from her place in the back room. Linen did most of the talking, and Joe Branch said almost nothing.

After a few minutes, Linen called her name. She came back into the room where the men sat. Ben saw Joe Branch staring down into the leather satchel. The bag was filled with stacks of ten-dollar bills. Steven Linen told Benedetta to come home with him. The leather case was left with Joe Branch.

And so she went. And it worked. This time, Joe Branch didn't come after her. She moved into a room in the servants' quarters of Steven Linen's big house, and Linen didn't even try to touch her. He let her be.

She was put to work in his kitchen, helping the cook. It was pleasant work — not at all what she was used to. She slept in a soft bed at night and she was happy. Until one night, when Steven Linen was hosting one of his parties, he came out to her room and woke her in her soft bed. Come on, he said to her. This is all part of the deal, he said.

Linen brought her across the lawn to the big house. There were a dozen men there. All very drunk. They were all well-dressed. Like gentlemen. Linen led Benedetta into a small room off the main dining room. There was a bed in the room only it wasn't a bedroom. There were also things. Tools and leather straps and binding things. It was a room where Steven Linen and his friends did unnatural things. Benedetta was made to take a part in this.

That night and again on other nights, Linen led Benedetta into this chamber, where he and his friends would take turns doing painful things to

Benedetta and to each other. It was very bad. The beatings that Joe Branch had given Benedetta had been loud, fast violent explosions, but this new pain was extremely slow and careful. The men performed like doctors. Silent and cool.

While Sprague tells me this part, Benedetta stands up and leaves the fire. I think I hear her crying.

Benedetta understood that she could not leave. Linen made that clear. Whenever, on mornings after his parties, he would notice a dark sadness in Benedetta's mood, he would stroke her arm and tell her: Joe Branch will never reach you here — just as long as I keep him away from you.

So Benedetta stayed with Steven Linen. For almost a year, she lived this way. He would host his parties once a week, and the rest of the time she would work in the kitchen. Beneath her starched servant's uniform, her body was scarred and bruised, covered in burns and slashes. On one occasion, she had bleeding from her woman's parts that was so severe that she'd had to spend two nights in the hospital. But when she'd recovered, Linen led her back into the chamber.

Ed Sprague came onto the scene one fine winter morning. He was on the bum, criss-crossing St. Paul and hitting on the finest homes for handouts. The butler sent him round back to the kitchen door. Benedetta gave him breakfast. She had him into the kitchen, where a table was set for him. They talked.

Ed Sprague had lived in the area all of his life. North, in a place outside Anoka. He had worked as a salesman for a seed company. Royal Family Seed & Grain. He never married, and he lived in the home he was born in. He shared this house with his one sister, who also never married. When his sister died in a fever in 1919, Ed "lost himself." He was committed to the state hospital, in the neurotics ward. It was here that he was introduced to painting, as a therapy.

The man who oversaw the salesmen for Royal Family Seed & Grain in that part of Minnesota came to Sprague's rescue. Ed Sprague might have spent the rest of his life in the state hospital if it weren't for this man. But the doctors seemed satisfied that Sprague was stable, and the Royal Family man promised to look after him, and so he was released.

But even at home, and even with his Royal Family supervisor looking in on him, Ed Sprague never again found himself. He lived alone, in the house where his sister had died, until the house fell to pieces around him. The bank foreclosed on the property and Ed took to the road.

He was never a common hobo. Sprague stood apart from the others in the boxcars and the church soup lines. He was an artist. He traveled with paints and canvases and sketchbooks, and he drew portraits for kind strangers and painted landscapes for himself. Prairie winter scenes and bayou sunsets and sun-parched Oklahoma highways. Traveling suited him, and painting eased his heart, and in time he became again a solid man. The "episodes" he suffered back in Anoka no longer debilitated him.

But when the Depression hit full-on, the trains and jungles and soup lines were all of a sudden filled with artists — and with mechanics and teachers and assorted other upright citizens — and so Ed Sprague was just another in the horde. I don't imagine anybody thought it very interesting that he painted pictures, or that he had lived a quiet, industrious life for years without so much as a single unkind word against his fellow man, or that he'd loved his one sister so deeply that when she died he lost his mind.

The morning he and Benedetta first met, they didn't talk about everything that was happening in Steven Linen's house, but they talked enough for Benedetta to be impressed by Sprague's friendly way. *She* saw that he was an uncommon man. He offered to sketch her portrait in exchange for the food, and he penciled her image on a piece of butcher's paper: Broad, sensuous Mediterranean features, black eyes, dark hair piled atop her head. He thanked her for breakfast and left, but came back a week later. He appreciated her kindness, of course, but he was also struck by something behind her eyes. She fed him again and he thanked her again. I'll be back, he told her.

So he began stopping by every week. For food and conversation. Who can say what she saw in him? Maybe he was the first man to ever *have* a conversation with her. And who can say what Sprague saw in her? What did he see "behind her eyes"? She was a pretty Wop servant girl with a kind heart. But why did Sprague think there was more to her than this? I can imagine him, a lonely man with a fragile mind, falling in love with the young girl who fed him and listened to his stories. But how could he think she would ever fall for him? What kind of heat sparked between them?

Benedetta *did* fall in love with Sprague. He doesn't to this day understand why, or how. But he trusts that her heart is true, and that it has remained true through all that her body has suffered, and so he accepts this truth. Sitting together at the kitchen table, they recognized the arrival of a love that was beyond sex or even romance; there was an honesty between them that was like a bolt of steel binding the two of them together. Stronger, even, than the bond of family.

After Sprague had been coming around for several months, Benedetta's full story came out all at once. One morning in the kitchen over cooling eggs and warm coffee. They talked for an hour, and Benedetta told him everything. Sprague wept and held her hands. Benedetta's face shone with relief at having unburdened herself. They both knew that she had to get away but Benedetta could not imagine how.

Come with me, Sprague said. And so she did. Just like that.

It makes perfect sense, in its way. He had nothing. Not three pennies in his pocket. He couldn't promise her anything at all but his company. And she needed nothing more than she needed this. She needed his company.

They walked out of the kitchen together — Ben had only a few personal things across the yard in her room, and she left them there — and they walked away. It was the end of May, the summer spread before them like an opened map to be pored over, explored. They were in love. Not like moving-picture star love. It's a love that I'd guess was too odd even for the fantasy-spinners of Hollywood: The strange old man with the broken mind, and the young wounded beauty.

They were two nights out, having made a kind of camp beside the lake in Como Park, when they stopped in a gasoline station to wash up and saw one of the posters that Steven Linen had just then begun spreading across the town:

Have You Seen This Girl?

Wanted For Questioning
With Regards To The Disappearance
Of Personal Property
From A Private Home.
Substantial Reward Offered
For Her Return.
Contact Mr. Steven Linen

Beneath the headline, Linen had made a lithograph reproduction of the sketch that Sprague had made of Benedetta on the first morning they'd met.

They spent the next few days sweating and frightened, watching every strange face for suspicious glances. The crowds in Como Park scared them. They moved on, but in every neighborhood they found themselves, they'd see the posters. Linen's men were covering a large area.

They crossed the river into Minneapolis, and they were on the east side, at Seven Corners, when the two of them talked and decided on the idea of the disguise. They picked up boy's clothes for Benedetta at a church handout. Sprague panhandled the price of a haircut and then took Ben to the barbershop. This barber refused to cut Benedetta's hair the way they asked. So they walked up the block to another shop. Here, the barber gave Sprague a look but shrugged and took up the scissors. He made Sprague show him the money before he'd start, and then he went to work on Benedetta's long, heavy curls.

Ben kept her eyes down and she didn't cry while the hair fell on her lap. The barber, a nasty man, maybe didn't like that Benedetta didn't cry, because he watched her face the whole time he worked, and when he finished cutting off all her hair the way Sprague had told him, he laughed a mean little laugh before he took up the hand clippers and swiped the clattering thing up the back of her head and over her ears again and again till he'd clipped her scalp clean as a penitentiary convict. Sprague finally told the barber to stop the haircut while there was still some bit of hair remaining on top. Ben stayed brave the whole time, but when she stood to leave she caught sight of herself in the mirror and then she covered her head with her hands and ran out of the shop. Sprague dropped the money on the floor, where the coins rolled into the dark pile of Ben's fallen hair, and he went out into the street after her.

They left Seven Corners, but they did not leave Minneapolis. Sprague had quit the road years before. He was nearing sixty now, and his body was no longer made for scrambling up track embankments and climbing onto moving freights, or for walking long distances in changing weather. He'd spent the last few years within the city limits, and even now, with Linen trying to find them, he thought it best that he and Ben stay close to ready shelter and food; though she was young, Ben had been living in hard conditions — her body was no more prepared for the strains of the road than was Sprague's.

It was Sprague's plan to head into downtown Minneapolis, to the Gateway district. He and Ben could live cheaply there and they'd be left alone. Eventually Linen would give up looking for Ben, and then they could try for more permanent settlement. The important thing in the short term was that they would be together. This was when I found them. Or when they found me. Whichever. On the Lake Street streetcar, they were trying to make their way west to the downtown line.

*

"Your eyes, watching us from the car, were kind," Sprague says to me now.

I'm holding a drumstick in my hand but I'm not eating. I stare at the blackened chicken skin. "Kind eyes?" I say. "I was just on my way to work. You two looked like you could use a handout."

"Any man on the car could have given us a handout, but nobody did."

I shrug. "So. I'm a saint."

"And no other man on the car even looked us in the eye," Sprague says. "It's a most troubling thing, I find. Being on the bum. People don't look you in the eye. But you did."

"Meaning what?"

"It's hard for me to express just what that meant to me and to Ben, that day. It meant a great deal. We were frightened. Do you know what it's like to be chased by people who want to hurt you?"

I keep my eyes on my drumstick. "I do."

"Then I think you understand," Sprague says. "A kind of panic. Irrational. Your small kindness calmed us, reminded us that we were not alone. None of us is alone, really."

*

Sprague and Ben decided to wait out the summer down in the Gateway. They slept in rooms at the Union City, or in cages they rented by the week, or outside under the hot stars. They settled themselves into the routine of poverty on the Gateway. But they were happy. Hell of a thing. Sprague and Ben walked those same streets that I'd walked, with the stink in the gutters and the filth underfoot, and they slept in cage hotels and spent warm-weather afternoons slumped on benches in the mists of the Gateway fountain, but they were happy there. Because they were together. They talked. That's all they wanted. They wanted to be left alone to carry on their conversation.

This is when I first spoke to them, the day after I arrived on Washington Avenue. Linen's posters had by now become almost a local joke. Everybody knew them. But it had been over a year since Ben had run away, and by now nobody really took the prospect of a reward very seriously. Linen, though, was still very serious. And he apparently decided to concentrate his efforts on the Gateway district in Minneapolis. New posters were plastered along Washington Avenue and outside the Great Northern depot. Ben and Sprague left the district. They camped on the grassy fields along the Minnehaha creek. They slept in church shelters on the north side. They spent a week at a camp the Communists had started out west, in the forests of Wayzata. Sprague finally made the decision to leave Minneapolis. They would go north. On the rails.

But the Minneapolis hobo jungle was a dangerous place. Sprague saw that the first night he went down to scope it out. He saw me beaten in a fight over a bottle.

It was Levin who finally got Ben and Sprague out of the Gateway for good. They knew Levin by sight, though they'd never talked with him. Levin helped people, and so Sprague approached him now for help. Sprague explained he and Ben's situation in only the most vague terms. Levin did not ask questions. He put them on Schneider's truck, heading west, where it seemed they might escape their pasts at last, forever.

They did not linger in the west as I had. From southwestern Minnesota, they rode a boxcar up into the north woods and the iron range. Sprague had ideas about painting lakescapes on the Superior cliffs. They eventually settled themselves, on the shore of a deepwater lake in this northwest part of the state, and for a while they lived peacefully where nobody bothered them. They ate berries and birds, and drank from the cold, clear water of the lake. It was, Sprague says, their paradise. But in late September, parties of men with shotguns began paddling in canoes past their camp site. Duck hunters. So they left. Sprague and Benedetta were heading west now, toward the Pacific coast, though they were going slow. They were avoiding the rails, and they would not try to cross the Rockies in winter.

Twenty-three

I drop my chicken bones into the fire and listen to the fat sizzle. Ben is still off away. Gone into the trees.

Terrible story. It's made my head hurt to listen to it. It's made me want to leave these two people alone. I guess it's like I'm kind of afraid their hard luck will come off onto me. And I've hard luck enough already, thank you. Or maybe what I'm feeling is not about the old man and the girl at all, but about me: sitting here with Sprague, listening to his story, all the automatic thinking that has driven me over the past weeks is chased away, and I'm all of a sudden caught up again in the bad thoughts and fears that had driven me back in Minneapolis. I give Sprague a look.

"Why did you let me sit and smoke with you?" I ask him.

"Beg pardon?" he says.

"When we met. You let me sit down there next to you, no problem. But you've just told me you were running. Scared. Afraid of everybody."

"Not afraid of you," Sprague says.

I don't like the way he says this. "Why not?"

"You spoke to us. You were open. Though you didn't have to, you offered us cigarettes. And the year before — remember? The kind eyes from the streetcar? You were different. You *are* different."

"That's a laugh," I say. "I'm not different from anyone. I'm a bastard."

"Are you?"

"I am," I say. And I don't like people like Sprague figuring me out one way or the other.

"I don't think so. I can generally judge a man's character, and I believe — "

"Well," I say, cutting him off. "You judged me wrong. Okay? Fact is, if I could get hold of Steven Linen right now, I might have a mind to turn the both of you in for the reward."

This doesn't have the effect I expect. Sprague smiles.

"Really?" he says.

"Really," I say. "Maybe. I just mean. Don't be so sure about me."

"I'll take that into consideration."

"You ought to. I'm a bastard. And when I met you I had money to live on, but now I don't."

"I'm sorry to hear that," he says, sucking grease off his fingers.

"Whatever you say, doctor. Fact is, now I'm broke and hungry and sick. If I was smart, I'd quit the road and go back to Minneapolis. I left a hell of a lot back there. You can bet on that."

"I'm sure," he says.

"Ah," I say, standing up. "Don't be so sure. Don't be so sure of anything. I feel like hell and I'm all turned over. You tell me a story like the one you just get done telling, and you sit there licking your fingers like a happy Republican after a Sunday meal. You got a girl there who's had nothing but dogshit dropped on her head from the day she was born. And you're looking at me like you haven't a care in the world. You've got nothing *but* cares, old man, and if you had an ounce of sense in you you'd rope a rock around your neck — and around the neck of that girl — and you'd both dive to the bottom of that pool right there and end your cares."

"And what about you?" Sprague asks.

"Maybe I'm next in line. Right behind you."

"You're letting life beat you," he says, shaking his head.

This, the little shake of his head, really sets me off.

"Damn right it's beating me!" I shout. "I feel like I'm already half in the pool with the weight tied around my throat. I'm in too deep. Too deep in life."

"There's no such thing as being in life too deep. We're all of us in it at exactly the same depth."

"I know that," I say, kind of stammering. "I mean. It's an expression. I was saying."

"I understand the point you're trying to make," he says. "You're in this life as much as I am. And as much as Ben. The one thing I've learned in my time on this earth is that life is never too deep, or too big, or too dark. There was a time in my own life when I thought it was. But I was mistaken."

I'm trying to take this in but then I have to stop myself and remember that Sprague is half crazy. He's an insane man. He told me himself that he went off his nut years ago, when his sister died. I'm standing here trying to understand his wisdom when he's nothing but a loon. This I tell myself. Then I have to tell it to myself again, because his words are kind of rolling over inside my brain.

Without my really willing it, my body has sat itself back down on a flat stone beside the fire. I feel my legs ache. Now I want to stay sitting down here for a long time.

"Ben," Sprague says, as Ben comes back to us. "Sit down. Please. There's more chicken. Eat."

Benedetta sits beside Sprague. I thought she was crying before but I can see that her eyes are dry and her face is calm. She takes up a chicken leg.

"I'm sorry," I say to her.

"Sorry?" she says. "For what?"

"Everything. The story Sprague told."

She takes a bite out of the chicken and chews it slowly. Her shoulders shrug inside her oversized shirt. "Everybody has a story," she says. She turns her big dark eyes at me. "What's *your* story, Mr. Powers?"

"No stories from me," I say.

"No?"

"No," I say, and I say it like I mean it.

"Fine," Ben says, turning her attention back to her food.

But, right away, I feel awful. "Okay," I say. "Listen. I'll just say this. I'm running. Like you."

Sprague stares at me. He looks like he's trying to hear something that I'm not saying.

"I'm running for my life," I say to him, because he doesn't seem to have got the point. "There are people who will kill me if they catch me."

"I'm sorry for that," Sprague says. But he's still staring at me in the same way.

"Listen to me," I say. "My name is not Powers. My name is Moon. My name is Horton Moon. There are people in Minneapolis who want me dead. I crossed some bad men. My fault. But there it is. My life is fucked." I give the lady a look. "Sorry, Ben."

"Your life isn't *fucked*," Sprague says. "A life can't be fucked. Just like it can't be too deep. It is a life, and it is a very precious thing. You must appreciate that."

"Sure," I say.

"Ed is right," Ben says to me. "It's true."

"I'll remember this," I say. "Right. Life is precious. I'll not forget this."

I stand up now and turn on my heel to leave. I don't know where I'm going. Maybe into the trees. I just want to get away from these two. Idiots.

"Mr. Moon," Ben says to my back. "We are only trying to help you."

"We aren't trying to tell you what to do," Sprague says to me. "But it is important that, wherever you go, you are clear on your path."

"And," Ben says, quietly, while I am moving away — I don't think she really expects me to hear her — "you don't seem clear right now."

*

It's afternoon and the chicken is digested. We're making to move. The sun is hotter now than it was in the morning, and the pool is looking good. But Ben and Sprague have gathered their things to go, and I'm going with them.

I don't know why, but they both think I'm something special. They're sure, even with my knowing the story, that I won't turn them in for the reward money. Maybe I'm touched by this trust they have in me. Or maybe I'm just tired of traveling alone. I've decided to follow them.

Sprague and Ben have dreams of the west coast and the vistas of the Pacific, and I go with them, though I'm going without any kinds of dreams. I wonder if Levin could have imagined when he sent us out, separately, from Minneapolis, that we three would find each other. There is no logic to the paths we've taken. Like insane birds, we have flown north with the coming fall. And now we will go together into the rising winds of the winter west.

Anyway. The badlands and the prairie in winter can kill as surely as the mountains, but Sprague has a plan. We're to go due west till we reach a place where Sprague says there is a large Indian Reservation. Sprague says that the Indians will put us up, free, for the winter. They're poor as homeless dogs, Sprague says, but they share what they've got and they understand people who are trying to disappear from the past. In the spring, we'll go on to cross the divide and make our way to the Pacific.

We can't stay here at the pool because Sprague says the local kids come here swimming most afternoons when their school lets out. And, as every hobo, tramp and traveler knows, kids are meaner than a troop of American Legionnaires. So we're leaving.

"When we reach the road, we'll head away from the gray house," I say. "I stole the birds from the fat farmer there."

"Right-ho," Sprague says.

"I wish you hadn't stole them chickens," Ben says.

"You ate, didn't you?" I ask.

"Yes. But. It only makes it harder, I think." She picks up her sack and straightens, arching her back in a stretch. "The news will be spread. We have enough trouble round here. Now people will see us coming and they'll think of thieves."

"They won't be so far off the mark then," I say. I laugh.

"You're a thief, Mr. Moon?" Sprague asks me.

"I am," I say. "At least when things are worth taking."

"Then you must do an awful lot of thieving," Sprague says. "Because this world is filled with things worth taking. If that's your bent."

"Well," I say. I want to back up a step here. "I'm not your real *bad* thief-type. I mean. I don't go for hurting people or robbing from those that can't afford to lose it."

"You've got morals?" Sprague asks.

"That's just what I've got. Sure."

"But morals can be slippery things," he says to me.

I kick at one of the flat rocks beside the dead fire. "Anyway. Stealing for food isn't really hardly stealing at all. And I haven't seen much lately in the way of diamonds or gold or heavy silver. So maybe my thieving days are behind me."

I begin to step over the flat stones to head toward the trail that leads out of the trees to the road.

"There's more in life worth taking than jewels and silver and gold," Sprague says. He takes up his pack but he stands in front of me so I have to stop and look at him talking. "A man can take and take in life and never even know what he's taking."

It makes me itchy to hear him talk this way. Crazy man. I don't like it. Maybe I'll catch his crazy just by moving in the same circles as him. And we have a lot of miles ahead of us to cover. I decide to shut him up.

"Old man," I say. "Don't give me any advice. You're off your nut. You told me as much yourself."

Ben pipes up, hot-voiced: "There's nothing at all wrong with Ed!"

But Sprague raises one hand and quiets Ben. He looks at me, his face all seriousness.

"Sanity, like morality, can be a slippery thing," Sprague tells me. "I grant you that. But you make a mistake if you ignore what I'm saying just because you don't respect the man who is saying it."

"Now," I say, "I did not say I don't respect you."

Sprague smiles a little. "*Off your nut* were the words you used."

"Sorry," I say. "I only meant that —"

"I know what you meant," he says to me. "I should shut my pie-hole and leave you alone?"

"Very well put," I say.

"Fair enough," he says, waving his hand. It's an odd gesture, and it's not clear to me whether he's waving away the topic or waving away me.

"Now, let's leave this place," he says. "But first, I need to duck away into the trees for a moment. Nature calls upon me."

He lowers his rucksack to the ground and goes off into the woods away from us. Ben and I stand far apart, awkwardly. Ben clutches at her pack, with both hands, in front of her. I travel light, without bags. I've got my hands in my pockets.

"Did I insult him?" I ask Ben, after a while.

"It's hard to insult Ed," she says.

"It's sometimes hard to *understand* Ed," I say.

Ben tilts her face. "What don't you understand?"

"Oh. That hooey about taking and stealing, for one thing."

"Matters of the heart," Ben says softly.

"Beg pardon?"

"It seems to me," Ben says, more loudly, "that Edmund was speaking of things beyond the physical. It seems to me."

"Sure. I get it," I say. I take in Ben. Now that I know the score, the baggy clothes and the haircut don't really hide anything. It all sort of only works to make her look better. If you know what I mean.

My body has been nearly ruined over the summer on the run. My spirit has been stripped of ornament. I've grown hard and kind of mean. But now, talking with Sprague — it's the first real conversation I've had with another human being in months — has stirred up my juices. I feel fluids working themselves up from the unused parts of my body, flowing like lubricating oils into my muscles and sinews and brains. And I've a belly newly filled with hot food, and I'm standing beside a girl, and she's a pretty girl, really, if you know how to look at her. I know how to look at her.

"You think Sprague is some kind of genius?" I ask Ben.

"He's not a genius," she says. "His mind is not particularly clever."

"But you think he's — what? — a great man? A holy man?"

"He's a good man," she says.

"Is he good enough for you?" I say, watching the way her trousers are bunched up, tied with a rope, at her narrow waist. "I mean, in the ways that count? You're a young woman. And he's an old man."

Ben raises her chin. "What are you asking me?"

"You know exactly what I'm asking you."

"Edmund and I are in love with one another," she says.

"Spiritually, like."

"In *every* way," she says.

"You've had a hard time, kid. Maybe — " I break off and turn my head to the trees, where Sprague has gone. I look back at Ben and I speak more quietly. "Maybe you never had it real. Never had it the way it's supposed to be."

Ben looks at me like I'm speaking Hungarian. "Mr. Moon," she says. "I've never had *what*?"

"Love," I say.

She smiles at this. But only like she's satisfied with herself for having finally translated the Hungarian.

"Do *you* know about love, Mr. Moon?"

"A bit," I say.

"I see," she says. She nods. "Can you tell me?"

"Words fail me," I say. "But I can show you."

"I doubt you can."

"Try me."

Ben gives me a long stare, like she's thinking it over.

"Ed said — when we first met you — that you looked like that man in the pictures. James Cagney? Only darker."

I nod. Is this good? "People have told me that, yes."

"I suppose you've had a very easy time with girls."

"I enjoy girls. And they enjoy me. Fun times."

"So. And now you are trying to make time with me," she says.

I ignore her tone of voice. "I'm not trying to make anything," I say to her. "But I like the way your eyes work in your face. And I like the way your skin shines when it's wet. I think you like me, too, and we're both young and alive. Sprague is a good man but he's old. You're young and you've got a young girl's wants."

She frowns at this. "Is that how you figure it?"

"It is."

Ben sighs and looks away from me. She pushes her fingers up into the short hair at the back of her head. "Ed thinks you're like us," she says. "He thinks you've been hurt but that you're right at the edge of discovering something important. But I believe that you're just a very stupid man who doesn't get anything. And you never will."

I've got to laugh. It's a slap in the face, but what the hell. It's not as if I thought anything was coming of this, anyway.

"So you and Sprague are on a voyage of discovery?" I say, crossing my arms over my chest. "Like Christopher Columbus himself, are you?"

"We *all* are," she says. "Whether you come out and recognize it or not. That's what this is all about: A wide, deep ocean we're crossing. Believing — even though there's no reason you should believe — that there's land to be found beyond the known horizon."

I grin at her. "Where'd you read that line?"

"I can't read," she says. "I never learned."

"No lie?"

"Truth."

"So Sprague taught you that?"

"Nobody taught me," she says, sounding for the first time impatient with me. "I just *learned* it. You could stand to learn a few things yourself, Mr. Moon. First off, things about women."

"Women?"

"The way you speak, I'd say you don't know anything about women. I suspect it's what has got you in such trouble that you've taken to the road."

I laugh. "I'd be a lucky man today if my only troubles were women troubles."

"I think," Ben says, "that all of your troubles come from the same place. Face that, and they all may fall into themselves."

"Ah," I say, smiling sweetly but making my voice a sneer. "Wouldn't this be a nice world if it were so?"

I turn from Ben. To hell with her. I move away from her and away from the bushes where Sprague is off taking a crap. I walk down to the edge of the pool and spit into the water. I step over the flat rocks along the edge and around to the other side opposite the splashing waterfall, to where the poolwater slips silently over a lip of pink stone and spills down away, continuing its course into a fast-moving creekbed. There's some kind of scrubby pine bush here, and I grab a fistful of needles off the nearest branch and start picking them into pieces, dropping the shreds into the water at my feet.

These two characters think they understand everything. What I can't quite get my mind around is why anybody would even *want* to understand everything. Aren't some things just what they are? Still. I guess what's really got my Irish up is what Ben said about me being woman-stupid. Women are the one thing in this life I think I understand. But, of course, the facts — as my old friend Peterson might say — don't support the conclusion. I tug at another sprig of pine but I don't snap it from its bough, instead letting the soft needles slip away over my fist.

I'm thinking again about the day I stood with Annie in the twins' bedroom on the afternoon of the winter thaw. Why didn't I take her into my arms? Was I afraid? I don't know if I can express this the right way, but when a fellow has been a bastard for so long, and has been told as much by so many people, the meaning of his actions just sort of wears away like sidewalk salt in a March rain. I've been untrue to my friends, and I've been bad to my family, and I've hurt my Annie and ignored my children. And I've heard the voices scolding me for these behaviors, over and over and over again. *You're a shit, Horton Moon.* Yes, I am. It'd got to the point where I'd worn my shittiness like a second skin. Or maybe like a tattoo is a better image to use; it was on me, in me, and — like it or not — there was no shedding it. Likewise, I've heard my Annie called a saint for so many years, I got to half-expecting to see a golden halo ringing round her head every time she came into the room.

But my Annie is not a saint, is she? She's a woman. And I am not a shit. I'm a man, am I not? Okay. Maybe I don't have all the angles figured out, woman-wise. But that's not the same as saying I'm a stupid man who'll never understand anything. That was a nasty thing for Ben to say. But I guess I brought out that nastiness in her. Maybe I shouldn't have said that about the way her skin shines when it's wet. I was only being myself. What's it they say about a leopard changing his spots? Still. I guess I've some choice in the matter. I am not a shit. I am a man.

I walk back to Ben, more slowly than I'd left her, and the two of us just stand there, a few paces apart, not looking at one another, not talking. Now Sprague comes back up from the cover of the trees.

"Let's be leaving here," he says, when he reaches the place where me and Ben are standing. He claps his hands together and speaks quickly. "There's a town about four miles south of here. If we walk an hour in the opposite direction, north, we should come upon a highway. We'll try to hitch a ride there. West. In three days we'll be among the Sioux."

Sprague's voice is full of hope and cheer. I can tell he didn't hear anything that was said between Ben and me. Or maybe he heard the whole thing, squatting in the sumac ten yards away, and he thought nothing was said that called for anything but cheerfulness. He's a crazy man. But, nonetheless, I find myself caught up in his enthusiasm. So let's go. Into Injun country.

We go. We step through the trees and over the brush, finding the trail that leads us to the road.

Where the cover of leafy branches parts above us and where the sun comes down bright, the patchy roadside grass meets the gravel meets the asphalt. We stumble out into the hot midday light, and there we see the men, standing up on the roadbed. They look like they've been waiting for us.

Twenty-four

"You the boys been stealing chickens?" one of the men asks.

I can't say which of them asks it. There are about ten of them. They are all very much alike. Mean-looking, wearing dirty, worn clothes. They are local farmers, but they look as broke and beat as railway hoboes. A few of them carry sticks or clubs.

Sprague is standing at my shoulder, having stepped forward ahead of Ben behind. I take a glance sideways at Sprague. His face is the color of a dead camp fire. His lip starts to wobble and words come out of him sounding all dry and weak.

"Chickens? What? Something about chickens?" he says.

"You got it, pops," the same voice as before says. Now I see who says it. Tall man. Yellow hair. The mob's leader, I guess.

"Some tramps stole some chickens this morning," Yellow-hair says. "We don't stand for such nonsense in these parts."

"Uh," Sprague says, his lips wobbling. "Uh — ugh — we — I can assure you — "

Sprague's a mess. It hurts me to see him this way. And I don't even want to think about Ben back there. All at once, I know what to do and so I do it. I make a move toward the men, holding up my hand as I come forward.

"I stole two chickens," I say.

"That so?" Yellow-hair asks.

"It is," I say. "These two morons don't know anything about it. I stole a pair of birds from the fat son-of-a-bitch, over yonder in that gray house up the hill."

Yellow-hair blinks at me. "That's my father's house."

I blink back at him. "Well. Your father is a fat son-of-a-bitch. And I stole two of his birds."

I let that sink in and then I jerk my thumb over my shoulder. "These two don't know nothing. The boy's a mental retard and the old man's off his nut."

"He's what?" Yellow-hair asks.

"Crazy. Insane. He thinks he's the Emperor Napoleon. But he's harmless. Anyway. I'm the chicken thief you fellas seem to be out to corner. It's me. You got me."

Now I raise my hands like in the cowboy pictures.

Yellow-hair and the rest of them are as dumb as cow shit. They just look at me and none of them moves. Sprague and Ben aren't moving either.

"You got me," I say again. But I guess this isn't the way Yellow-hair and his buddies thought their afternoon was going to pan out, and they don't know what to do about it.

Now one of them, a rat-faced Mongoloid standing closest to Yellow-hair, leans his body over toward his boss. "If this is the guy, we should take him in."

"Yes," Yellow-hair says, after seeming to think it over for a while.

"We can bring him in to the cop house."

"Yes," Yellow-hair says again.

"Don't seem right to bother with the other two," Rat-face says, eyeing the club in Yellow-hair's hand. "Let's just take the one into the cop house. Just like that."

It's quiet, and a few boots start to shuffle in the dust on the road. Somebody coughs.

"Let the cop take care of him," a voice says, from the back of the gang. I give the lot of them a good look. They're a sorry bunch, and a few of them try to kind of hold their clubs and ax-handles behind themselves, like they're embarrassed. One young kid looks away from me when I catch his eye. When he looks back up at me, I nod at him.

What the hell. You never know how anything will turn out, but this is just fine. Thirty days in the local workhouse. Maybe sixty. Spending the winter with a lot of smelly, half-starved Indians didn't sound too appealing, anyway. The workhouse means regular meals and a roof overhead. And it looks now like they're going to let Ben and Sprague go on their way.

"We'll bring him in to the cop house," Yellow-hair says, staring at me. The other men make agreeing noises. "Skogie'll lock him up proper. Keep him away from chickens for a while."

This is apparently a joke, as Yellow-hair shows his big teeth and a few of the other men let out little barks of laughter.

"Yes, sir," Yellow-hair says. "No more chicken-stealing for this one."

Yellow-hair keeps staring at me but the rat-faced Mongoloid waves his arms toward Ben and Sprague.

"You two get out," Rat-face says to them. "County line is that direction. Head toward it and don't stop till you cross it. And don't stop *then*, neither. Just get out of here for good."

"Yes, sir," I hear Sprague's voice say behind me.

"And you," Rat-face says to me, "you're coming with us. Come on."

I go to him but Yellow-hair steps up now, shoving the rat-faced Mongoloid to one side.

"You insulted my father," he says to me, and he lets go with the ax-handle, swinging from his shoulder like a baseball hero. I see the blur in the air between us, then bright white, then it's lights out.

*

I wake up and it feels like my mouth is filled with cement. My head throbs and it seems hard to keep my skull balanced up on the top of my neck, and so I don't sit upright. I open my eyes. I'm covered with vomit and blood.

I'm in a small room. It's a jail cell, I can see now. One wall of iron bars. An overhead lightbulb hangs from a cord and fills every corner of the room. The place stinks of my vomit and somebody else's piss. And, now I notice, cigar smoke.

I turn my head, painfully, and I see a big man standing up from a chair. A cop. He walks over to me and stops a few feet away from the wall of iron bars. He puffs on his cigar and blows smoke my way.

"Hey," I say to him. It takes a great deal of effort to croak this word out from deep in my throat, and when I do manage the sound, it sets my whole upper body burning. Like I've just coughed up a hot coal.

"Prisoner," he says to me, nodding.

I realize that I'm not able to talk. There's something wrong with my face. Something wrong with my whole head. I stare at the cop and I hope he can see in my eyes that I'm saying to him something is wrong with me and I need help. Does he see this?

He puffs on his cigar. "Don't take this the wrong way, Prisoner," he says to me through the smoke, "but you smell like an ill-kept barn. The cigar helps. But I can't get too close to you. You feeling okay?"

I try to shake my head, *no*. I don't know if I do it. I don't know if the cop has seen me shake my head.

"You're banged up bad," he says. "Broken jaw, I guess. Though I'm not a doctor. Lew Cleary, he's a doctor. He'll come by to check you over later. Today's his daughter's wedding. Lew Cleary ain't gonna leave his own daughter's wedding to come check on a prisoner in the jail. You can understand that. But Lew Cleary will come round later. He'll fix you up."

A broken jaw. That explains my face. That explains why I can't talk or move. The whole thing from my ears down is a mess. But the rest of my head is clearing.

The cop is a big man. He looks like the kind of cop who wouldn't smack a fella around. That's about all you can ask for in a cop.

"My name is Skogstad," the cop is saying. "If you want to be by-the-book about it, it's *Captain* Skogstad. But we don't have to be by-the-book. Just Skogstad. I don't know your name. You got no papers. No nothing. And you're not talking. So."

He takes a puff at the cigar and then he leans a little forward toward me. "I guess you can't talk. On account of the jaw. I understand. Just take it easy. Bet you're wishing you never took a poke at David Tomaski. That's the blonde fella. Knocked you flat. I've known David all his life, and the boy wouldn't swat a fly if it was biting his ass. So you must have really gone at him to get him to lay you out like that. Well. Your mistake."

I groan. I know I can't really talk, but I feel like I've got to make some protest over this.

"Relax, you." Skogstad looks at his cigar. "Stealing for food is one thing. Times are hard and, if a man is going hungry, a man has to do what he has to do. I accept that. But you stole the chickens and then got belligerent on poor David. That I can't abide. Serves you right he busted your jaw. Shut up, now. Relax. I imagine it'll only hurt you worse if you try to talk before Lew Cleary comes to doctor you. Relax. I'll do the talking for both of us."

Now the cop, Skogstad, goes back and collects the chair he'd been sitting in before. He carries it, slowly, across the room and he sets it in place just outside my cell. He sits down.

"You know what it's like? Being a peace officer in a town like this? Dull. It's farm country. Churchgoing people. People don't break laws. Not much drinking. I don't handle much of anything but the occasional fistfight. Last summer I had to drag a body out of Cooper Lake. Suicide. Old German farmer. *That's* the most excitement I've had in sixteen years. Otherwise. Dull. Dull, dull, dull. It's all I've ever done. My daddy was the constable before me. I'll do this till I can't do the work no more. It's dull as hell."

I watch him work the cigar in his mouth. Okay, I want to say, I get it — it's dull. A dull life for a cop. It's breaking my heart.

"So now you're here, bleeding and throwing up all over my cell. I'll have to clean all this up, you know. Disgusting. I've got to hold you till Judge Gislequist comes in. He's at Lew Cleary's daughter's wedding, and then he's leaving tomorrow morning for a duck shoot north of here. Judge won't be in to set your terms till four days from now. So get comfortable. Anyway. I'll tell you right now, you won't stay here. We don't have the space or the money to hold no prisoners. Had a workhouse the next town east of here but we broke that up. Too many honest men in need of work these days to be giving it away to prisoners and miscreants. So rest up now. In four, five days, Gislequist will send you off. Probably to the state pen. Yes. Sorry about that. But we can't keep you round here. And, seeing how you assaulted one of my citizens, I suppose the state penitentiary is the right place for you. Ten years? Maybe less. I don't know. I'm not a judge. But we'll ship you off. You'll leave me here. Leave old Skogstad here in his dull little town with nothing to do and nobody to talk to."

Ah, shit. What is this? What have I stepped in here?

I make myself sit up, pressing my back against the wall. I brace myself and look at Skogstad. I try to make my eyes friendly. I'm pleading. God, I'm in pain.

"Whoa. Look at you. You feeling stronger? Good. Glad to see it. So. Like I was saying, things here are dull. I'd give anything for a little action. Don't get me wrong — I'm no kid, and I don't want life to be like the G-man movies. I ain't talking about shoot-em-up machine-gun battles with St. Paul gangsters or nothing like that. Just a little action. A little change. A little *interest*."

Skogstad's tune is starting to get stale for me, and my head does hurt so. I close my eyes and let him do his talking and I just work on getting the waves of pain to stop splashing against the inside of my eyeballs. State pen. Mother of God.

"I'm not an educated man. I don't read books and novels and such. I never went to school. I'm a *cop*, you know. But I'm not a stupid man, either. I know there's life going on out there, beyond this little town. I get hints of it. Bits and pieces come in. Like this. Look at this. Hey. Prisoner. Open your eyes. Look at this."

I open my eyes. Skogstad is holding something in his two big hands. It's a newspaper. No, it's a poster. I make my eyes focus. I can see it now.

"What do you make of this?" Skogstad asks me. "It's something, isn't it? Do you know who Steven Linen *is*? Do you? I do. He's a bigshot down in St. Paul. His daddy started a chain of gasoline stations that runs from Iowa to Canada. Millionaire. And look at this beauty. On the run. Girl like that, how do you think she could move around the country? I placed a call to Linen's folks, just as an interested peace officer. She's traveling with an old hobo, they think. But wouldn't they make an odd pair? If you saw them together? An old hobo and a young pretty girl? It makes you think, don't it? It makes *me* think."

Skogstad sucks on his cigar. It's dead. He makes a face, then re-lights the cigar, taking his time. He puffs for a good thirty seconds after he's got it lit, until he seems satisfied with the way the cigar is drawing.

"It makes me think," he says again. "I think about this. But that's me. Life is dull in these parts, and I've got nothing but time for thinking. You know. Now, if the girl was changed. If she didn't look the same. Then maybe. But — here's my thinking — even if the girl peroxides her hair blonde and dresses in dirty rags, she's still a young girl with an old hobo. And that's tough to blend in. Right? But. Maybe she really changed. Maybe everybody's looking for a young girl," Skogstad gives the poster a snap, "when they should be looking for something else entirely. You follow me. Do you? Do you?"

I move my head up and down.

"I thought you might follow me on this. Maybe the key to making this Steven Linen fellow happy is not to find this girl in the drawing, but to find something else. Like a young girl all made up like a boy. You understand what I'm saying? Of course. You understand, Prisoner, *exactly* what I'm saying."

Skogstad smokes and stares at me. Maybe he smiles at me. I can't tell. He's doing something with his mouth, but maybe it's just the way he's smoking the cigar.

"The boys that brought you in here told me you were *with* an old hobo and a young boy. They said the kid was a little Guinea-looking thing. Retard. Mute. They sent the two of them off away. They brought you in alone. They let your friends go."

I move my head back and forth, painfully.

"No?" Skogstad says, impatiently. "No, they weren't the couple in question? Well. I can't say I'm going to accept that as an answer."

He stands from his chair and looks down at me. He rolls the poster up, distractedly, making it a tight tube.

"See, Prisoner. I know for a fact that the couple in question has been spotted in these parts. Sheriff John Hope, from Becker County, up north, is a friend of mine. Few months ago, he pulled a load of tramps off a train for delousing and he found one of them to be a lady dressed up like a boy. She was traveling with an old man. Sheriff Hope sent them out of his county, in my direction. He told me to keep an eye out for them coming. Mind you, this was all before I got wind of Mr. Linen and his interest in the matter," he said, wagging the rolled poster at me behind the bars.

"David Tomaski and his gang, them that brought you in — they don't know nothing about this poster. And that's fine with me. They're good boys but they're not bright. You and me, Prisoner, we're the only ones who need to know about this for now. I want you to think about this. Where are your friends heading? Where are they now? Where can I find them? I know you can't talk right now, but you'll be able to talk sometime soon. Maybe you'll be able to talk before Gislequist comes back from his duck shoot, before Judge Gislequist can pass sentence on you."

He draws on his cigar and lets the smoke out slowly. "Maybe you won't still *be* here when Gislequist comes back. Think about this." Skogstad squints through his cigar smoke at me. Now he smiles. No mistaking it this time. "I'm bored here almost out of my head, but I believe something very exciting has dropped into my life. I believe that *you*, Prisoner, are going to change *everything* for me."

Twenty-five

Skogstad boils the soup at the iron cookstove in the corner of his office. I wish he wouldn't boil the soup. It's not bad soup — beef and potatoes, made up by his mother a few days ago — but the man puts it on the flame and leaves the pot till the soup boils, and then it's too hot to eat.

I know some folks gripe about cold soup, and I know I'm a prisoner in a jail, and I know I shouldn't complain. But still. If you're going to feed a man soup, feed him soup. With my face all busted up and swollen, it's just that much harder for me to sip at this scalding broth that Skogstad brings me every day.

I sit in my cell and watch Skogstad burn the soup. It's the third day I'm here. My head is completely cleared up now. The doctor, Cleary, fixed me up with some kind of sutures inside my mouth, so that when I talk my words come out mumbly. But I can talk enough to be understood.

I'm here three days and I can see why Skogstad declared his life dull. He's here all alone, all day. Arrives with the papers at eight. Reads (slowly) through the morning. He goes out at one point, I guess walking around the town outside, and then he comes back and sits. Post comes just before lunch. Skogstad boils soup for me and for himself, then he takes his time cleaning up, and then it's back in the chair for the rest of the afternoon. A couple of times the telephone has rung. Skogstad answers brightly but always sounds kind of disappointed at whoever it is on the other end of the line. Nothing ever comes of these telephone calls. He falls asleep sometimes in the afternoon. At supper time, he boils more soup. After I eat, he takes away my bowl and spoon and washes them clean for tomorrow. Then he leaves.

Now he comes to my cell, carrying a tray of soup and bread. It's noon. Skogstad takes out his key, a single shiny key — doesn't look much used — and he jiggles it into the hole in the cell door. He swings the door open, the key still in it, and he steps into my cell and crosses with the tray.

"Hot stuff," he says.

"As always," I say.

Skogstad does a take like a movie-house comedian, his mouth agape and his eyes bugging. "What's that? You're talking?"

"I'm not saying anything you'll want to hear," I mumble back at him.

He recovers. We've been through this routine before. "Suit yourself, Prisoner. Anyway. Here goes. Hot soup."

"Thank you."

"Most welcome," he says.

Skogstad is stopped, standing in my cell with me. I'm not sure I like this. He usually leaves right away.

"How old are you, Prisoner?"

"Go fuck yourself," I say.

He shrugs. He seems to be thinking of something to say, but then he shakes his head and goes out of the cell. He closes the door and pockets the key.

"Just trying to be friendly," he says.

"I know full well what you're 'just trying,'" I say.

"Ten years in the state pen is a damn shame. That's ten good years in a young man's life. And to think you could be out wandering free. Riding the rails. Answering to nobody. Making your own way."

"I'm not playing this, Skogstad," I say to him. I try to sip at my soup but the stuff is so goddamned hot that the steel spoon, standing in the both, burns my fingers when I touch it.

Skogstad goes back to his chair. I'm not playing this game, but I don't know just what game I *am* playing. I don't think Skogstad's bluffing about this judge and the time he'll give. Ten years. Even five years would be hell, in the pen. If I lasted that long. The Minneapolis syndicates have people in Stillwater. Everybody hears these stories. They'd find me out in a minute. I've been thinking about this for the better part of three days.

I'm not going to say I'm a saint and that I haven't considered ratting out Ben and Sprague. I could, easily. Big Indian Reservation. How many of those are there out here? If I wanted, I could find them, I bet. I could lead Skogstad there. Easy. So why don't I? I'm not a saint. Why start pretending I am? I don't know. I really don't know.

Maybe it comes from what Ben said to me. About how I'm a stupid man who doesn't know anything and who never will. When a person makes a statement like that about you, it comes back to snake around through your brain after a while. It's been snaking through mine. What *do* I know? I mean, beyond the obvious things. I suppose I know, looking at Ben and her old man, Sprague, that the couple of them are the closest I've ever seen to two happy people. You don't have to be a saint to see it's wrong to steal away a happiness like that. It's just plain wrong. Lord knows, I've already ruined the happiness of enough people to last me till judgement day.

Sprague says we all have just the right life. It's up to each of us to make peace with that. Ben has made her peace, and so has the old man. Me, I haven't any peace. Maybe I never will have any. This life of mine seems to have reached the end of the streetcar line. Tomorrow the judge comes, and then it's off to the pen for me. Delivered to the north side gang. So where does sainthood get me then?

The soup still hasn't cooled. Damn. I slouch back on my hard mattress and take in the miserable little jail-house.

The hot light overhead never changes, except when it's turned off at night when Skogstad leaves. There's no window in the cell. There is a window up near the desk where Skogstad is sitting, studying a magazine, but it is covered by a shade that he always has pulled down. Skogstad's desk is cleared of papers, as clean as a dining table. There's a calendar hanging on one wall, and a brass clock hanging on the opposite wall. In the corner, on the wall above the cookstove, Skogstad keeps his gun belt. It's an antique-looking thing, with a holster holding a big Colt revolver, like something out of a cowboy matinee.

Skogstad all of a sudden jerks his chair backwards and stands up fast. He's not really been reading the magazine, I guess. He clomps across the floor toward me, and he grabs onto the bars of my cell. His big hands choke at the iron bars covered in chipped paint.

"I'm gonna find them, you know!" he says. "With your help or without. I'm gonna find them two and bring them down to St. Paul and get the reward money. Alls I'm asking you for is help."

"Fuck you," I say.

"No, fuck *you*! I've been looking for them on my own, every night, when I leave here. I've been looking. I've been checking the hobo camps all around here, I've been checking the train yards."

"Keep it up," say to him.

"I will. I will," he says, his breath coming hard.

"Only," I say, "I gotta tell you, you are wasting your time in the rail yards and hobo camps."

*

Skogstad's grip on the bars loosens. I see his fingers relaxing.

"What do you mean by that?" he asks me.

"Rail yards and hobo camps," I say, and I slowly shake my head side to side. "Not there."

"Prisoner," Skogstad says, his voice barely a whisper. "Are you talking to me?"

"I am," I say.

He stares at me for a long moment, trying I guess to read if I'm fooling with him or not. He wets his lips and nods.

"Go on," he says.

"It's just," I say, but I don't finish. My head goes to one side and both my hands go up to my throat. I breathe hard, shallow breaths and I rock on my mattress. I double over, my face near my knees. I'm making sounds that aren't words. Desperate sounds. Pleading for help.

"Prisoner!" Skogstad shouts at me. He slaps at the bars with open palms, then he curses. I hear him shuffling in place, then I hear his key in the lock of my cell door. I hear the door swing open.

"Prisoner!" Skogstad's voice is loud, just above me now.

His big hands grab my shoulders and force me upright. He is standing in front of me, staring at me, wondering what is wrong. I reach sideways for my lunch tray. I take up the bowl of scalding soup. With a flick of my wrist, I toss the soup into Skogstad's face.

He screams and he's still screaming when I get outside the cell and close the door and turn the key in the lock. When I go to the wall above the stove and take down the big Colt revolver and I come back toward the cell with the pistol pointing at him on the other side of the bars, Skogstad has stopped screaming.

"God damn, boy. God *damn*!" he says, holding his hands to his face. "I mean, God *damn*! Did you have to throw soup at me? I'm asking you. Did you have to?"

"Shut up," I say to him. "Take off your clothes."

"What?"

"Take your clothes off. No clothes."

He looks at me like this is some kind of parlor game. "Why?"

"Because I've got a gun pointing at your chest and I told you to. That's why."

"Okay, okay. You're in charge now," he says.

"For all I know, you've got an extra key, or a Derringer in your trousers pocket. I don't want any funny business like that."

Skogstad manages a small smile. "A Derringer? No. This isn't that kind of neighborhood. But still. Good thinking."

He gets his things off and passes them through the bars to me. He sits on the edge of the mattress.

"Okay if I sit?" he asks.

"Sure," I say.

He touches his face with his fingertips. "Damn. My mother *made* that soup. So this is a jailbreak. Never been through one of these."

I shrug with the shoulder of my gun hand. "Neither have I."

"So what's next?"

"I'll need a car."

"A car?"

"An automobile. Yes." And I lift the pistol a bit, reminding him that he's not in a position to question my needs.

"I've got a car," he says, his voice going flat. "A Ford. Out front."

"I'll be taking that."

"I see."

I stoop and pick up his trousers, feeling through the pockets till I've found an automobile ignition key and a clip holding seventeen dollars. Skogstad sits glaring at me.

"Word of advice, Prisoner," he says now.

"What's that?" I ask.

"Don't get caught. Because if you get caught, it'll be a rough time for you."

"I imagine you're right," I say.

"Sticking up a peace officer," Skogstad says gravely, shaking his head at me. "Assaulting him with the soup his own mother made."

"I'm sorry about the soup," I say, and I mean it. "It couldn't be helped."

"I understand. But still. Stealing chickens and punching at white-trash farmers is one thing, but playing with guns is another altogether."

"I understand that."

"Okay," he says, giving me a sad kind of stare. "I suppose you do. You know what you're doing."

"I believe I do. Yes."

"You'll not get away with this. And if you're caught you'll likely be killed."

"Well," I say. "Let me offer *you* a word of advice, Captain Skogstad. Give up your search for Steven Linen's girl. She and her hobo are halfway to Chicago by now, I imagine. They're heading east, heading as far away from that pervert, Linen, as they can get. In a week they'll be in New York."

"That so?"

"Yes. That is so. And as for me, I have no intention of getting caught *or* killed. I'm just going to get lost."

And with that — which, you've got to admit, sounds like something Ronald Coleman himself might spout — I turn and walk out of the jail house. I'm surprised outside by the sunlight, and by the chill in the air. But then there's the Ford, waiting out front just like Skogstad said. And with a nearly full tank of gas.

Twenty-six

It's a shit town. Two streets, a half-dozen wood-frame buildings. The afternoon is cool and sweet with the taste of autumn, but all the windows in the town are clouded over with summer dust. I can't leave the place fast enough. I drive the Ford to the edge of the town, then circle back the other way. Then I have to drive out in a third direction before I find the rails. I circle around a bit in a neighborhood of grain towers and wind-beaten shacks until I get the lay of the place and I find the rail yards.

I scoot the Ford a half-mile further out and I drive it into the tall grass at the edge of a drainage canal beside the highway. I leave Skogstad's Colt pistol on the front seat of the Ford. No reason to carry that kind of trouble with me. I walk back, fast, to the rail yards.

When I reach the lot behind the rails, a big locomotive comes *schlugging* into sight like it was ordered for me. The train stops, coughing smoke and steam and sparks, and I watch the men clamber up the water tower to swing the valve around to fill the engine's tank. It seems to be taking them longer than it should, and for the first time since I left Skogstad I'm starting to feel itchy with nerves. But in fifteen minutes, the train men finish up their business and hop back into their places, and then the whole thing starts up moving.

Like a building suddenly come to life, the impossibly big locomotive shudders and shakes and slides away from in front of me, the afternoon sun glinting off its greasy black surfaces through a haze of smoke and steam. Trailing behind, it looks like a mile of boxcars.

Away. I'm going away from here. But the long, long freight train is only the first leg of my journey. I've decided. My destination is not westward, not toward the clean, bright plains of Dakota, not to some imagined prairie from an earlier century; I'm going to the ground I know belongs to me, and I to it. Home. I lied to poor old Skogstad when I told him I was going to become lost; I've been lost too long already. Have I changed? I don't think I have. Having become no better, no worse, I return only because I know that my place is there. Whatever that may bring.

I'm watching for dicks but there's none to be seen except for the two in the car just behind the hopper. Too good to be true? Or maybe it's just the luck of the Irish, coming back to me after a long absence. I skip forward across the yard and catch onto one of the boxcars before the train makes too much speed. Swinging up into the shadowed insides, I drop and roll backward away from the open door.

I'm alone. Got the car to myself. Wait. Check that. There's two others, way over there in the far corner. I give them the once over, though they don't seem too interested in me. It's a fat-bellied hobo, a lifer by the looks of him, and a young colored guy in good clothes. I stand up and walk over to them, getting my legs under the rocking of the car.

"Hey there, fellas," I say. We're picking up speed and already the noise is getting too much for real talking. The old hobo looks up at me but his face is dead. Maybe he's drunk. But the well-dressed colored guy raises one hand.

"Hey yourself, boss," he says.

"Where's this rig heading?" I ask him.

"Heading south, I guess. Southeast. Heading into St. Paul."

"Glory be to God," I can't help but say.

"I hear that," the man says, grinning. "St. Paul is my kind of town, sure."

I try to smile back at him, but my mouth is in awful shape and I can't imagine what sort of face I make at him. His grin goes away fast — he looks put off.

"You have any idea of the time?" I ask him. "You know when we're due into St. Paul?"

He frowns. "No idea whatsoever. Why? You got an appointment to keep with the governor?"

"No," I say, just as the noise from the tracks rises up and drowns all our talking out. "I'm not in any kind of hurry at all."

*

In St. Paul, it's a cold morning. There's frost on the wooden slats of the boxcar. I stand the last two miles in, hopping from foot to foot and trying to get the devil out from my bones. The colored guy, whose name is Bates, is standing beside me and we're watching out the door at the stockyards and at the clumps of dirty-looking houses hammered into the hillsides.

"St. Paul!" Bates shouts, with a wave of his hand. You'd think he's viewing the glories of the Venetian canals. "This is *my* town!" Bates says, giving me an elbow in the ribs.

"Welcome to it," I say.

He laughs at this. He's a decent fella. "Good to be back. Good to be back," he says. I get a look at his face and for the life of me I can't read what he's seeing as he looks out on this miserable scene. I guess a lot of it has more to do with what he saw back out there, on the northern plains.

Bates and I have talked over the past few days. He spent the summer on a Montana cattle ranch, riding horses like a movie cowboy and getting paid in pennies and beans and coffee. The boss treated him alright, but some of the other cowhands were real bastards. They didn't care that he was a nigger so much as they hated him for being from the city. They slapped his horse and stole his food and put sand in his bunk roll. Bates, finally, was left with no choice but to settle accounts with the biggest and meanest of the ranch hands. Bates made his argument with a razor. He'd had to leave quickly, hopping freights across the Dakotas until he got himself on the St. Paul train where I found him.

The old hobo I'd first seen Bates with is named Greene. He is not a drunk at all, but his brains are dashed from a run-in with club-wielding rail cops. Greene sleeps a lot. Bates has taken it on himself to help Greene get down to St. Paul. Greene says he has a brother who works for the water company.

Now our train is slowing to a crawl, and we can easily step off any time we want. I look at Bates and I look back into the car, where Greene lay. "Should we wake him up?" I ask.

"I think so, yes," Bates says. He goes to Greene and shakes him. Greene opens his eyes and stands up, stretching silently like a dog. "Here we are, Greene," Bates says, guiding the hobo forward toward the door. "St. Paul."

"Gateway to paradise," I say, sweeping my arm out to indicate the muddy stockyards, which stretch before us now as far as we can see.

"It's cold," Greene says.

"Yes," says Bates. "Fall has arrived. And so have we. Goodbye Mr. Powers," he says to me.

"Goodbye, Mr. Bates," I say. "Goodbye, Mr. Greene."

He takes Greene's arm and then he and Greene drop off the boxcar onto the brown ground and go slipping away between the fenceposts and cattle shoots, but I stay in the car for another ten minutes, until it has entered the rail yards.

*

I use Skogstad's money to feed myself a meal at a diner three blocks in from the rail yards. My jaw is bad and so I order soup and hash and a pot of coffee. The waitress stares at me while I order.

"And what are you looking at that way?" I ask her.

"You," she says.

"What of me?" I ask her.

"You look like you been dragged through the yards face-first, that's all."

"You don't look so hot yourself, lady," I say.

"You don't have to get nasty," she says.

"But you do?" I ask.

"I wasn't being nasty. I was saying."

"You was saying, alright. Be a dear and just get me my food, okay?"

She goes off and I'm left sitting there thinking. I suppose I do look like hell. I touch my swollen face, covered with a beard. My clothes smell like a boxcar. And I also smell faintly, I notice, of Skogstad's cigars. I'm not dressed for the weather and when I hold up my hands I can see they're red as raw steaks. I run both hands over my hair, smoothing it back. Then I have a coughing fit that I can't stop till the waitress comes back with the coffee.

"You on the road?" she asks me.

I start to give her a look, but her voice is kind and her face is dumb and harmless. "I was," I say. "I'm heading for home now."

"Welcome home," she says, as she pours me a cup of the coffee. Then she leaves me.

I take my time with the food. Partly because my mouth isn't working properly and so I can't hurry things, but partly also I guess because I've been moving for days now and I'm feeling pretty good to be still at last. Sitting still in a warm room.

I pay for the food and I leave the waitress a half-dollar. I feel bad for having crossed swords with her about appearances. I get change at the cashier's and, even though I've got enough cash in Skogstad's clip to hire a limousine, I walk over to the streetcar line and hop the streetcar west toward Minneapolis.

It's late in the morning and the working people are all deposited in their jobs, so the car is near empty and I find a seat in the middle for myself. It's queer to feel the familiar seat around me, rattan-smelling and soft. The heat-vent on the floor is just at my feet, and with the sun coming in the window, warming my face, and with the electric heat coming up my legs, and with the comforting rock and wheeze of the car as it clatters along, in no time at all I drop off to sleep.

I wake up on Lake Street, coming off the river bridge. Now I stand up, though the car is still almost empty of passengers. I stand in the aisle and hold the pole, letting my knees bend to keep my balance. I've come home. But my home is a complicated place, badly built, a fragile structure; there's bad weather blowing in on my back that may shake the whole damn place loose from its foundations. I know that the first thing I've got to do against these coming storms is to close the doors I've left ajar. At Columbus Avenue, I step off onto the old paving stones. I cross in front of the stopped streetcar and step quickly across Lake Street to the opposite side. I go to the barbershop and get a shave and a haircut, and then I walk down the block toward Caroline's apartment building.

*

Audrey answers the door. She doesn't say anything for a long time. Then she steps out into the hallway with me, closing the door behind herself.

"Well," she says. "Hello, you."

"I've come back," I say.

"So I see."

"Caroline. Is she— "

"She's here. She's in bed."

"Is she sick?"

"She's not well."

"The baby?"

"She's had a hard time. The doctor wants her off her feet. She stays in bed most of the day now."

"What about her job?"

"She lost her job two months ago," Audrey says. "I lost my job, too. If you care."

"I'm sorry," I say. I look Audrey in the eyes and I want her to understand this. "I'm sorry. I've come back."

She doesn't make a move. "I'm not sure you're welcome back," she says.

"But Caroline."

"You've hurt that girl pretty badly."

"I've come back to help her get better."

Audrey stares at me and I think I see something getting softer in her eyes. But she still doesn't move from blocking the doorway.

"What happened to your face?" she asks. "Your voice is all funny when you talk."

"My jaw is broken. And my ear is fucked up. And I've got a cough I can't shake. But I think I can be of some help here."

Now I see for sure that her stare is softening. She smiles at me and rubs at her nose with the back of her hand. "Ah. Hort."

"Yes?"

"Why'd you go?"

"I had to. I'll explain it someday. But now I've come back. I had to."

"She's not good, you know," Audrey says, glancing back to the closed door.

"What is it?" I ask.

"She's had bleeding. She's weak. The baby's still coming, but Caroline can barely move. It's been hell."

"I'm sorry. Let me in to see her. I need to see her."

Audrey nods now and steps sideways, opening the door.

"C'mon in, Horton. Welcome to the real world."

Twenty-seven

Caroline has lost weight and her hair has lost its shine. She wears a braid that sits on the blanket like a length of rope, dull and pale, almost white. Her eyelids are pink and her lips are chapped and cracked. She cried when I came in the room. And then she laughed. And then she cried again for a long time. Now she is calm and she's not crying or laughing.

Audrey's gone out for cigarettes, and when she comes back she's also picked up a bottle of bourbon.

"Can I pour you one, Hort?" she asks me.

"I don't think so, no," I say.

Audrey drinks alone, and I sit in the hard chair beside Caroline's bed and I hold her hand. We talk a little, awkwardly. Mostly we just look at each other. After an hour, Caroline falls asleep.

Audrey clears her throat behind me. "Horton," she says.

"Yes?"

"You really should bathe. You smell something awful."

"Yes," I say. "I suppose I do."

So I go into the bathroom behind the kitchenette and I fill the tub with hot water. I empty my pockets on the washstand and take my clothes off to pass them to Audrey, so she can take them to the laundry. But my shirt collar is blackened and my trousers are worn through. I open the door a crack and hand Audrey instead a pair of Skogstad's bills. She leaves to buy me new clothes.

I settle into the tub for a long soak, but in five minutes I'm out, rising to answer Caroline's moans.

Covered in a towel, I hover at her side.

"You're here," she says.

"I'm here," I say.

"I thought I'd dreamed it."

Which hurts my heart. I close my eyes and touch her hands.

"Try to sleep some more," I say. "Audrey says the doc orders it."

"Horton," she says. "Your face is knocked all sideways."

"It is. I'm a mess."

"You're not a mess. You're not."

"I am. But I'll get better. I'm recovering."

"And you'll never go away again, will you?"

"You need to rest," is all I say to that.

"I know," she says. "I need to rest."

"You do. You do."

I'm sitting now in the chair beside her, and she closes her eyes and sleeps. I lay my head on the bed next to her braid, and I fall asleep, too.

*

Audrey's bought me ditch-digger's clothes. Dungarees and a heavy, denim-cotton shirt. It was all she could find to fit me, off the rack. I don't mind. My shoes are worn and broken, and covered with mud and dust from my travels. Tomorrow I'll go buy a new pair.

"I'll take that drink now, Audrey," I say to her.

Caroline is asleep again. She woke for supper — fried liver and toast and cold milk — but she fell off as Audrey was washing the plates in the kitchenette's sink. I'm still sitting in the hard-backed chair beside the bed.

Audrey fills me a short tumbler and hands it to me.

"No ice," she says.

"None needed," I say.

If you've ever gone weeks and weeks without a drink and then had a sip of good strong bourbon from a clean, heavy glass, I don't have to tell you what I'm feeling now. Just right, up in the place behind my nose.

"She sleep this much every day?" I ask Audrey.

"Some days more. Some days less." Audrey dries her hands on the dish towel and leans her ass back against the countertop. "She's not been well."

I let this go between us. There's nothing to say to that. It's what old Peterson would call an obvious fact beyond contention. I drink up my bourbon and hand the glass back to Audrey for another. She pours me another and this time pours one for herself.

"What are your plans, Horton?"

"I'm still making them," I say.

She shifts her weight against the countertop. "I was afraid you'd say that," she says.

"Well," I say.

"The girl needs you," Audrey says, and she's got a bit of an edge to her voice.

I touch the side of my jaw carefully. "There's a lot of people need me right now, Audrey."

Audrey's narrow face looks like a basketball with the air going out of it. "I thought you said you came back for Caroline."

"I said I came back. I came back for my own reasons. The fact of the matter is, I only came here tonight to say goodbye to Caroline."

Audrey's face goes ugly, like I've told a joke on her.

I hold up my hand, before she can say anything. "I know, I know. It's not coming off the way I'd planned. But when I came here, I didn't expect to find the girl in this kind of shape. Something went from me. I lost my nerve. But I do need to say goodbye to her."

Audrey is quiet for a short while. When she speaks again, it comes out fast and hard. "You really are a bastard. You come here — for what? — to make yourself feel better? You want Caroline to give you her blessing and send you back to your wife across the park?"

"Audrey, I — "

"You know what?" she says, fighting to catch her breath. "She forgave you. She was done. When you left, the poor kid, she thought it was her fault. She thought you were doing the right thing to go back to your family. She thought you were a prince."

"But I intended then to come back," I say. "I mean, I didn't leave her forever. I meant to come back. I did."

"It doesn't matter," Audrey says, shaking her head. Her voice catches with a bitter little laugh. "It doesn't matter what you intended. Don't you get it yet? This isn't about *you*. Look at her. She's hurting. You did that to her. Don't you feel anything? Don't you understand anything?"

"I'm only trying to figure it all out," I say, my voice low.

The radiator in the corner starts up banging and hissing. The air in the small room is too warm, and it's heavy with the smells of fried liver and unclean bed linens. I need to clear my head. Brace myself for what I have to do when Caroline wakes. I stand up from my chair.

"I'll be back," I say. "I'm going out for about an hour. You'll be here?"

Audrey doesn't answer me, but I leave her there.

The air is cold off the water of the Powderhorn lake and it feels good in my mouth. Night is falling, though it's not late in the day. I cross under the oaks and kick up the leaves that have heaped on the pathways.

Up ahead, I see Tim Young working with a crew. They've raked up a big pile of the leaves and they're setting them on fire.

I call to Tim from the path.

"That you, Hort?" he says, from his fire.

"It's me," I say. The firesmoke is a lovely smell and I'm feeling Audrey's whiskey.

"You've been away," Tim says.

"I'm back," I say, and I make a little bow and then I do a sort of jig, skipping away from him up the path.

At the Frenchman's, Davis is on. It must be Tuesday. I'm sorry I've missed Elsen.

"Give me a beer and a bump," I tell Davis, when I've got my elbow on the bar.

He just stares at me like I've asked for a glass of blood and a plate of eyeballs.

"A beer and a bump," I say again. "Please?"

"You got it," he says. He's snapped out of whatever spell he was suffering. I've never liked Davis.

He brings me my drink and he stands above me.

"You're back in town," he says.

"Who said I was *out* of town?" I ask him.

"Well. You ain't been around."

"Maybe I just found someplace else to drink," I say.

"I heard you were out of town."

"You heard from who?"

"Ah. People talk."

"Yes," I say. "I suppose they do."

Davis isn't leaving me. Time was, I couldn't get him to look my way. Now he's studying me like I'm a celebrity blown into his joint.

"Where you staying?" he asks me.

"I'm sleeping at your mother's," I say.

He leaves me alone.

I look to one end of the bar and it's nothing but strangers. I look the other direction and I see Scotty Boyle, coming across the room from the can.

"Scotty," I say. "Come over here and let me buy you a drink."

Scotty brightens and slaps my arms and gives me a round of how-the-hell-you-beens. When Davis brings him his beer, Scotty and I touch glasses.

"I was hoping I'd see Peterson in here tonight," I say.

Scotty gives me the eye over his beer glass. He lowers the glass slowly.

"You ain't heard?" he says.

The sounds of that gives me what we used to call bees in the breadbasket. "I ain't heard nothing," I say.

"Peterson's dead," Scotty says.

"How?"

"Piano wire round his throat. They found his body in Loring Park. Beginning of the summer."

I don't say anything. I just nod.

"You heard about his cousin?"

I nod again.

"Same thing. Murdered. This was just a few days after the cousin. They think it was the same guy. It was in the papers."

"I bet it was," I say.

Scotty takes a drink and shakes his head. "Papers said the two of them were mixed up with something. You know."

"Sure," I say. "I know." I drink my beer but it kind of sticks in my throat.

Scotty is a happy guy and he doesn't like to dwell on bad news, so he changes the subject and he tells me about his sister, who won the parish raffle in July. She bought Scotty a box of dollar cigars and paid the next year's school tuition for all four of Scotty's kids. Then he tells me about Elsen and how he took a week off from the Frenchman's in August and went up north fishing and came back with a muskie the length of your arm, mounted on a board. He hung it over the bar but someone stole it last month. Imagine that? Stealing a man's fish from behind the bar. How'd they pull that off? Then Scotty tells me a story about baseball. I can never follow baseball stories and this time it's worse than most. I notice that I haven't touched my bump and so I empty the shot into my mouth and I almost gag on it.

"You find work yet?" Scotty says, when he's finished the baseball story.

"Who said I was out of work?" I ask him.

"Now. Nobody *said*, Horton. I just guessed."

"Why'd you guess that?"

He makes a sympathetic face. "The collectors."

"What collectors?"

"They came around the Frenchman's. Asking after you. I mean, I *figured* they were collectors. You know." He makes a motion with his finger at his face, drawing a long nose.

"Jewish fellas," I say.

"Yeah. Blood-suckers."

I keep my voice very steady. "They came round here?"

He nods. "More than once."

"Recently?"

"They been around. These people never let go."

"You talked to them?"

Scotty curls his lip at me. "Horton. *Nobody* talked to them. Don't worry. We all been in the same boat with those loan-sharks."

"Right," I say. "Right."

But all I'm thinking is about Davis and what a shit he is and how he looked at me when I came in and how he asked me where I was staying. Where I was *staying*. What the hell kind of question is that to come from Davis? I all of a sudden want to talk to Davis, very much, only now I notice he's nowhere around. A young drunk at the end of the bar is rapping his beer glass on the bar impatiently. But there's no Davis anywhere.

"Scotty," I say. "I've got to go now."

"What?" he asks. "Just like that?"

I stand up quickly. "Yes. Just like that."

Twenty-eight

These people, as Scotty said, never let go. So be it. I guess I'm not surprised. It's one of the storms that's blown in behind me, coming home from the north. *One* of the storms, mind you, but not the only one. I'm going to walk across the park to Caroline's apartment now and I'm going to say goodbye to her. I know that it'll be bad. The easy thing to do would be to just leave it alone, to just never return. Audrey says she forgave me when I left in July. So what have I done? What have I done over these months, hiding and running, going without food and drink and the people I love? I thought I was doing it for her, for them, but now I find Caroline let me go in July. I should have known that. Another man might have known that. Or he would have done something, said something, reached out to her someway, to make her know what he was trying to do in leaving her. What was in his heart. I thought I was being strong and noble, but the awful truth of the matter is I was afraid then. I was always afraid.

Anyway. No more. It's going to be misery to try to tell her things tonight. I know that. Easier to just go now. But I'm through with easy things. Audrey may say I think it's all about me, but that's not true. It's for Caroline, too. She needs to know what's happened to us. I owe her more than a cap left on her bed. I'm going to try to tell Caroline what I know, what I've learned, how I've changed.

We have this one life, each of us, and all you can say for sure about any of it is that this once around is ours and ours alone to live. The least a fella can do is open his eyes and recognize that much. You can try to smooth out the rough edges of the truth with philosophy or religion or even the drink, but — rough edges or no — the main shape of it remains unchangeable. Benedetta, in the forest, told me that I was a stupid man who would never understand anything. She's a better woman than I'm a man, and she might very well be right, but I think she's wrong.

Maybe I am a freak of nature, and maybe I can love two women equally, at the same time. But I can make a proper life with only one, and my one is my Annie. It is only my bad behavior that has cut through that life, and through that love, like a sharp knife. I don't know if I can heal this wound, but I can most certainly stop cutting the flesh anew. I've hurt Annie terribly and it's going to take a lifetime for me to make up that hurt. And a lifetime is something I just no longer have.

Because that much is obvious, isn't it? Look at it from any angle you like and it all comes back to this: returning to the Powderhorn is a death sentence for me. These people never let go. But what I've figured out is that running away from my Annie is another kind of death, and one that I fear more than the quick and final one that we're all born to meet. Annie's love is not easy, not mine without effort, but it is a love that is in me — and me in it — in a way that can't be ignored or denied. I cannot say that Annie would be better off without me, and I know that without her I will be sunk away from the light like an iron railway spike dropped into the cold waters of a deep lake. I understand that I need to run home to Annie, no matter whether that will be my end or my beginning.

So where does all this understanding, this *awareness*, get me? You tell me. Maybe, by rights, I should drop to the pavement, paralyzed with fear and regret at the prospect of the words I need to speak to Caroline. But that's not happening to me. I'm feeling something like the opposite of that. Skipping along the pathway at the edge of the Powderhorn, I've come alive. I'm anxious to act. I'm happy to be conscious. I'm not ruined by remorse but shot full of piss and vinegar. I'm braced with Audrey's bourbon and with the drink from the Frenchman's, and with the good, cold October air, and maybe even with the thought of the northside gang closing in. But there's something else at work here, shaking me awake. I don't know *what* it is. That's what I mean: you tell me. I don't get it.

But whatever it is, it's part of me now as surely as the awfulness I'd worn like a tattoo had been part of me in the past. I'm changed now. I need to make it clean with Caroline. I need to make her know that I love her but that our lives must go on separately. I don't need her blessing. I only need to speak the truth aloud. I'm going to take care of everything.

At the door to Caroline's apartment building, I'm almost knocked sideways to the pavement by the old Polock neighbor. I mean, I guess that it's the old Polock neighbor; when he knocks me sideways, I've never before seen him — him being the one that never left his rooms in all the time I'd been coming around the place — and I don't know *who* he is. He's a small, old man, but he's moving fast and he catches me when I'm unsteady.

"Hey there," I say to him. But his eyes are wild and he only gives me a short, hot glance before he rushes off away into the night. I enter the building and right away I hear it. Caroline screaming. And other voices, shouting. I run the length of the hallway to her apartment.

The door is opened. Audrey is standing at the foot of the bed. A man is standing at the head, near Caroline. Caroline looks like she's trying to sit upright and the man is pushing her back down onto the bed. Caroline and the man and Audrey are yelling at one another. I see blood. The sheets are dark and wet with it.

"Mother of Christ," I say, stepping into the room. I say it almost under my breath, but all at once everyone stops their shouting as if I've burst into the room with a scream. It's quiet now. "What's this?" I say.

The quiet lasts just that long, and then Caroline starts up wailing and screaming something awful. I'm staring at the blood-darkened sheets and Audrey is coming across the room at me. "Hort. Get out," she says.

"What is it? Who's that?" I ask.

"He's the doctor. Get out."

"What's happening?"

"Get out," she says again. She's been shouting and her voice sounds raw, but she speaks evenly to me. "There's nothing you can do here. Get out."

"But Caroline," I say.

"We're trying to help Caroline."

"Is she going to die?"

Audrey blinks at me like I've just asked the weather. "I don't know the answer to that," she says.

Now the doctor shouts over at us. "Who the hell *is* that?" the doctor asks Audrey. "Get him out of here!"

"The father," Audrey says back to the doctor, while pointing a finger at me. My eyes are on that finger. Blood under the nail.

"You. Father," the doctor says to me, and I look up from Audrey's pointing finger. The doctor's face is shining and he bares his teeth at me. "Ice. Go get some ice."

Audrey turns back to me. "You know where to get ice, Horton?"

"Sure," I say. "Ice."

I step away, through the doorway, and Audrey closes the door behind me when I go.

I guess I walk the hallway to the doorway, and I guess I go out and make my way on the sidewalk toward somewhere I think I'll find ice. I say "I guess" because all I *know* is that I kind of snap-to, like out of sleep, and I'm walking along Columbus Avenue and it must be twenty minutes since I've left Caroline's. Something about the blood and the shouting, and about Caroline laid out on her bed that way, has really shaken me. But I come out of it now, and I think I'm all right.

Ice. In the stories, they always yell for hot towels, don't they? But the doctor said ice. What do I know? Annie and I never had one at home. So I'll get ice.

I light a cigarette. I'm to go for ice. Right. Only the thing is, I came back to her place from the Frenchman's tonight just to say goodbye to Caroline for good. Nobody knows that. With all the fireworks going off back there in the room, even *I* forgot it. I forgot everything.

Maybe that's what my problem is. I'm made stupid when I should be stirred into my most clear thinking. Or I'm filled with piss and vinegar when I should be crumpled with guilt for the horrors I've made. It all comes from the same thing: I'm a man who can't work by a plan; I make it all up as I go along. I'm not unconscious of my surroundings, but I can't ever deny the whims of my spirit. Each of us, I know, is called away from life by these distractions. But — here's an idea — might it not be that some of us are just born with distracting spirits that are more persuasive than those of other men?

Take me now. I'm whistling in the night when I should be running with tears in my eyes. I walk and I worry about Caroline, but all the while I'm feeling like it's one of the most glorious nights I can remember. By that I don't mean all that's occurring — I mean just the night. The air and the quality of the light. The clouds are breaking up under a full moon and there's a wind that's blowing. It's always something special when the wind blows at night. I can smell Tim Young's park fires on the wind, and other fires, too. Maybe somebody's burning logs in a fireplace somewhere. There's a sharp thing in the night wind that, if you sniff hard and think about it the right way, smells like snow.

It's weather, the best kind of weather there is, that whispers away the times you are living in and tells you secrets of other nights. God, the Octobers I've known. When I think. As a kid, the cold air at night made us wild, so we'd run in packs and throw coal at the beer wagons. When I was sixteen, I remember taking a horse blanket out on the Powderhorn lawn with Lorna Shawn, and she was scared and just kind of bunched up her skirts but I stripped naked as God made me. *That* October night, the cold raised bumps on me, and the grass and hard-packed mud beneath me felt as frozen as the Canadian tundra. Now, walking, I can come up with a hundred more October nights, just like that

— remembering girls in wool coats, and whiskey bottles passed between reddened hands, and boys shouting for me to kick a football, and bonfires on the Powderhorn, and the cool lips of a pretty redhead blubbering round my earlobes in the dark down at the bottom of the river flats.

I ought to be ashamed. Caroline, my Caroline, most likely dying as I walk, and all I can think of is the fine air of the October night. Mother of Christ. I'm off to fetch ice.

I turn down Caroline's block. At the Greek's, I duck in for ice. I pay for five pounds and I have the boy at the counter chop the ice for me, breaking it up so I can carry it out in the canvas sack. When I reach Caroline's building, I hop up the steps of the stoop and pull open the door. It's quiet now.

When I reach her room at the end of the hallway, it's still quiet. I open the door.

I've never seen the place this lit-up. Every lamp in the room is on, and even the big ceiling globe that Caroline never uses is shining harshly. I come into the room and I see that it's just Audrey, alone. She's bent over the bed, doing something with the sheets. Caroline is lying on the bed very still. Her nightgown is bloodied and her legs are uncovered. There is a clump of stiff-looking sheets on the floor, stained dark brown.

"Caroline?" I say.

Audrey turns from the bed. "She's gone."

This doesn't mean anything to me. "Where's the doctor?" I ask Audrey.

"He went out for a telephone."

"He's left her like this?" I say.

Audrey opens her mouth. Then she closes it.

"She's gone, Horton," she says finally. "She's gone."

"Gone?" I say, though I'm not really asking for clarification. I'm staring at Caroline on the bed and I can see that her skin has gone the color of cigarette ash. I understand what Audrey has said. She's gone.

And how do I make sense of this? I know nothing about people dying. Scotty Boyle said that Peterson was dead. But that's different. This is Caroline. My Caroline. If I try, right now, I can remember exactly the way her breath tasted in my mouth. And now she'll never breathe again. Dead. It makes no sense to me. Though maybe this is just a trick my brain is playing on me. A trick of kindness. Maybe it'll all make sense five minutes from now, or in five years. But just now, I'm befuddled.

I look at Caroline's face and I can see that she's not sleeping. Her face, when she's sleeping, is serene. I know, when I look at her sleeping, that she is dreaming happy dreams. Now her face looks pained. And there's the color. She's gone from me.

"I thought," Audrey says, and she takes a few deep breaths. "I thought you left again. You didn't come back."

"I've brought the ice," I say. I set the bag down on the floor beside me. "I'm sorry I didn't come back sooner."

"There's nothing you could have done."

"No?"

She shakes her head. When she starts to cry, I have to look away. I've never seen Audrey cry before. I can kind of see, from out of the corner of my eye, that she's standing in a queer way, her arms out toward me, and I realize she's wanting me to come over there and hold onto her. But she's crying and I've never seen Audrey cry. I stay standing where I am.

"Who is the doctor telephoning?" I ask.

Audrey can't stop crying and I think she doesn't hear my question, but after a minute or so she catches her breath and she answers me: "He's calling the hospital people, to come take them away."

I nod. But I don't get something. "Take *them* away?"

"Caroline. And the baby."

"The baby," I say.

Audrey motions with one hand toward a place on the floor beneath the window, where a blanket is folded into a square and something is sitting atop this square. A small bundle, wrapped in one of Caroline's ruined sheets.

I can't look at the thing and I don't want to see Caroline's lifeless body on the bed and so I stare, in a very focused way, at Audrey's face.

"Where will the hospital people take them?" I ask.

Audrey's swollen eyes flicker and roll. "I don't know. I suppose Caroline will be sent home. To her family."

"They won't send the baby," I say.

"No," Audrey says, "probably not. Caroline hadn't told her family. She hadn't told them anything."

When Audrey cries, her forehead goes white as paste and her nose and eyelids go red. The dark parts of her eyes get darker through tears. Her skinny lips swell up. She doesn't look at all like the Audrey I'd known before. I'm staring at the line on one of her cheeks made by a tear sliding down, drying now and fading away.

I let my eyes snap sideways at the thing on the folded blanket.

"I'll take the baby," I say to Audrey.

"You'll *what*?"

"The baby. The body," I say. "The hospital people won't deal with it properly. I'll take it away."

"No you won't, Horton."

"I will."

"That's morbid," she says. "Leave it for the hospital people."

"It is mine," I say. "My son? My daughter?"

Audrey wipes at her face with her hands. She looks at the wrapped baby on the floor and her face seems to compose itself. "A girl," she says. "Your daughter."

I watch the color in Audrey's face begin to go back to its normal balance.

"I'll take my daughter," I say.

So I do. Audrey doesn't say anything else, but she finds a clean bath towel for us to cover the baby with. She bends over the thing on the floor and begins to remove the wrap, but I stop her. I tell her to just bundle the towel around it as it is. I don't want to see the dead baby. When Audrey hands the body to me, I'm surprised by how heavy it is. But that's how it's always been with my babies.

I leave the apartment. I'm hurrying, thinking that the doctor is going to return and try to stop me. But nobody tries to stop me.

Twenty-nine

The park house where Tim Young keeps his equipment is down the slope near the north edge of the lake. Tim Young and his crew are gone for the night, but they've left the door to their park house opened. I find a spade and I carry it out in my left hand. I'm cradling the body against my right side, like it was a live baby.

I go away from the park house and climb the slope, to a place up from the lake where the land levels off and a stand of tall cottonwood trees grows. Beyond the cottonwoods is a baseball field. The pathways that Tim Young and his men work so hard to keep tended wind wide around these trees from the fields to the lake. Nobody comes through here much.

The electric lights that they've been raising throughout the park don't shine here, and if it weren't for the full moon it'd be black as a night in the country. Even the city sounds are far away.

I put the body down gently, as if afraid I'll wake a sleeping baby. Out of habit, I guess. Then I dig. The earth breaks easily here, and it's not long before I'm cutting through roots four feet down. I dig a foot or so further. Just to the tip of the spade handle.

I don't know what I expected, but I'm shocked by how difficult it is to lay my dead child in the ground. Shocked, I mean, like I was working without thinking through the planning and the digging, but now that I've actually taken up the body and I'm standing over the hole, I'm shocked into thinking. I'm breathing hard and I can feel sweat between my shoulder blades, from the effort of the dig. I'm holding it — holding her — in two hands now and I'm standing with my feet astride the black deep beneath me.

But I've got to do it. I lower myself, dropping on my ass at the edge of the grave. I let myself down into it. It's a small hole, just big enough, and there's no room for me to really bend and set the baby down right. So I have to kind of stoop as low as I'm able and then I drop her down.

I pull myself out fast and I fall over sideways into the pile of soft dug dirt beside the grave.

I'm shaking hard. In a sick way. I've had the shakes this way before, in a fever. Only there's no fever now. I'm healthy as hell. My shoulders are aching and I think it's from something I strained in the dig, but then I begin to think the ache is from the way I'm shaking. Then I realize I'm crying.

I've never had a cry like this before and I don't know where it's come from or where it's taking me. I lose my idea of time and of where I am, and when I taste the soil of the Powderhorn in my mouth and I come to with my face in the mound of dirt I've dug from her grave, it's like I'm waking up from a deep dream.

I sit up and I spit out the dirt and I wipe it away from my nose and eyes with my hands. I look around me and then I find a cigarette in my shirt pocket and I light it. I stare into the blackness of the hole at my feet.

It's got to be finished. I know. I smoke my cigarette and let my heart get back to normal, and then I stand up. Things need to be said. Even in a situation like this, without a proper burial mass, words need to be spoken.

I throw my cigarette away behind me and I cross myself. "Hail Mary, full of grace. The Lord is with thee. Blessed art though among women, and blessed is the fruit of thy womb, Jesus. Holy Mary, mother of God, pray for us sinners, now and at the hour of our death. Amen."

I take up the spade again and shove it into the pile. After the first load has been dropped in, the sound of it falling isn't so bad. I work quickly and I finish fast. When I'm done, I leave the spade and walk away. But then I think the spade will give the site away, and the police or somebody will come digging her up from her place. I don't want anybody to bother her ever. So I go back and get the spade and I carry it down to the lake and I throw it out as far as my arms can manage.

I leave the lake and go up the grass to the path, and I walk the path across the Powderhorn. Now the city noises have come back to me, and the electric lamps are glowing over the path, making the pavement look blue. I'm walking without knowing where I'm heading for a while, but then I stop and turn around and begin walking in the opposite direction. I can still taste tears and dirt in my mouth, but my eyes are clear.

I see the lights of the big houses at the edge of the park, and I walk a little faster, turning off the blue-lighted pathway and cutting across the darkness of the night lawn. The big oaks grow here, and they block out the moonlight. I can hear dry leaves swishing up in heaps beneath my feet, but it's too dark to see them when I look down.

I know, without my seeing it, that there's a moon above in the cold black sky. There's a white moon glowing, the color of bone, up beyond the heavy limbs of oak that spread their shadow over me. I know that the moon shines tonight on Ben and on Sprague, left alone together in their love somewhere on the western plains, and the moon's cool light falls on my still, spent Caroline, and on the grave of the daughter we made, and on my lonely wife Annie, with her hungers unresolved, and on my children asleep in their beds in a home without a father. The moon shows its light on the lost souls of the Gateway square, and on good, godless Levin and his fallen-away nun. And the October moon, I realize, is just now showing itself to a hundred thousand million others whose names and lives and joys I'll never know, whose nights will pass without me, whose mornings will follow whether I'm here beneath our shared moon or not.

Something in this last thought stirs me and lightens my heart. It's not even a thought, really. A thing blowing through my brain like smoke on the October wind. Not a thought but just an emotion.

"Now, where did *that* come from?" I ask myself, aloud. The sound of my voice makes me start. But where *did* that come from, that quickening emotion? What do I care of anyone else's passing nights and coming mornings? Because haven't I known all my life that, when all is said and done, nobody looks out for Horton but me myself — and that, likewise, it's every other man out there for himself and himself alone? Yes, I've always known that, and I've always been satisfied with the arrangement. Still. What of these others? These strangers. Are we a line of identical tragedies playing out under the moon, destined each of us to break the same heart in a different place? Will there ever be a one that passes his time properly? Might not someone, somewhere — maybe even one of my own, maybe Frankie or Ralphie or Bridget or small Richard or new Stanley

— might not some one man or woman live a life without it all coming down to nothing but sadness and regret?

But, anyway. Why should I hope? And why, now, should I suddenly take comfort in this idea of other, imagined souls and in their imaginary tomorrows? Why should I be taking any comfort at all?

"I mean, who am I," I ask the dark, "to be feeling anything but misery on a night like this?" I shake my head. I move forward through the dry rasp of the fallen leaves.

"Oh, my girl," I say, not caring that she can't hear me. And the brief, queer lightening of my heart — my October smoke emotion — is snapped apart and scattered. A sadness spreads through me, dull but even more complete than the sharp crippling sorrow I'd felt back at the graveside of my buried daughter. Because, really, there is no comfort to be had in hoping for the imagined, no consolation in dreams of other moons that might or might not come.

"My girl. My dearest girl. It's too late after all, isn't it?" I say, slowing my steps through the leaves. "What have I done with this one chance we had? What have I done? My time's been a great banging and rattling, like the wagon of a scrap-tin collector, but has there been anything *there* beyond the noise? I don't know. I wish I could say yes. But.

"Like the philosophers say, we have only this once around, any of us, and then we're a long time dead. I didn't take up my part. I hadn't been in too deep. I was never in deep enough. Such a pity. Such a damned pity."

But I've never been good at feeling sorry for myself. I take a lungfull of the sharp October air and I straighten my shoulders, and I even throw a small, private smile toward the butter-colored lights in the windows of the big houses at the approaching edge of the Powderhorn.

"Ah. Well," says I. "Given another lifetime, my girl, we two could have been the happiest couple in Christendom."

When I reach the end of the green where the sidewalk runs along the roadside, a big black Cadillac sedan pulls up to the curb, fast, and brakes hard six feet from where I've stopped. Two men stand up out of the front doors. They are big and solid-looking, and they wear expensive overcoats and new fedoras that shade their faces against the lamplight. It's about how I expected it to be.

"Horton Moon," one of them says.

"Himself," I say.

"There's someone wants to talk with you."

"Yes," I say. "I understand."

So it's all over for me, and I go toward the Cadillac.

Thirty

One of the big overcoats holds the rear door open for me, which seems a little formal for the circumstances, but there you have it. I stoop and slip into the rear seat. It smells of Turkish tobacco smoke and strong cologne.

"Uncle Jack," I say, seeing him there and struck too stupid by the shock of it to say anything more sensible.

Jack Morrison, seeing I guess the look on me, lets out a little laugh and draws on his cigarette.

"Hello, young Horton. Long time no see."

He's spread out over the seat like a king on his throne. Silk suit. Gleaming tie pin. Cigarette burning in an ivory holder. He's a Minneapolis alderman but he could pass, in a Hollywood casting office, for a successful gangster. Which is exactly what he is, of course.

"I've been away," I say. The car door closes behind me.

"So I gather. You've been very hard to find," he says, and he gives me a long look. "People have been trying."

"Yes," I say. The car starts moving.

"They're not any more," Jack says. "I mean, the people looking to find you are not looking for you any longer. You can relax."

Looking out the window of the Cadillac, I can see that we're driving away from the Powderhorn, heading to Lake Street. North. In the front seat, the two large men sit still as stones. One of them's kept his fedora on. The other, driving, has a sleek, shiny head the size of the walrus's in the Como Park zoo.

"Oh," I say. "I'm relaxed as hell."

"Do you know the name Moses Rivkin?" Jack asks me.

I swallow. "Don't believe so, no."

"Mr. Rivkin. He's the gentleman whose money you stole."

"Ah," I say. "Now, Jack. I can explain that."

"Leave it," he says, waving his cigarette. "Nothing to explain. Mr. Rivkin is an associate of mine. A kind of friend, you might say."

Shit. So it's like that. I am being turned over by my own.

Jack gives me a small pat on the knee with one of his big hands. Then, like the subject of Rivkin is now dropped between us, he launches into this:

"D'you know the improvements to the Powderhorn? It's going to be a showplace. We've got quite a lot of federal money coming into play. We're laying new ballfields. We're planting a grove of flowering cherry trees. It'll be a grand place in time. And the new bandshell? Have you seen the plans for the new bandshell? It's been in all the papers. But, I forget — you've been away, haven't you? Probably haven't seen the papers. Anyway. We're building a spanking new bandshell, with a picnic pavilion attached. Place for families. A friendly place. There'll be a bar that'll sell soft drinks and popcorn. And vending machines. For the kids to buy candies and gum and whatnot. Oh, the plans we're making for the place!"

Jack Morrison tilts his head back, cigarette holder between his teeth, and he grins at the ceiling of the Cadillac. Looking like Franklin D. Roosevelt himself, really. His hand is still on my knee and he gives it a squeeze. "You needn't worry about Rivkin and his people, young Horton. They're working with *me* now. They want their little vending machines in the Powderhorn, and I run the Powderhorn."

"I get you," I say.

Sweet Jesus. I breathe and I feel like I'm letting out a breath I've held for a week. Even Jack Morrison's strong cologne and his Turkish tobacco smoke come at me like the scents of the flowers of Eden. I stare out the window of the car at the street going away past me and I probably even let out a little laugh. Without being able to help it. Jack smokes and sits on his end of the big bench seat and neither of us says anything. It's only after a minute has passed like this that I notice Uncle Jack still has his grip on my knee.

"Horton," he says at last.

"Yes?"

"You abandoned my niece, my Annie."

"No," I say. "I've come back for her."

"Don't bullshit a bullshitter," he says quickly. "I know exactly what you've done, what you've come back for."

"I came back for Annie," I say, trying to make him hear me. But how can I make him know that I'm not lying to him? I mean, really, how can I make known the truth of my heart to a man like Jack Morrison? He doesn't want to believe me. I came home for Annie, and I was willing to die for that if it meant dying on my way to reach her. But even if Jack believed me, what would it matter? I get the feeling that this conversation is not about my heart and its truths.

He lets go of my knee and he bends forward to the silver ashtray at his door. He mashes out his cigarette, removes the butt from the holder, and slips the ivory holder into a pocket of his silk suit.

"I've saved your ass, boy," he says, turning to me. "D'you understand that much?"

"I do."

"And do you understand why? Why I did it?"

"I think I do, yes."

"Do you think you matter a glass of piss to me?"

"No. But Annie."

"You're goddamn right, 'but Annie.' You're a little shit and you're good for nothing, far as I can see, but you're my Annie's husband and you're the father of her babies. She's too young to be a widow and the children don't deserve to be orphans. You're going back to her —"

"That I am, Jack."

"Shut up. Don't say anything. You're going back to Annie and you're going to settle down and be a proper husband and father. No more of this fat blonde cunt, and no more of this playing Dilinger. Do I make myself understood?"

"Perfectly," I say.

Because what else could I say? He is Jack Morrison. Nobody can touch him. Even the northside Jews let go when he says to let go. I am going back to my Annie — not for his reasons but for my own — but I understand that this is his show. The whole south side is his show. He's the hero of the Powderhorn.

Jack settles himself again, leaning back into the soft leather of the seat cushion.

"I've got you work," Jack says.

"A job?"

"A proper job. On the city books."

I let the car glide a half block of Lake Street before I ask, "What kind of job is it, Jack?"

He glances sideways at me. "If it's cleaning the mayor's toilet with your bare hands you'll be happy to have it."

"Of course," I say.

"It's a good job," he says. "Minding the booth on the river bridge."

I lean my head against the cool glass of the window and close my eyes.

"Thanks, Uncle Jack," I say. "It's a good job."

*

Clickety-click. So it goes. I'm in the booth. It's a small place, only a little bigger than a telephone booth, with a hard seat and a plank run across under one window where I can set my insulated jug of coffee and my newspapers. Like a telephone booth, there's glass up to the ceiling on two sides; in the day the sun would come in and warm me. But I'm here nights.

I click the clicker that I hold in one hand. Counting traffic. The cars get a click each. The big beer wagons get two. When a truck comes over pulling a trailer behind, I give it three. Even the milk wagons, drawn by horses, get a click. On the hour, I check the counter and record the numbers on the sheet in the clipboard. In the morning, I hand the clipboard over to Fagen, the supervisor, and he carries it on downtown where they're making up a survey. Clickety-click. It's my job.

The nights are cold, but I've got a kerosene heater burning on the floor at my feet. When the wind blows very hard off the river, the drafty glass around me rattles and the kerosene heater is no good at all. I wrap myself in mule blankets and stand up from my seat and I step from one foot to the other and keep the brass clicker held inside one of my woolen mittens.

These cold winter nights go on. I mean, they seem to last longer than any night should. The air outside my booth is black and dead, the freeze killing off even the smells of life that normally would be moving through the midnight. I wait through the dead dark in the close atmosphere of my room, the kerosene stink turning my stomach and my eyes blurring from reading and rereading the papers under the bare lightbulb on the ceiling. Traffic is light in these hours. I can usually make my count without even looking up from the newspaper, just listening for motors and feeling the way the bridge span wobbles slightly under the heavier wagons. Left alone nights with only the newspapers for company, I've become more acquainted than I'd ever wished to be with world affairs and with Hollywood gossip and even with college basketball scores and the standings in the Canadian hockey league. I, who never cared for sports and games, now study newspaper box scores to chase away the silence inside. For two weeks the papers all lead with the sensational story of Steven Linen, found in the bedroom of his Summit Avenue mansion, murdered, after one of his parties. At first the papers hint vaguely of lurid, scandalous goings-on, then later change their tone, calling it a simple crime of passion — reporting that Linen was involved in a love triangle. But the father of the teenaged boy who killed Linen has even more money than Linen's father, and so in the end the whole matter is dropped before it is brought to trial. The story just disappears from the pages of the newspapers. I go back to reading about film stars and New Deal farm subsidies.

Memories of my dead wear me, the way they say the landscapes of the north were shaped long ago by the weight of ancient glaciers, forming and retreating.

When my shift ends in the morning, it is still dark. I normally exchange a few words with Lewis, coming on for the morning shift — he's a pleasant fellow, his lungs and nerves ruined in the war, but quick to laugh at a joke — and then I take up my emptied coffee jug and my dinner pail and I walk across the way to the corner for the streetcar.

The sun is rising by the time I reach home, and I come into the kitchen to find the kids eating hurried breakfasts while Annie scolds them toward the door on the way to school. Some mornings I sit at the table and smoke a cigarette while the twins stuff toast into their mouths, or I try to answer Bridget's questions about arithmetic. Small Richard is learning riddles, and sometimes he tries them out on me. Other mornings I pass through the kitchen quickly and I go to the bathroom, where I fill the tub with hot water and soak my cold bones till the children go and the apartment beyond the closed bathroom door is quiet.

Annie and I don't say much to each other.

I don't know what she knows about my time away from her, or why I left her at all, or the role her uncle Jack Morrison had in my making it back to her alive. Maybe she knows it all, and maybe she herself made my case to Uncle Jack. Or maybe she doesn't know a thing except that her husband left her and went away for a summer and then came back sorry and sick. I turned up with my busted face and with my cough I couldn't shake, and I begged her to let me back in. I promised her I would never leave her again, and I even tried to explain something about what I thought I learned from leaving, but I couldn't really tell her much.

She said that I was a good talker, but that she'd known that about me all along. She told me she didn't need me to talk anymore, about anything. This I understood.

I mean, I understood that I could talk till the breath ran out of me but that I could never tell my Annie what she needed to know about me. About why I'd come home to her. Something in Annie had died when I'd gone away, died like a fire reduced to cooling ash. There was no way I could speak to her, or touch her, that would make that heat and light start up again anew. All I could do was to stay here with her, and go to the job her uncle had made for me, and bring her my pay money every week. And so I do this.

There is a rhythm in my days that I'm beginning to find comfort in. I work the night shift six times a week. When I go to my bed, Annie has made it up, smoothed the spread, fluffed the pillows, cleared our bed of any sign of herself. I sleep from nine in the morning till sunset. When I wake up I sit with my children at the supper table and I drink coffee. In the evenings we listen to the radio together and then I help the older children to bed while Annie settles baby Stanley. Annie goes to bed shortly after the children, and then I sit up alone in the parlor with my cigarettes and the radio until it's time for me to go to work.

One morning I go to the bedroom to sleep and I find that Annie has not made up the bed as usual. She has left the covers turned back, the sheets rumpled, the feather pillow with the impression of her head still in it. I think that she must have forgotten, or been distracted by the kids fighting with one another more than usual before school. I settle between the sheets and, for the first time in months, I can smell where my wife has slept in the night. I spread my hand over the folds of her pillow.

But it is not a mistake or an oversight. The next morning, the bed is left for me like this again, and the next morning as well. Now it is like this every morning. I come home to sleep in the bed where she has been. One night, Annie's washed her hair with gardenia-scented shampoo, and in the morning I fall asleep with her pillow pulled close to my face.

A bitter February cold comes, turning the river hard as granite and dropping workhorses dead on the frozen cobblestones of the downtown streets. I've come home from a night in the booth worse than most, and I take my hot bath and go directly to bed without speaking to the children. My muscles ache from shivering through the night. In bed, I kick my feet under the covers, unable to make myself feel warm even after the soak in the bathwater.

I'm restless and I'm still awake when the kids have gone off to school. I hear Annie pushing the sweeper in the hallway outside the bedroom and so I call to her.

She comes, opening the bedroom door and standing there with one hand on the knob.

"What is it, Horton?" she asks.

"I'm cold," I say to her.

"It's a cold morning," she says.

"It was a colder night."

"I bet it was," she says, picking a speck of lint from the front of her housedress.

"Not that I'm complaining, mind you," I say. "I know I'm lucky to have any work at all in these times."

"Yes," she says.

This is the most we've said to one another in four months.

The blackout shades are drawn down against the bright sunlight outside, but that light is bouncing like mad off the snow and off the ice on the sills, and the bedroom glows, only half dark. I can't sleep. I sit upright and shift my pillow up behind me against the headboard. I'm turned toward Annie in the doorway.

"Were the kids warm enough?"

"Yes," she says. "Warm enough. Bridget wore Frankie's old quilted coat over her heavy raincoat. And I made up one of your jackets, the blue one you don't wear anymore, into a vest for small Richard."

I touch the covers over my lap with both hands. "You're a good mother, Annie."

She tosses her head at this, making a face. But she's let her guard down, and I can see a change in the way her dark brows arch slightly.

"Ah," I say softly. "As if you need me to tell you as much."

We both hear Stanley now, letting out a yelp from the twins' room.

"Baby's awake," Annie says, speaking toward the floor.

"So he is," I say.

She steps backwards away, and she's pulling the door closed behind her.

"Annie," I say. "Wait a sec."

She regards me through the narrowed opening.

I don't say anything but she doesn't look away from me. Baby Stanley is growing louder behind her, but Annie doesn't turn away. We're looking at each other, and for the first time in too long Annie is seeing me. She's not got a hard face on her for protection. She's just standing there, open to me as she used to be in the old days, before everything. It's a wonder, a beautiful moment, and it's only going to last a second or two longer. I don't even need to say anything. But I do, I always do. I can't help myself.

"Annie," I say. "Do you think, even given a lifetime, I can ever make known to you the deepest parts of my heart?"

Her eyes go liquid but right away she tightens her mouth and holds everything together. "Oh, Horton Moon," she says. "You are a poet, aren't you? Alfred Lord Tennis-ball himself's got nothing on you for words."

And at this, her joke, she smiles. She's a small mouth, though nicely formed, and it's a mouth made for nothing so much as for smiling at quiet jokes in the morning.

We nod at one another, our eyes coming together in the old way, easily. She leaves me, pulling the door closed softly behind her. I'm alone in a soft bed and the room is darkened, and my bones are sore and my body is weary to the point of exhaustion from the long, cold night I've just passed. And yet I cannot sleep. How can I? I am fallen in love, again, and this has set me trembling and tense like with an electric charge. I tell you, love does this to me. It pounds through my body and my head in ways that are painful. It's a curse, indeed. I lie there staring at the ceiling, unable to sleep.

Outside, the cloudless midwinter sky opens up above my roof, above my neighborhood, above the Powderhorn. The sky is high and blue, the color of one of small Richard's paintings of a sky. Its blue is dry and cold and without the slightest smear of pale cloud that might promise spring showers; these are weeks and weeks away still, and none of us really has any choice but to wait with patience for the seasonal thaw that will bring warmer air, and shorter nights, and the rains that make green things grow.

I returned to Minneapolis thirty-four years later, in March of 1969. Ed had died eighteen years earlier. I still wasn't over it. He and I had a good long time together. We lived in Oregon, outside Portland. I worked as a governess. Rich family. Lumber money. Two boys that I raised and loved like they was my own. Ed helped the gardener a bit, poking around the grounds with a hoe, but he mostly just worked on his painting. We lived in a little cottage down the hill from the big house. Ed made some swell pictures of the mountains. I still got the paintings. But I missed Ed.

Anyway. I flew back to the Twin Cities for a visit. One of my boys, one of the boys I raised, was a college professor then. He'd got a position at Macalester College, in St. Paul. Jim — that was his name — Jim was good to me. He had me out and he put me up at the Radisson Hotel in downtown St. Paul. I wrote Horton Moon a letter before I came out, and we met for lunch at the Dayton's department store, downtown Minneapolis. He was pretty quiet. I did most of the talking. I told him about the family I'd worked for out west. I told him about my boys. I told him about how Ed painted and painted, right up till the end. I told him the boys had called Ed "Uncle Edmund." Moon seemed glad to hear about Ed and how well he lived in his last years.

I don't think Moon was a happy man. He seemed distracted. You know what I mean. When he was listening to me, and even when he was telling me about himself — he'd gone to night school and taken drafting classes, he'd found a nice job in the offices of an engineering firm, his kids were all grown up and married and making grandkids for him and Annie — he was kind of faraway in the eyes, with a look on his face like there was a bad taste in his mouth.

I got an idea we should take a trip down by the river. I asked Moon was he up for it and he said, sure. He kind of got a smile on his face and said, "Sure, Ben. Let's go check out the old stomping grounds."

Moon hadn't aged so well. He was grey the color of candlewax. His body looked all bent and beat up and his lungs made a whistling sound when he breathed. We decided not to walk, and so we took a bus. The streetcars were long gone from Minneapolis. We sat in the back of the big smoke-belching bus, above I guess where the diesel engine was, and the bus wheezed and groaned so that we couldn't really make ourselves heard in conversation. At the Washington Avenue bus stop, Moon held the door open for me and let me step out ahead of him.

It was gone. The whole neighborhood was gone. The pawnshops and the saloons and the rooming houses and the sandwich counters and the mission flop-houses, all were gone. There were parking lots. Blocks and blocks of parking lots. All full. Nothing to see but a thousand cars, from Marquette Avenue to beyond First.

I looked at Moon and he was laughing. "Welcome to the old neighborhood," he said.

I turned around and around. I couldn't quite believe it. It was like seeing a trick by a clever magician. How had they done this? Of course I had seen the work of the wrecking ball and the bulldozer before, but this was on a scale I couldn't wrap my mind around. How did they do this? I wondered at the marvel of an entire city wiped away. Where had the Gateway district gone? Where had the rubble been carted to? Where on earth was there a place to contain the tons and tons and tons *of brick and concrete and broken glass and iron rail and stone gargoyles, the pipes and plumbing and wiring, the tile and woodwork, the stuff of an entire small city knocked to dust and taken away in truckloads? The whole project awed me, and I asked Moon to explain how,* how, *but he was unimpressed by the how of it. He just grinned with that kind of bitter look on his face. "They" had had their reasons. Somebody, Moon said, was getting paid. Behind the smirk, though, there was in Moon's voice a note of approval, admiration even. I got the sense that he wished he himself might have had a hand in this, the scraping clean of the messy landscape of our past.*

He lit a cigarette and we walked together along the edge of the parking lots. In three blocks, we didn't see another person walking.

At the foot of Nicollet Avenue, a new building stood, a modern thing that looked like a space ship dropped down in the middle of all the parking lots. Moon and I walked the length of an iced-over reflecting pool alongside the spaceship structure, and then we sat on a bench in front, facing an empty basketball court. I had to laugh at this. Where were the children who would play in this park?

Moon smoked his cigarette down and lit another.

"Do you know where we are, Benedetta?" he asked me.

I looked at the parking lot beside the spaceship. I looked at the parking lot on the other side of the basketball court. "Not really," I said.

"This is where we first met," Moon said. "Right on this spot. The Gateway fountain used to stand just there." He pointed his cigarette toward one of the rows of chrome and steel and windshield glass.

"Oh," I said. "You are a sentimental old man, aren't you?"

He laughed softly. Out here, in the winter sunshine, Moon seemed more free with his talk than he had back in the Dayton's dining room. He told me more about his kids. He talked a little about his work. He started recalling some stories from the old days in Minneapolis. Moon told me about an uncle of his wife's who'd been an alderman. A scoundrel, but a character. Taken down when Hubert Humphrey cleaned up the city back in the Forties. Moon told me how Dave Levin had quit the Union City mission, married a nice, smart Catholic girl, and moved out to the Arizona desert. And Moon talked about himself, spinning out for me this theory he had about his unusual heart and how he could fall in love — still, nearing sixty now — more frequently and with greater intensity than any normal man. He fell in love with Annie every day, he said, but there were other women, too. Still.

And then Moon told me about burying his own daughter back in the Powderhorn Park in the autumn of 1935. The way he told this story, I got the idea that Moon had spent too much of the rest of his life remembering that one October night — mourning the dead in an out-of-balance way that, I know, can let the living get away from a person.

I don't like sad stories. Never have. And the Portland coat I was wearing really wasn't right for a March afternoon in Minnesota.

I stood up off the bench. "I'm cold," I said. "Let's walk."

We left the spaceship building and walked uptown, away from the parking lots. Headed back to Dayton's, where I could catch a taxicab to drive me back to my hotel in St. Paul and Moon could board the city bus heading out toward his home near the Powderhorn Park.

"It's the damndest thing," Moon said to me, walking slowly up Nicollet Avenue. "But I think she might have been the one. That baby girl. Don't ask me why I think that. Maybe it was her mother. Her mother was remarkable."

Was Moon telling me that his buried daughter was the one love of his life? Or the one something else? Whichever, it's a pity. To think of a man living into old age with a crazy notion like that. I guess it explains his distracted way. The set of his mouth. You see what I mean. How must it have been for him, to live forever either swelling with new passions or retreating into bitter memories of a lost past? Anyway. I think Moon's theory, about him falling in love too much, was off. His condition was not that simple. Or maybe it's not that complicated. I think of the old joke: Forget about the falling — his curse was that he never learned to land in love.

I wished Ed were here. Ed would have known what to say. Ed always saw right through things. I myself didn't know the right words to say, and so I didn't say anything. The two of us just walked slowly along Nicollet Avenue that way, not talking at all, Moon I guess thinking about his stillborn daughter who could have been the one, and me thinking how I should have packed a proper coat for the weather.

Joseph McInerny was born in 1962 in Minneapolis, Minnesota. He has made his living as a vintage-clothing store clerk, a night watchman, a proofreader, a delivery driver, an advertising copywriter, and by selling pretzels in the Greenmarket of New York City's Union Square.

Powderhorn is his second novel.

CPSIA information can be obtained at www.ICGtesting.com
Printed in the USA
LVOW01s0812070913

351414LV00015B/540/P